E.C.T.

CUCUMBER SANDWICHES

AND OTHER STORIES

Cucumber
Sandwiches

and Other Stories

J. I. M. STEWART

New York

W · W · NORTON & COMPANY · INC ·

CONTENTS

Laon and Cythna

PART ONE

I

LET ME BEGIN by recording something which was within my own knowledge at the start. Arthur Holroyd, although an active and, I believe, eminent member of the Parapsychological Society, has never been interested in ghosts. Of course he will always maintain in public that in the insecure state of our knowledge—the near-infancy, as it still is, of psychical research—it is necessary to keep an open mind. But privately he has assured me more than once that he disbelieves in the survival of human personality after bodily death, and in consequence in the possibility of veridical phantasms of the dead. He admits as a plain fact that people—even groups of people—do occasionally experience apparitions. But these must be explained, he says, without recourse to the notion of disembodied spirits revisiting (as Hamlet has it) 'the glimpses of the moon'.

Shortly before the perplexing events I have undertaken to relate, Holroyd had become interested in a subject very remote from demonology. This was psycho-kinesis, or PK, a term which will perhaps bear a passing comment. A conjuror affects to possess this power when he makes mystic passes before a cabinet with the result that a lady vanishes from its interior and reappears in an alternative receptacle at the other side of the stage. A hysterical girl, it may be said, actually achieves psycho-kinesis if she generates that kind of 'poltergeist' phenomena in which vases tumble off mantelpieces and sundry petty levitations take place. And a similar force may be declared operative when, in a *séance* with a 'physical' medium, a tambourine or parasol is hurtled across a room.

Except in the case of the conjuror, who is doing no more than play a clever trick on us, it is difficult to arrive at any well-founded view of such happenings. Holroyd's interest was in the possibility of controlled experiment. Has the human mind any detectable power to influence the movement of material objects at a distance?

It certainly *believes* it has. As my friend pointed out in a paper contributed to his Society's *Proceedings* some years ago, when a football has been powerfully impelled towards the mouth of the goal at a populously attended match, the spectators to a man strenuously 'will' its passing either over or under the bar according as their partisanship dictates. On bowling-greens and putting-greens, similarly, players may frequently be observed contorting their bodies under the stress of frantically 'willing' a psycho-kinetic effect. Would nature, it may be asked, have developed so powerfully in us this particular mechanism of the mind while at the same time decreeing that it should have no biological value whatever? Or is there in man a power, whether vestigial or rudimentary, a full exercise of which might very notably conduce to his survival—deflecting, for example, the arrow as it flies? As a step towards answering such large questions Holroyd had devised a small machine.

It is very difficult to be certain that one is succeeding in making physical events behave in a random manner—a fact well known to, though not much publicised by, those charged with constructing and operating the 'electronic brains' and the like used in the conduct of state lotteries. Holroyd believed he had succeeded, having simply perfected something already in use in other laboratories: to wit, a contrivance for tossing three dice on a table. Actually it did a little more than that, since it was capable of picking them up again and continuing the process indefinitely. The agent in the experiment would sit watching the machine through a glass partition, and would over a substantial period of time endeavour to dictate some specific course of behaviour to the dice : that they should produce, for example, what Holroyd (who is a Classical scholar) calls an *Aphrodite,* meaning three sixes, or a *dog,* meaning three aces. It is a very boring sort of experiment, one would suppose, particularly as it has to be conducted for weeks on end before enough data can be accumulated to make valid statistical analysis possible.

I mention all this because it is important to get clear the kind of thing that Holroyd had come to think of as modern psychical research. He is not a fanciful or imaginative man, but he is a pertinacious one. It certainly needed pertinacity to persevere with O'Rourke.

How my friend came upon O'Rourke I do not know, nor does it matter, since the man is without significance for my substantive narrative. He was an unemployed Irish labourer, and it appears that he was accustomed to earning occasional free drinks by some sort of card-guessing exhibition in pubs. Something, I have forgotten what, about the technique of this suggested to Holroyd that O'Rourke might be a suitable man to address his mind (if the expression be appropriate) to those tumbling dice. So he hired O'Rourke, and O'Rourke spent long hours concentrating, or professing to concentrate, upon the task entrusted to him. So far as his personal habits went, he was not an ideal collaborator. Holroyd has described him to me as drunken and smelly. He was also resourcefully profane, and when he chose to feel some particular recalcitrance in the dice he would curse them through his glass window in the most appalling manner. The first run of results, however, was declared by Holroyd's mathematical colleagues to be encouraging, and the experiment went on.

Unfortunately, O'Rourke's success presently appeared to be of the flash-in-the-pan kind with which psychical researchers are only too familiar. His results fell off, and soon the laws of probability alone seemed to be at play upon those falling *tesserae*. Perhaps fearful that he was going to lose his comfortable if incomprehensible employment, O'Rourke made prodigious efforts to reassert himself. The veins stood out on his temples, Holroyd asserted, and his objurgations became so vehement that it was feared lest the delicate mechanism of the dice-casting machine might be affected. In vain. O'Rourke did not cease from mental strife against the brute insentience of matter. His efforts were now wholly unrewarded.

But the man might—Holroyd doggedly told his colleagues —simply have struck a bad patch. They must carry on, even if it meant ordering in another firkin of ale (for it was with copious potations of this wholesome liquor that O'Rourke recruited his flagging energies as he laboured at his honourable if humble assignment as a scientist). And this determination was eventually rewarded. O'Rourke's results transformed themselves from being *merely* bad to being *significantly* bad. The dice, after what may be termed a brief honeymoon period, had taken to ignoring him. They were ignoring him still, but now they appeared to be taking orders from some other intelligence instead, and the effect of this was to depress O'Rourke's score below the mere probability line.

Whose was this other intelligence, or whence came this new and alien force? It was Holroyd himself who found the answer. In the sense that he had been suspecting, no fresh factor had entered into the affair at all. O'Rourke's will, and O'Rourke's will alone, was what had once more defeated blind chance by imposing itself upon those small rolling objects. But it was O'Rourke's will as that will had been directing the dice not at the time but twenty-four hours *later*. The dice had been taking their orders neither from O'Rourke present nor from O'Rourke past but from O'Rourke future. It seemed almost necessary to endow them with a precognitive faculty.

There were those who at once told Holroyd that he had conducted himself into a realm of very great nonsense. I have little doubt that he was inclined to agree with them, since he is (I must emphasise) a most sensible man. But at least the mathematics of the thing could be checked again from start to finish, and perhaps a new series of experiments devised. He must have been all agog to try. Yet when at this moment it so happened that he was asked to go down to Vailes he agreed at once.

Nothing could have been more characteristic of the conscientious nature of the man. I have said that he wasn't interested in ghosts, and that this was because he didn't believe in survival. Well, it wasn't a ghost that had turned up at Vailes. Not yet. But it *was* the prospect of material with a bearing on the problem of an after-life. No doubt the well-known caution of the Parapsychological Society is reflected in its having been Holroyd, more than neutral before such a conception, who was invited to act. It was also relevant that, although a much younger man, he had been an acquaintance of Lord Lucius Senderhill's.

Vailes has belonged to the Senderhill family ever since it was built by that family's founder, one Humphrey Senderhill, in the reign of Henry VIII. It is a Chinese egg of a place. Were one to remove—what would not be difficult— the Gothicizing screens of the later eighteenth century there would be disclosed an imposing early Georgian mansion by Leoni. If this in turn were demolished a Jacobean house would emerge, and within that again would be found the original Tudor dwelling. Not much of this last, indeed, might stand up long enough for inspection, but the ground-plan would at least reveal that through some four hundred years Senderhills had been moving around much the same not very conveniently planned rooms and corridors. The gardens give a similar impression of the superimpositions of successive phases of taste. What has left most impress is a cunningly contrived largeness of romantic reference. But a little scratching around would reveal the lines of forecourts, terraces, fountains, waters formally confined, and long walks once shadowed by yew hedges and fantasticated topiary towers.

All this had been good enough for the Senderhills until the mid-nineteenth century, at which time Robert Senderhill, the third Marquess of Melchester, having made a pioneering marriage with an American heiress of the first order, removed himself and his household goods to a seat of his own designing, celebrated as the last edifice of anything like its size to be achieved by a private individual in England. Henceforward no Lord Melchester lived at Vailes. It became the residence, first, of the third Marquess's second son, Lord Otho Senderhill, and, second, of Lord Lucius Senderhill, who was the third son of the fourth Marquess. It is as well to be precise about such matters, although they smell a little of Debrett.

I see, incidentally, that I have fallen into a small inaccuracy here. The Lord Melchester who deserted Vailes did not in fact take *all* his *lares et penates* with him. Being of a modern and forward-looking turn of mind, he left behind him a good deal in the way of worm-eaten furniture and darkened family portraits, together with whole vistas of mouldering volumes in quarto and folio, and even a muniment room which had evidently been no more than hastily run through for documents of surviving legal importance. As a solicitor drawing his clients in the main from the class of society—the 'landed interest', as we used to say—which the Senderhills represent, I am bound to deprecate such casual behaviour. It will be found, incidentally, to have some significance for the chronicle to which I have committed myself.

For that chronicle I have now more or less set my scene—except that a word must be said about Lucius Senderhill himself, since his death must be regarded as my starting-point. Ever since the first flourishing of the original Humphrey Senderhill, the family has been accustomed, generation by generation, to play some part in the public life of the country. It has produced one or two statesmen of major stature, as well as innumerable political figures of virtually no stature at all. It has produced bishops and admirals, generals and judges in regulation fashion. There have been eccentric Senderhills who became artists or writers—including, for example, that Timothy Senderhill who made a bold bid for the laureateship with his *Poem on the Late Promotion of Several Eminent Persons in Church and State* (of whom a number, as it happened, were Timothy's uncles and cousins). There have been a few really versatile Senderhills, who have combined the achieving of political eminence with undeniable distinction in one or another purely intellectual field.

Lucius Senderhill was one of these last. 'He divided his time,' his obituarist in *The Times* informed us, 'between the political arena and the study'—with the result that he almost became Prime Minister in 1922, and had already by that date gained a high reputation as a philosopher. Whether anybody now reads Senderhill's *Structure and Growth of the Mind* I do not know; perhaps it is at least not quite so forgotten as his kinsman Timothy's poem. But the book's title is important. Senderhill took a profound interest in psychology, and in his earliest twenties had written a brilliant review of William James's *The Varieties of Religious Experience*. Moreover he did not hesitate to support those who were at the time pressing ahead into new areas of research and speculation. And this brings me back to my friend Holroyd's Parapsychological Society. Lord Lucius was one of its founder members.

The Senderhills are a long-lived family. (Or they are so when their natural life-span is permitted them : I shall come later to one who met a most tragic death at an early age.) Lucius Senderhill had lived to be eighty-five, by which time his active career was far behind him. All sorts of 'climates', as they are now called, had changed during his later years, including that in which this business of psychical research is conducted. There was a period during which it exercised a peculiar appeal in aristocratic circles of the more intellectual kind, and in great houses like Vailes there was much solemn holding of *séances* purporting to be 'scientifically' controlled, and much ingenious thinking up of techniques for communicating with the dead. I am inclined to believe that this interest was dropped by the fashionable world when modern methods of mass slaughter produced enormous numbers of socially unassuming persons suddenly and unnaturally bereaved, with a consequent proliferation of spiritualist churches and the like. Since then, psychical research at any intellectually reputable level has tended to professionalise itself. Holroyd's dice may appear fairly crazy. But a great deal of his sort of thing—statistically oriented enquiries into extra-sensory perception and so on—now falls within the sphere of orthodox experimental psychology.

As a young man, Holroyd had been perfectly at home in Senderhill's circle. He is an Anglo-Irishman of the Cromwellian settlement, and has much of the Irishness that these invaders seem to have picked up since that time. His light-blue eyes glitter like a madman's, so that you are surprised by his academic manner (he has in fact been a Professor of Latin since a very early age) until your impression is abruptly modified by his producing an explosive burst of laughter. This is the more startling in that it is susceptible of easy phonetic analysis. Holroyd appears simply to be saying 'Ho-ho!' very loudly, and being so pleased with the result that he repeats it with a deepening resonance several times. The effect of this mere vocalising of a printed symbol of mirth might be conjectured not really to suggest overwhelming hilarity. But it does. The experience of Holroyd's laughter is disconcerting at first (after 'Ho-ho!' you rather expect him to add 'and a bottle of rum') but wholly agreeable later. It co-exists mysteriously with his underlying almost chilly intelligence and complete sobriety of judgement.

I always enjoy my encounters with Arthur Holroyd. So I was both surprised and delighted to be greeted by him under the main portico at Vailes only some ten days after Lord Lucius Senderhill's death.

2

'Ho-ho!' Holroyd said. 'Ho-ho, ho-ho! So you are to be on the rummage too.'

'My dear Holroyd, this is a great surprise. I had no idea you were to be at Vailes.' I stood beside my suitcase, and watched the cab by which I had been transported from a fairly remote railway station retreating down the drive. 'How very pleasant.'

'No idea, you say? I hope that doesn't make my position irregular, eh? Are you our late friend's executor, or anything of that kind? The Society got me here because there was a letter from a local solicitor, transmitting some expressed wish of Senderhill's recorded a long time ago. But don't let us stand around.' Holroyd dived with surprising speed for my suitcase, getting his hand on it triumphantly before me. 'You'll want to wash, my dear chap—and then we can perhaps get some tea.'

'I never acted for Lucius Senderhill in my life.' It seemed best to get my position clear. 'But Lord Melchester is a client of ours, and he's rather anxious about some of Senderhill's papers. He fixed up my coming down, I imagine, with the same local man who contacted your Society.'

'Ho-ho! A joint rummage, as I said. Now come along. I've been here only since this morning. But I'm beginning to know the ropes. Mind these steps. They're a bit slimy. Some kind of lichen, I'd say. Mixed up with last autumn's beech-leaves.'

'I see one has to be careful.' It had already become apparent that this main entrance to the solidities, indeed the splendours, of Vailes was not precisely swept and garnished. I made an unsuccessful attempt to take over my suitcase. 'Aren't there any servants?' I asked.

'All departed.'

'What an extraordinary thing!'

'Well, all except a Mrs Uff. She may be called a house-keeper in the Victorian taste. And I believe she has a daughter, although the child has not yet manifested herself. How many other servants there were—whether within or without this sizeable mansion—I don't know. Probably not many. And they've all been packed off. Quick work. One supposes there isn't too much money to spare.'

'I see.' We were now standing in a hall, delicately oval and massively marble, within the confines of which it would have been possible to mark out something like a tennis court. In sundry niches sundry Senderhills, dressed in togas, stood like ball-boys attentive to an invisible game. 'I suppose,' I said, 'that it will be made into some sort of reformatory. It was a grave folly in the third Marquess, turning Vailes into a mere bolt-hole for younger sons. *Une folie des grandeurs.* No good could come of it.'

'No doubt, no doubt. A responsible family solicitor's view. But the immediate problem is, where are you to be put up? Mrs Uff hasn't mentioned expecting you, but she is a reticent woman, so you must not lose hope.' Holroyd showed signs of saying 'Ho-ho!' again, but thought better of it. 'If we walk on into the saloon, it may be possible to ring a bell.'

At this moment, however, Mrs Uff appeared unsummoned, and proved to be a competent if commonplace woman in middle life. Moreover she had been properly apprised of my arrival, and presently led me up an imposing staircase to the chamber prepared for me. It was an enormous room, and was fitted with proportionately enormous radiators of the sort to be found in houses which pioneered the luxury of steam heating at some time during the earlier reign of Queen Victoria. A glance told me that I had no hope of them, and I was glad that we were enjoying a mild spring. With a certain restrained showmanship, Mrs Uff opened the door upon my bathroom. This was excessively lofty, was sheathed in what might have been massive bits and pieces of marble left over from the hall below, and contained a tub which struck me as adequate for the ablutions of a small elephant. The various shower and douche mechanisms were particularly elaborate. I wondered whether any hot water conceivably ran to them.

'My daughter will bring up some hot water,' Mrs Uff said, resolving this question. 'And tea will be at five. It was his late lordship's hour.' Mrs Uff appeared in no doubt that, in the persons of Holroyd and myself, it was a species of half-gentry that had begun to descend on Vailes. 'And the vicar,' she added somewhat unexpectedly, 'is coming to dinner at eight. It will be in the steward's room.' Mrs Uff paused, as if some faint dubiety had after all assailed her. 'Because I can light a fire there, sir,' she added, and with well-trained noiselessness withdrew.

The room being of a sort tolerably familiar to me, I glanced round it only absently. It contained no less than three telephones, all of them standing on the floor, and all looking as if they had been purveyed to some long-deceased Senderhill by an emissary of Mr Thomas Edison or Mr Graham Bell (as indeed they probably had). On a table beside the bed lay a bible, an excellently preserved copy of *The Wonder Book of Trains,* and a slim pink volume which might have been the *Thoughts* of Chairman Mao, but which proved to be the *Golden Sayings* of Marcus Aurelius. Only the wallpaper was Chinese, and enriching it were a few faded water-colour sketches by departed Senderhill ladies. It was evident that the intellectual interests of the late Lord Lucius had not extended to impressing themselves upon this apartment.

The thought of Lord Lucius made me reflect on the nature of my own mission to Vailes, and I decided that there was no reason why I should not communicate this quite fully to Holroyd. It was simple enough. Although he lived and died a bachelor, Lucius Senderhill had been normal in his sexual tastes, and in a discreet way by no means a stranger to women. But not, perhaps, quite *always* discreetly. There had been a couple of entanglements, known within the family, the publicising of which would be distinctly mortifying. Lord Melchester, as the family's head, was fearful that some record of these might be extant in his kinsman's papers, and had formed the somewhat irrational notion that a search should be made for them. In order to have this carried out, he needed (or believed he needed) nothing but the permission of the Trustees of the Senderhill Settled Estates. (I need not explain this. The trend of social legislation being as it is, people like the Senderhills have to protect their property through all sorts of curious inventions.) Having gained his point, he promptly called on me and asked me to undertake the job. It was, of course, very much employment for a

responsible confidential clerk. But Lord Melchester was
pressing; there seemed nothing particularly objectionable in
what Holroyd was now cheerfully terming a rummage; and
I had agreed to spend a short time at Vailes. I was not
uninfluenced by the recollection that the place was supposed
to shelter historical records going back far beyond Lord
Lucius's time, and that it might therefore be possible to
gratify certain mild antiquarian interests of my own.

There was a knock, or rather a bang, on the door, and a
young girl who I knew must be Mrs Uff's daughter entered
the bedroom. It was a singularly gauche entrance, for she
was a lumpish and awkward creature, and apparently proud
of the fact. I am not certain, indeed, that this was my sole
first impression of her. Knowing what I now know, it is easy
to persuade myself that the child (for she was little more than
that) carried some other and indefinable suggestion about
with her. But certainly she was largely unattractive.
Although somebody, presumably her mother, had
endeavoured to dress her neatly, she herself had managed—
I suppose by a toss of her hair, a twist to her dress, a wrinkle
in a stocking, the flopping carpet slippers on her feet—
to express a kind of slovenly and sullen discontent. She was
carrying a copper hot-water can of the old-fashioned sort,
and as she crossed the room without glancing at me or
speaking she contrived the further manifesto of slopping a
good saucerful of water on the carpet.

Rather oddly, it was this girl's appearance in my room
that gave me my first and only vivid sense that Lucius
Senderhill was indeed dead. (I hadn't, after all, known him
at all well.) During his lifetime, even in his last years, it
would have been impossible that so graceless an apology for
trained service should have made itself visible to a guest at
Vailes. This child—whom Senderhill's mother, if not Senderhill himself, would have described technically as an

'encumbrance'—would never have ventured beyond some baize door in the inferior regions of the mansion.

Naturally enough, I at once reproached myself for this uncharitable judgement upon a child who was only helping out her mother as well as she could. It certainly wasn't her fault that whatever footmen or housemaids there may have been' had departed. Probably she would have further unaccustomed tasks when it came to that dinner in the steward's room. In any case, I ought to try to be pleasant to her.

'Thank you very much,' I said, when she had put the hot-water in the cavernous bathroom and appeared again. 'You are Mrs Uff's daughter? What is your name?'

'Martha, sir.' The girl's expression, as she glanced at me fleetingly for the first time, was suspicious and perhaps hostile. But there was something not unattractive about her voice—and it wasn't at all that her mother had been working at her articulation in the fond hope of preparing her for good service. Her mere accent was hideous. Apart from this, she didn't improve on further scrutiny. And she certainly didn't want to cultivate my acquaintance, for she was edging in an ungainly fashion towards the door. 'Will that be all, sir?' she asked. This time, the phrase was certainly something she had been taught.

'Thank you, yes, Martha. I shall be quite comfortable.' As I uttered these words, the curious persuasion came to me that this child was frightened—more frightened than was to be counted for by her having been promoted to perform unwonted services for a stranger. It was as if she suffered a dull but burdensome apprehension that I was dangerous. So I made a further effort to get on terms with her. 'Have you and your mother been long at Vailes?'

'I never see'd nothing, nor I never done nothing!' This inconsequent reply came from Martha Uff with explosive force. Following it, she stood silent and gaping, as if shattered by her own outburst.

'My dear child,' I said, 'I think you must misunderstand me. Why—'

'Yer the police, aren't yer?'

'I'm certainly nothing of the kind!'

'But my mum says yer 'im as puts the law on people.'

'I am what is called a lawyer, Martha.' I saw that either Mrs Uff's expository power was singularly defective or that her daughter was what is euphemistically termed mentally retarded. 'But that doesn't mean I have anything to do with the police.'

' 'e'd take me into the dark to show me something.' Miss Uff again spoke with panic inconsequence. 'But 'e never managed it, 'e didn't. I never see'd nothing. I never done nothing, I say.'

I should have been a poor lawyer had I not felt at this point cogent reasons for bringing my conversation with Martha Uff to an end. On the other hand, I was not very clear that I had not a duty to proceed. The latter view—or perhaps mere curiosity—prevailed. I asked her who had been by way of taking her into the dark.

' 'im. 'is lordship. 'e'd took something into 'is 'ead, 'e 'ad. But I never—'

'All right, Martha. Perhaps we shall talk about this again. But I don't think you should speak of it too much—except, of course, to your mother. I suppose she knows about it?'

But to this I got no reply. Martha Uff had exhausted either her will or her ability to communicate. She gave me one brief look—which this time seemed less alarmed than abruptly apathetic—and slip-slopped out of the room.

Ten minutes later I quitted it myself, and as I made my way downstairs I wondered whether I ought to recount this odd episode to Holroyd. I decided to get a clearer notion of his own business at Vailes first. It seemed unlikely that some senile impropriety on Lucius Senderhill's part (for this was presumably what I had been hearing about) would be relevant to my friend's inquiries.

The steward's room proved to be rather like my own office—only somewhat larger and better appointed. Mrs Uff brought in the tea. The china and appurtenances were of a very modest sort, and it amused me to notice that Holroyd found this circumstance irritating. I was chiefly concerned, however, to take a better look at Martha's mother. She had been a good-looking woman in her day, I thought, and she was well-spoken in an upper-servant's fashion. The uncouth articulations which overlay that indefinably attractive quality in her daughter's voice probably represented the child's only substantial acquirement at the village school. I had failed to discover whether Mrs Uff had been made acquainted with Martha's adventures with her employer. If she had, she must be congratulating herself that Lord Lucius was safely dead without any positive scandal having transpired. That kind of thing can be disadvantageous to one in superior domestic employment.

Over my first cup, and between unenthusiastic nibbles at a piece of cake which seemed to be composed mainly of caraway seeds, I gave Holroyd a brief account of my mission. It was greeted with a very pardonable 'Ho-ho!'

'You think,' I said laughing, 'that I have taken on a ludicrous assignment out of an odious obsequiousness before the higher nobility.'

'No, no—nothing of the kind. Or ludicrous, yes. But your acquiescence is a matter of courtesy, my dear fellow—or, at the most, a proper deference to a former Minister of the Crown.'

'I don't think Melchester was ever anything of the sort.'

'Well, well—you know what I mean. But of course you won't find anything. Compromising outpourings in a diary?

Threatening letters from outraged husbands? Senderhill would have destroyed anything of the sort.'

'I rather agree. And even if there was anything lying around, it would be discreetly dealt with by whoever comes to do the routine tidy-up. But, on a larger view, some of the Senderhill papers may be interesting. It's said that Vailes still shelters some of them from centuries back.'

'Ho-ho! So that's it.' Holroyd was delighted. 'Then you're likely to be one up on me. Mine is going to be a wild goose chase pure and simple. It's those damned, old-fashioned cross-correspondences, you know. And similar hoary dodges. They're all more or less invalidated anyway, now that we realise the alarming range of precognitive telepathy. Nothing to prevent the living Lucius Senderhill in 1940 dropping something into the mind of somebody in 1960 or 1980.'

'Even if that person wasn't born until 1950?'

'A good question.' Holroyd was now perfectly serious. 'But let me tell you one of the things that I'm supposed to find here, and that the Society is supposed to judge significant.'

'Significant of what?'

'Of Lucius Senderhill's continued personal existence in a hereafter. He has undertaken to demonstrate it if he possibly can. And there's a notion he's picked on Mrs Gladwish. You understand me? The *deceased* Lucius has picked on the *living* Mrs Gladwish.'

'He seems not to have lost much time. But who the devil is Mrs Gladwish?'

'A highly reputable non-physical medium. Just the person to be nobbled by a lord. And she's said to have picked up some of the bits and pieces. I'm supposed to find the others—impressively under seal—in this house. It's very simple. Heroic couplets.'

'Holroyd—I think I'm right in believing that you don't
believe in all this?'

'Not in—well let's say not in the heroic couplets. If we
survive, then presumably we also *pre-exist*—and I'm blessed
if I've never been able to swallow that one. But let me *tell*
you about the heroic couplets. Here at Vailes, in the solitude
of his august library, Senderhill composed a sizeable run
of them. Or he *may* have done, for it's by no means certain
that the project ever realised itself. But say he did. He then
memorised his poem—'

'It was to be a coherent poem?'

'Certainly, but of a not too simple sort. He memorised
the thing, and then he copied out either the first or second
line of each couplet. He sealed up that copy, stowed it
somewhere or other round this house—'

'Why on earth didn't he deposit it with your Society?'

'Some notion of minimising the operation of clairvoyance.
It's all *bien vieux jeu*, as I say. And then, of course, he
burnt the original poem. You can see what is meant to
happen.'

'Mrs Gladwish falls into a trance, and produces sundry
disconnected lines of decasyllabic verse. After that has taken
place, whatever you find here at Vailes is opened, and what
is found is more lines of decasyllabic verse. Somebody does
a little piecing together, and the result is the reconstruction
of Senderhill's original rhyming poem. And half of it can
only have come, *via* Mrs Gladwish, from beyond the grave.'

'That is certainly the idea, and I won't say it isn't a clever
one. Whether there are not some soft spots in the logic—
well, that's another matter.'

'Does Mrs Gladwish realise that verse is required of her?'

'She's not supposed to. In fact, and to be fair, I think it
highly probable that none of the few people who know
about the project has *told* her. What may have seeped
around in a commonplace extra-sensory way it's quite

impossible to tell. Anyway, Mrs Gladwish *has* been producing verse.'

'The deuce she has!' As I uttered this exclamation I
felt—it is honest to record—a certain *frisson* down my spine.
It was occasioned, I believe, by the odd conjunction in
Holroyd of an icy scepticism about human survival with a
matter-of-fact acceptance of modes of mental operation
unacknowledged by orthodox science. But his voice here
was coming to *sound* like that of orthodox science. I wondered for a moment what very odd verities even an elderly
person like myself might be obliged to acknowledge before
he died.

'I have to look out for other things as well—with an
account of which I needn't trouble you. It may all take
some time.' Holroyd picked up the teapot, the spout of
which was defective. 'I shall have a word with Mrs Uff,'
he said. 'She must be apprised of our consequence.'

'I shall be interested to see if you succeed.' Although my
friend had not accompanied his remark with his familiar
laugh, it didn't occur to me that he was serious. 'Are your
small expectations of anything significant turning up a
matter of your impression of Lucius Senderhill? I have a
notion you knew him quite well.'

'It wasn't really a close acquaintance. But I have my
picture of the man.'

'He lived to a notable old-age.' I hesitated—and when I
went on it was with Martha Uff's imperfect revelation
in my mind. 'Did he become any sort of nuisance in his last
years?'

'Not that I've ever heard of.' Holroyd looked at me in
surprise. 'Although it's likely enough that he was tiresome
in some ways. You must ask Mrs Uff.'

'I don't know that it would be very proper to do that.'

'Then you must ask Tommy Hartsilver. He's the local
padre, and I've invited him to dinner. Mrs Uff has taken it

quite well. Hartsilver and I were at King's together. He saw a lot of Senderhill, I believe. We must pump him hard.'

'I'll be delighted to meet him.' I had put down my cup and walked to a window, and it was only inattentively that I produced this conventional response. Nor did I much heed Holroyd's vision of the two of us as remorseless investigators. What occupied me was the prospect with which the late Lord Lucius's steward had been in a position to refresh himself. There was nothing about it that could be described as in any grand manner—by which I mean contrived vistas closed by artificial ruins, or classical belvederes, or bridges of Palladian elaboration conducting over artificial waters to columns and obelisks commemorating forgotten grandees. The hand of man was not immediately evident either upon the margins of the lake which lay before me or in the glades which opened amid the woods surrounding it. Here and there a simple wooden structure crossed a small tributary stream, and in the foreground there was a boat-house so plain that it could scarcely be described even as of rustic character. In some of the gentle declivities leading to the water a mist was gathering—for the greater part transpicuous and faintly luminous, but in places thickening to a texture not penetrable by the low light of late afternoon. 'It's hard to see where art comes in,' I said to Holroyd, who had joined me. 'But such compositions aren't just achieved by chance.'

'Behind that sort of thing, I suppose, are the painters called the *Romantiques*. Corot, eh? The indifferent tranquillity of nature is very much a creation of the mind. But wait till after dinner, when you see it as a nocturne. Not that it isn't extremely pleasing now.' Holroyd's appreciative note was a shade perfunctory. 'Attractive, I agree.'

'Precisely that. It draws one. If one had once known it well, one would always want to return to it.'

'Ho-ho! Haunt it, would you say? Let us be off to the library, my dear chap, and decide where to begin.

'Very well.' But for a moment I lingered by the window—chiefly because in a clearing beyond the lake (which lay some eighty yards from the house, and was itself at this point perhaps eighty yards wide) there had appeared a couple of fallow-deer, delicately grazing. They were, I think, does, and in the fading light their still unspotted winter coats made their presences scarcely distinguishable. They too were *romantique*, and I wondered whether they belonged to a considerable herd. I also wondered whether there was a practicable path round the lake. I would explore it, I told myself, on the following day.

3

Dinner happened in a candle-lit dining-room, after all, and I wondered what Holroyd had done to bring this about. I suspected him of having amused himself by communicating to Mrs Uff not his own respectable connections but what he could invent of mine. However this may have been, the change of plan was far from conducing to our comfort, since the dining-room at Vailes proved predictably vast, chilly, and bleakly august. Nor, I imagine, did it conduce to Martha Uff's comfort either. She had conceivably been admitted at times to wait upon the late Lord Lucius's steward, but it is improbable that she had so much as been inside the awesome room in and out of which she now had to scurry with plates and dishes. The poor child had been bereft of her carpet slippers, and had even been thrust without verisimilitude or impressiveness into an apron and cap. It was hard not to let some feeling for her sufferings—although these indeed continued to be of a sullen and un-appealing sort—impose a note of constraint upon the meal.

Fortunately Holroyd's friend Hartsilver turned out to be a conversable man. He even extracted a word or two from Martha—whom it was no doubt incumbent upon him to acknowledge as a parishioner as well as a servant. And when the girl had brought in some tolerable coffee and departed for good, and Holroyd had mysteriously produced cigars, I found myself much at ease with the vicar.

'You must have realised,' I said, 'that Holroyd and I are both here more or less as what are called private enquiry agents. It's a lowly calling. Holroyd says we must pump you hard.'

'He was the most unscrupulous man of his year.'

'Ho-ho! What about your grandmother's funeral on Derby Day, Tommy?'

I had to listen for some time to exchanges of this sort, but eventually the talk came round to Lucius Senderhill. I cannot imagine that he could have been in any sense a believing Christian, and indeed within Vailes itself there was a totally derelict private chapel to prove the point. It appeared however that some inherited feudal feeling had made him exact in public observances; that he had from Hartsilver's first appearance in the parish shown him what Jane Austen would have called every proper attention; and that in his last years the vicar had been as close a companion as he had. I couldn't very well—or not yet—enquire whether Senderhill had latterly formed the undesirable habit of taking young girls into dark places. But I could find out something about the general character of the man.

'Psychical research,' I said, 'isn't my affair. But Senderhill's addiction to it does interest me. What made him go in for it?'

'I can answer that one.' Holroyd, who had been very scandalously investigating sundry sideboards, commodes, wines cases and spice cabinets, triumphantly flourished a bottle of brandy. 'Tommy,' he said, 'will you get some glasses from over there? The answer is straight intellectual curiosity. Senderhill was one of the ablest men of his time, and he took all sorts of speculative and experimental interests in his stride.'

'I question whether that's the whole story,' Hartsilver said. Quite as unblushing as Holroyd in his depredations, he had set three substantial goblets on the table. 'Are individuals any longer described as psychic, Arthur? It used to be a common term when I read about such things.'

'It's a perfectly useful one, no doubt. The jargon changes. The "psi-factor" is all the go now. "How's your psi-factor this morning?" Ho-ho! But some people are undoubtedly more susceptible to paranormal experiences than others. Not Lucius Senderhill, though. His interest was entirely objective and from the outside.'

'Are you quite sure of that?' It seemed to me that the vicar was faintly amused by his old friend's dogmatism.

'Certainly I am—unless he prevaricated about it. He always insisted that no psychic experience had ever come his way.'

'Then he *was* prevaricating—unless he once prevaricated to me.' Hartsilver hesitated. 'He hasn't been long in his grave. Is there almost a breach of confidence in this talk?'

'My dear Tommy, we'll drop it if you think we ought. It's just that one wants to get, if one can, at the truth of certain matters.'

'To be sure. And, after all, there's no scandal in the thing.' Hartsilver consulted his goblet contentedly. 'I suppose that with all of us there are things that used to happen, and that now happen no more.'

'Wordsworth,' Holroyd said.

'Yes, yes—a very good illustration. But what about something happening to a man just *once*? There are plenty of records of that too—some of them carrying the highest spiritual significance.' The vicar was silent for a moment. 'And other perceptions, other ecstasies. Just once.'

'Um,' Holroyd said cautiously.

'Or something, not clearly meaningful in itself, the mere isolation of which in a man's experience renders it tanta-lising, haunting, over the rest of a lifetime. One might readily turn cagey about such a thing, and be reluctant to acknowledge it as motivating—well, say intellectual enquiry into the nature of apparitions, hallucinations, ghosts, and so on. Arthur, you would agree?'

'Yes, of course.' Holroyd was almost in danger of letting his cigar go out. 'And you're describing Senderhill—on the strength of something you know about him?'

'On the strength of something he told me, and apparently never told anybody else. Which makes this a little awkward for me, Arthur.'

'Yes, yes.' Holroyd controlled himself. 'It's a subject that you might perhaps think of coming back to another time.'

'Well, say just a little later.' Hartsilver turned to me. 'Do you feel, may I ask, the present emptiness of this vast house? Almost, I mean, as a physical oppression?'

'I certainly do.'

'If there's a soul beside the Uffs, it will be merely a woman brought in from one of the cottages to wash up. Of course, when Senderhill was alive, there were other servants as well—and a number of outdoor people whom I used to think—particularly in any sort of bad weather—rather largely indoor too. Still, there's been this empty feel about the place for a long time. Senderhill himself became aware of it.'

'I don't know why he should,' Holroyd said. 'Not with a whole staff running around, even if no longer on an Edwardian scale.'

'Perhaps,' I suggested, 'he didn't count servants. When he

was without relatives or guests here, he regarded himself as
quite alone.'

'The empty palace,' Holroyd said a shade informatively,
'is a potent symbol in the unconscious mind. But so is a
commonplace empty house. I believe it's easier to feel
menaced by solitude in an untenanted building than in a
desert. But, Tommy, has this anything to do with some
psychic experience Senderhill had—once and once only?
That's what you were getting round to.'

'Yes, indeed. But the lonely mansion is only relevant, as
a matter of fact, to his having confided in me. That, I think,
was a matter of his sense of solitude here. The time had
come when he was too old and ill to retain old associations
on an intellectual plane, or much in the way of social
associations either. An extreme old age without family ties
is bound to be a solitary affair, and living on in a great
place like this can only enhance the condition. That's why
Senderhill took to talking to me a good deal. He was
uninterested in religion, I'm sorry to say, and he was reticent
on personal matters, so we tended to discuss literature and
philosophy. We weren't at all up to date. Bradley, Moore,
Whitehead. Gissing's novels, Meredith's poetry. Then—
quite suddenly one evening, and in this very room—he
made me a curious confidence. Which *was* very personal!'
The vicar paused, and remembered his brandy. Then he
glanced across the room. 'Arthur,' he went on, 'do you
know, I've a fancy to have those curtains drawn back? The
moon must be up by now. Let us add its illumination to
that of Mrs Uff's candles.'

Buried in Hartsilver, I can now see, was a certain instinct
for the theatre, and the next few minutes were given up to
a kind of innocent stage management. We had been permitted a little warmth from an ancient electric radiator on
a trailing cord, and Holroyd so arranged this that it

continued its office when we disposed our chairs in a half-
circle near the window. Before us now was a great sheet of
glass in which the candle-flames behind us were reflected
only as small smears of light : they might have been phos-
phorescent streaks, fire-drakes, Jack-o'-Lanterns far out on
the surface of the lake. Holroyd had promised me a nocturne,
and here was his friend the vicar providing me with it. These
faint lights which seemed to hover deep in a silvery greyness
ought to have provided, indeed, a nocturne in the manner of
Whistler. Yet the effect was not at all of minor artistic
delectation. It was mysteriously disturbing, as if the scene
were oriented not quite within the spatial dimensions of
common experience. I can only think that the mere disposition of its planes—the horizontality of the lake, the
several obliquities of glade and valley and beech-wood as
the moonlight softly bathed them beyond—fortuitously built
up a formal relationship having the power to create some
out-of-the-way, perhaps some atavistic, reverberation in the
mind. Even so, the prospect remained by night, as it was
by day, steeped in a tranquil beauty.

'A peaceful spot,' Hartsilver said, much as if echoing my
thought. And then he added : 'Which makes Senderhill's
experience the more surprising.'

'Speak up, Tommy. There's no going back on it now.'
Holroyd appeared to cast round in his mind for further
encouragement. 'And it sounds like something that my
highly respectable Society should know.'

'He didn't think to communicate it to you, all the same.
Perhaps that was because it begins with a love-story.'

'A love-story ! Senderhill ?'

'Yes, indeed. I know what you are going to say, Arthur.
Lord Lucius was tolerably well known to his own circle as
having kept clear of women except at the level of—well,
call it cold pleasure. But that was a consequence—this is
the gist of what he told me—of the burnt child dreading

fire. As a young man, and only shortly after he came to live at Vailes, he fell very much in love. Who the girl was, or what the circumstances, I don't know. Even in this sudden confidence he made me, he managed to preserve a great deal of reticence. What he insisted on was the force and depth of his passion, and the absolutely catastrophic manner in which the affair was brought to an end.'

'The girl jilted him—or died?'

'Once again, I don't know. But he was a man of powerful intellect, as you have said, and also with what one imagines to have been a strength of character that would stand up to a good deal. So one must suppose something pretty stiff, since it had the effect of never again letting him risk giving his heart away. It induced immediately an acute nervous illness—the kind of attack which in those days was called brain fever. When he emerged from that it was into a deeply depressed state. So he was sent round the world—it was the regular thing—and either that or the mere healing touch of time got him reasonably straight again. A year after his calamity he was back at Vailes and leading a normal life. And not yet a lonely life; his political career was opening before him, and he was making his way impressively among the *savants* as well. A sister came and presided over his household from time to time, so that he was able to do a good deal of entertaining on the scale judged appropriate in a house like this before the Kaiser's War.

'The second anniversary approached—the anniversary, I mean, of that death, betrayal, dire revelation, or whatever it may have been. Senderhill took it into his head to confront it alone, here at Vailes. His sister was abroad, he emptied his house of bachelor guests, the very day came round.'

'So there was an actual day?' Holroyd asked. 'His disaster could be pin-pointed like that?'

'Apparently so. The day came round, and it closed with

Lucius Senderhill sitting where we are sitting now—looking out over that lake, which was illuminated by just that moon.'

'Really, Tommy—'

'Please listen. I'm not, I promise you, telling a tall story. It was a calm night with a clear sky, and in the air there was still the warmth from what had been a hot summer day. Senderhill got up and threw this window wide open, stood looking out for some moments, and then sat down again. He became aware of a deep nervous perturbation, which reminded him of the onset of his illness two years before. He told himself that he was in a fever—and then suddenly he felt very cold. It *was* very cold. He had a curious certainty of this as an objective fact, and there flitted through his mind the prosaic idea of summoning his butler to discuss with him so unusual a climatic phenomenon. Then he saw that he was no longer looking at the lake—or not at the lake as it had been a moment before, or as it it is for us now. He was looking at a sea-storm, at a tempest, at waves which could be called mountains high.'

'Was it a noisy storm?' Holroyd asked. His tone was casual, but his blue eyes had even more than their accustomed brightness. 'A howling gale?'

'Nothing of the kind. It was like, he said, a silent movie. There was obviously a great hullabaloo, but you had to imagine it on your inner ear. He rather thought that the sky had darkened, or that clouds were scudding across it and casting a dramatically changing chiaroscuro over the scene. But he couldn't be sure. Because, after a first couple of seconds, his attention was entirely riveted on the ship.'

'The ship!' I exclaimed. My gaze had happened to be on the little boathouse, which was in part outlined against the motionless and moon-blanched water beyond. It might contain, I supposed, a dinghy, a punt. 'He saw a ship?'

'A barque, he called it—and he intended the word in its

technical, not its poetic sense. Its mizen mast was down, and
on the fore and main masts there was only a tatter of canvas.
Suddenly the barque's stern went up in air, and she sank
rapidly beneath—well, call it the sea, the lake, or what you
will. Senderhill believed that he cried out, or tried to cry
out. And then it was all over. He was looking again at
what we are looking at now.'

There was a momentary silence in which, having withdrawn my gaze from the lake, I glanced curiously at Hartsilver. It was certainly true that he had been without the
intention of telling us a tall story. But what about Senderhill himself—had he perhaps been amusing himself by
pulling his vicar's leg? I judged it improbable. Senderhill
might conceivably have fabricated a tale of the supernatural;
it was impossible to think of him beginning it with the
avowal of a non-existent—or even existent—tragic love-
affair.

'Well?' I heard Holroyd say.

'That was Senderhill's entire narrative.' Hartsilver
sounded puzzled. 'Do you expect a sequel to it?'

'Yes, of course. The experience bears all the marks of
what is called a crisis-apparition. One would expect it to
prove to have been coincidental with some actual shipwreck
somewhere around the globe, probably involving a person
or persons known to Senderhill.'

'He made that point himself. But nothing of the kind
was ever heard of.'

'Then we are in the region of fairy-tales. Some family
legend of a stock supernatural manifestation, intermittently
turning up in an unvarying form for centuries, and presaging
sudden death or what-have-you.'

'There is no family legend. Senderhill could connect it
with nothing at all. And nothing whatever succeeded upon
it.'

'It ought to have been investigated at the time.' Holroyd
had shrugged his shoulders. 'Nothing can be done about it
now.'

'But, speaking of investigation,' I asked, 'was this vision
the prompting occasion of Senderhill's interesting himself
in psychical research?'

'Certainly it was,' Hartsilver said. 'Even although some
deep reserve made him refrain from bringing forward the
actual circumstance to his fellow-investigators. And I come
back to what I said earlier. That isolated and utterly
unaccountable experience haunted him for the rest of his
days. He craved more of the same thing. He felt *entitled*
to more of the same thing, and yet he couldn't come by it.
Does that sound a little mad?'

'Not in the least. It's common enough.' Holroyd had got
up and was pacing restlessly about the large tenebrous
dining-room. 'Only it doesn't often express itself in wide-
ranging intellectual enquiry and experiment.'

'Like the composing of your blessed heroic couplets,' I
said. 'There's not much connection between *that* and a
spectral shipwreck.'

'Perfectly true.' Holroyd halted abruptly. 'I suppose there
were still plenty of barques sailing the seven seas when
Senderhill was a young man?'

'Good lord, yes!' I said. 'Barques and schooners and
clippers and whatever you like.'

'Looking much as they'd looked for centuries?'

'I wouldn't quite say that.' I realised what was in Holroyd's mind. 'No doubt if a ghost turns up in doublet and
hose one notes the fact as having chronological significance.
And if it had been, say, a seventeenth-century shipwreck
that appeared to Senderhill he'd probably have been
conscious of the craft as belonging to a past age. But
nothing of the sort might be apparent if his marine drama
belonged even to the earlier nineteenth century.' I turned

to Hartsilver. 'This affair made Lucius Senderhill a foun-
dation member of the Parapsychological Society. But do you
happen to know whether he went in for enquiry and
experiment in a purely private way? And locally?'

'Well, to the end of his life the lake held a fascination
for him. There can be no doubt about that. He was for ever
prowling restlessly round it. He regarded it as numinous, I
suppose, or as a spot where some mysterious revelation was
peculiarly likely to take place. He would have wished to
believe that if he gazed out over it long enough—and
particularly at night—a second and more meaningful preternatural experience might be granted him. But it wasn't. So
he came to believe that he himself commanded only a very
limited responsiveness to such things—or perhaps with the
passing of the years had ceased to command any at all. He
just wasn't "psychic" in the sense we were speaking of. And
he very much wanted to find somebody who was.'

'Do you mean,' I asked, 'that he would bring down
mediums and other psychically well-accredited persons to
gorp and gape at that lake by moonlight?'

'He well may have done. But it was rather his idea—he
explained this to me—that somebody with the right sensitive-
ness should have a *spontaneous* experience here, just as he
himself had done, long ago. He thought, for example, that
an adolescent—' Hartsilver broke off in perplexity. 'My
dear sir,' he said to me, 'have I been so very amusing?'

It was true that I had produced a laugh not much less
explosive than Holroyd's own—for I was oddly relieved at
having a small squalid notion thus dissipated.

'I'm sorry,' I said. 'But it happens that you have restored
the late Lord Lucius in my regard. I now know why he
took Mrs Uff's daughter into the dark, with vague promises
of showing her something.'

'Showing her something?'

'Yes—but she never see'd nothing.' I controlled my

hilarity, and glanced at Holroyd. 'Poor Martha's psi-factor is negligible.' I paused, rather expecting that my friend would be as amused as myself. But his response surprised me.

'Do you know,' he said, '—and I speak as what you might call an expert in such things—that I'd rather suppose it wasn't that way with the girl at all?'

'My dear Holroyd, you've scarcely had a word with her.'

'Very true.' Again Holroyd shrugged his shoulders. 'But one gains these impressions rather rapidly at times.'

'I must be off to the vicarage.' Hartsilver had got to his feet. 'How fortunate that I don't have to cross the lake! I'd hate to be tempest-toss'd after so very tolerable a dinner.'

We saw the vicar through the saloon, past the blind gaze of the toga'd Senderhills in the chilly hall, down the hazardous steps beneath the portico, and into his modest Mini car. Then we watched him down the drive, and returned into the house.

'Tomorrow,' Holroyd said a little grimly as we parted for the night, 'we get to work.'

4

And indeed we went to work faithfully enough. For my own part, I quickly came to see that I should remain long at Vailes only under false pretences. The papers left by Lord Lucius Senderhill bore no reference to his private life; they were exclusively scientific, or philosophical, or of a sort to interest political historians of the earlier twentieth century; and they were destined for the library of Senderhill's old college at Cambridge, where they would be available to all properly qualified persons. Lord Melchester's apprehensiveness was entirely unjustified.

Arthur Holroyd, too, looked like drawing a blank or

near-blank. The poem in heroic couplets had never got itself
written, and a brief jotting in one of Senderhill's scientific
notebooks simply gave reasons (of which Holroyd approved)
for abandoning the project as invalid. I am bound to say
that I was amused at the thought of Mrs Gladwish conjuring
her decasyllables from the void in vain.

This particular negative result did not quite licence my
friend to pack up and go. There is a theory, it seems, that
the mind or personality may survive *for a short time*—
disintegrating slowly, so that its final dissolution is postponed
weeks or months beyond the period of bodily death. For
some reason which did not become clear to me, this made
desirable an immediate and rapid survey of such of Senderhill's papers as were devoted to psychic matters. The task
was going to take several days. Perhaps I may so far run
ahead as to say that here, too, nothing material was to
emerge—or nothing beyond those marginally and dubiously
significant data with which I understand the annals of
psychical research overflow.

It is, in fact, fair to warn the reader that I have reached
a point in my narrative at which Lord Lucius Senderhill
must a little retreat into its background—although to make
way, indeed, for other, and earlier, Senderhills. His sole
substantial link with what I have now to reveal is the vision
once mysteriously granted to him through his dining-room
window.

That vision—or the vicar's account of it—had increased
my own disposition to explore the lake, but Holroyd's very
proper insistence on 'work' had the consequence of a couple
of days having passed before I was able to do so. On a
bright and rather blowy spring morning the scene, naturally
enough, held nothing of the haunting quality that moonlight
had shed on it. There was now a sparkle over the surface
of the water, which was stirred by the breeze to a semblance

of tiny breakers feeling their way, not quite noiselessly, through the pebbles which here and there lay in a tumble below the bank. I wondered whether, if one lay flat on the turf and cultivated a Lilliputian eye, one could magnify this into such a sea-storm as Senderhill had glimpsed, and even see as cliffs of foam the willows whitening on the farther shore, and as great inland mountains the beech-woods lying beyond.

The path I followed was to some extent overgrown; there was meadow-sweet to trample down, and here and there a trail of bramble trammelled the foot. Yet I saw signs of recent passage, so that I wondered who now came this way, and whether even in the last days of his life Lucius Sender-hill had managed to frequent the lakeside. There was a beguiling abundance of water-fowl : coot, mallard, pintail duck—some with their young already in their wake, pro-gressing with the just perceptible jerkiness of small mechanical toys. Ahead of me endlessly distraught lapwings quartered the air, wildly crying.

I saw that the lake, although narrow, was not much less than a mile long, and that the mansion, with its offices, outbuildings, and little boathouse, lay at one end of it. There was no reason why, if the path permitted, I should not make the complete circuit in an hour's stroll, so I put the unconvincing Gothic front of the house behind me, and set off.

I have sketched the scene, and I have no doubt that my appreciation of it was lively enough. Yet I was not half-way down the lake before I had fallen into an abstraction effectively diverting my attention from my surroundings. At breakfast Holroyd had said something about the Census of Hallucinations, by which I supposed him to mean an ordered and classified record, no doubt compiled by his Society, of just such experiences as Senderhill had recounted to Hartsilver. I wondered just how common such visitations were. I had myself never contrived to do more than (as I think Shakespeare has it) suppose a bush a bear, nor could I recall anyone recounting to me anything more than momentary aberrations of a similar trivial kind. I wondered whether by any chance Senderhill himself had ever been on a sinking ship, or whether perhaps some ancestor of his had been lost at sea. There was scope for inquiry here, I thought, and I resolved to discuss the matter with Holroyd.

I tried to create for myself the experience of suddenly being confronted with a tempest more magical than Prospero's. What would one chiefly feel? I recalled reading somewhere that supernatural apparitions seldom rouse terror —and sometimes not even surprise, let alone disbelief—at the actual time of their occurrence. But surely Senderhill must have been unnerved—and not least by the unnatural *silence* in which the fated ship went down? Yet, I remembered, such is supposed to be the general way with hallucinations; they are seldom accompanied by auditory phenomena. What about olfactory sensations? There is something peculiarly primitive about the sense of smell which one might rather expect to be exploited in psychical experience. Through that dining-room window, and in that balmy summer night, had Lucius Senderhill's nostrils been suddenly assailed by the tang of a salt ocean air?

I had got so far in these mere ruminations when I found myself abruptly at a halt. Something sharp-scented had caught at my breath, and for a second I really believed that it was the odour of the sea.

In fact it was quite different. I had passed the end of the lake unnoticing; the terrain had in consequence slightly changed; the smell was of wild mint crushed beneath my feet. There is nothing briny about wild mint, and I was amused by the false association my absorption had prompted. Turning round, I had a view up the length of the lake, with the small boathouse just visible in the distance, and behind it one wing of Vailes itself—the greater part of the house being from here invisible behind a clump of trees in the park. I saw that the route by which I might return along the farther bank was a regular bridle-path, which in the other direction wound away through beech woods on a line approximately continuing that of the lake itself. I was now as far afield as I had intended to go, but the continuing path somehow invited further enterprise. So I left the lake behind me, and plunged into the wood.

Wherever the trees thinned a little there was a carpeting of bluebells and pink campion, and at one point the path passed through a hawthorn copse in which the buds were still sealed close amid a foliage of brilliant green. Presently I was aware of a larger clearing, the ruins of a cottage in the middle of it, and a woman riding past it, rather bumpily, on a bicycle. I was a good deal surprised to find that my encounter was with Mrs Uff.

She dismounted as I approached, and I saw that she proposed to speak to me—a civility which I took as a further token of the success with which Holroyd had persuaded her of what he called our consequence. I made a remark about the quality of the day, and Mrs Uff further indicated her respect by precisely concurring in my estimate of it. I then said something about the trouble we must be giving her in view of the fact that she and her daughter were now virtually unsupported at Vailes. She replied to the effect that she relished a little professional labour, since it helped to occupy her mind in this melancholy period after his lordship's decease. And she volunteered the information that her present expedition had been a marketing one in the interest of that evening's dinner.

Although a full basket on the handlebars of Mrs Uff's bicycle substantiated this claim, I found myself oddly persuaded that here was not, at least, the sole explanation of the house-keeper's presence on the spot at which I had come upon her. Wherever she had been collecting her poultry and fruit, it seemed improbable that so rough a path represented her best return route. Rather more than by this, however, I was struck by a certain constraint in the woman, as if she were uneasy at having been encountered where she had. And there was something yet further. One cannot have worked for long as a solicitor without coming to know when a client or acquaintance is hesitating on the verge of making a confidence or seeking counsel in a difficulty. And some instinct told me in what general direction any problem of Mrs Uff's was likely to lie.

I remarked that a capable girl like Martha must be a great support to her, and then offered the sage conjecture that the girl was no doubt holding the fort for her at Vailes at that moment.

'No,' Mrs Uff said, 'she's not at the house.' And suddenly she added, 'As a matter of fact, sir, I have an eye open for her now.'

'Ah, Martha likes rambling? Well, it's a very pleasant part of the country for that.'

'Yes, sir.' Mrs Uff hesitated, as if uncertain whether to construe this casual rejoinder favourably. 'She goes off, and that's the fact,' she said. 'Sometimes by day, and sometimes in the dark.'

'And it worries you, I see.' The word *dark* had naturally put me in mind of Martha Uff's recent history : both my suspicions about Lucius Senderhill's nocturnal occasions with her, and the respectable if eccentric explanation these had proved to carry. I hadn't the least idea whether Mrs Uff knew that her late employer had cherished the hope that her daughter might possess psychical or preternatural powers. But it was possible that she might be attributing Martha's unsettled behaviour to Senderhill's concern with her—and if this were so it seemed to me that she ought to have made clear to her what the nature of that concern had been. So I resolved on a certain measure of frankness. 'Do you think,' I asked, 'that Lord Lucius had anything to do with setting Martha wandering?'

'Yes and no.' Mrs Uff, although startled by my question, rose to it with what I could see was relief—the relief of having taken a plunge. 'It may be he ended by putting things in her head, sir. But she was a strange girl before that. And it was her being strange that made him interested-like.'

'I see.' I noted, as rather touching, that the idiom of the folk was likely to return to the superior Mrs Uff under stress of strong feeling. 'But just how was Martha strange in the first place?'

'She wasn't right at school, sir, for a start. They said that if she was to learn her reading and ciphering, it would have to be at some special place. His lordship acted very generously, as soon as he learnt about that—and it was before he took his queer kind of special interest in her. He offered to send Martha to a boarding school that wouldn't be any kind of national school at all. A school where the gentry send their children of Martha's sort. He said more could be done for her in such a place, where there would be plenty of teachers and equipment and money. And it would be all at his lordship's charge.'

'But you didn't agree, Mrs Uff?'

'It would still have been a place for defectives. There would have been talk.' Mrs Uff was silent for a moment, while I registered in myself a certain respect for her thus taking a stand firmly with her own order. 'And I thought perhaps I could take her through a bit more than her A.B.C. myself.'

'I quite understand your feeling, Mrs Uff. Is Martha an excitable girl?'

'She didn't use to be. But when her womanhood began

to come to her, then she did start having her hysterical times.'

'I'm sorry to hear that. But it's something that is likely to pass away later.' I am no Arthur Holroyd, but I did now recognis: in Martha Uff a psychological type which turns up often enough in the field in which his interest lies. 'Would you say that Martha—' I broke off, conscious that Mrs Uff's attention had momentarily strayed from me. And it had strayed to the small and unimposing ruin close to where we stood. 'Is this,' I emended, 'one of the places Martha wanders off to?'

'Yes, sir—here and round the lake. It was her liking the lake that first struck his lordship, you see. But it was mostly here she used to come. She'd bring her work to near this ruined cottage, and sit with it all day long. And so she will still. It's one of the things I dread about probably having to leave Vailes, sir—that it will upset Martha so. She can do very fair plain sewing, Martha can; and it's here she does it. Mr Hartsilver—who dined at the house last night— encourages her at that. He says her work is just right for some of them in Africa.'

'I'm sure it is.' My own gaze in turn had now strayed to the ruin. The stone walls of the cottage nowhere rose more than a couple of feet above the foundations, and for the most part hemlock and nettle and thistle obscured what remained. There was nothing romantic about it. And such feeling as it might evoke—the pathos inherent in any memorial of humble life long passed away—seemed of a kind to be experienced in maturity rather than by a child. Had it been the mouldering mass of a mediaeval castle that confronted us, I could better have understood Martha Uff's haunting the place. 'Do you know anything about this ruin?' I asked.

'No, sir. But it looks to have been like that for a very long time.'

'I agree—perhaps for a hundred years or more. It must be on the Vailes estate?'

'Indeed, it must be. It's still Senderhill land here, these many miles around. A keeper's cottage, this might have been. Or it might be a water-bailiff's.' The altitude of Mrs Uff's domestic service seemed to come through in her familiarity with a term like this. 'But I never heard tell any stories about it.'

'Mrs Uff, would you call your daughter a secretive child?'

'As the grave.'

'I think there are things she is afraid to tell.' I had been startled by the sudden vehemence of Mrs Uff's speech, and my professional instinct to speak in a measured way was aroused. 'All in good time, it might be desirable to win her confidence, and hear about them. Do you think Lord Lucius first became greatly interested in her because of something she told him?'

'No, sir, I don't. It was just her loving to walk round the lake, and gaze at it.'

'And to come and sit in this clearing, beside this ruin?'

'Not that, sir. I don't think his lordship got to know about that. You see, it was the lake that he had what you might call a thing about. Or so I thought.'

'I happen to know that you are quite right, Mrs Uff. Lord Lucius hoped your daughter might see something on the lake that—well, that not many people would see.'

To my considerable surprise, Mrs Uff crossed herself. And she must have noticed my remarking the fact, since she offered an explanation at once.

'Yes, sir—I was brought up in the old faith, and I remained with it when married. But in my way of service, if you can't be with the Catholic gentry, it's convenient not to mind taking up with the local thing.' Mrs Uff paused, but not through any consciousness of having smartly characterised the Anglican communion. 'We knew, of course, all

of us at Vailes, that his lordship had his interest in matters
that, like enough, are not meant for man to know. But quite
harmless, it seemed to be. Nothing to do with witches or
black magic or the like—which is what some in rural parts
get mixed up with. It went into books for the learned, did
the manner of inquiring into such things that his lordship
had. Or so Mr Hartsilver has told me. That would be right,
sir?'

'Oh, most decidedly. But tell me, Mrs Uff.' I had resolved
to put one question boldly. 'Is it your belief that Martha has
indeed—well, seen things?'

'Now, sir, that's not easy to answer.' Mrs Uff had given
me a wary look. 'But I'm sure she hasn't seen what his
lordship wanted her to see.'

Since it would have been awkward to trot beside Mrs Uff
on her bicycle, and not too easy to sustain a conversation
had we proceeded together on foot, I returned to Vailes on
the side of the lake by which I had come. Like Mrs Uff, I
kept an eye open for the errant Martha, but to no effect.
I went over in my mind my very brief conversation with the
child on the afternoon of my arrival, and endeavoured to
compare it with what her mother had told me. The implication of Mrs Uff's final speech had been that Martha,
although she had proved unavailing for Senderhill's purpose,
was to be suspected of having had some positive uncanny
experience of her own—which, however, being secret 'as the
grave', she had determinedly kept to herself. What I myself
had received from Martha had borne the appearance of a
comprehensive denial of having 'seen' anything at all—as
also, indeed, of having 'done' anything. But she might have
been telling the truth about herself vis-à-vis Senderhill while
being less than candid about some other matter. She had
been alarmed, and had talked about the police. There had

also been about her—I now recalled—an indefinable air of
guarding or protecting I didn't at all know what.

But what might a country girl 'see' that would make her
apprehensive of the local constable? A crime or deed of
violence was one answer; had Martha been the witness to
such a thing and failed to speak up about it, she might soon
come to feel that her silence constituted implication. Or
might the unlawfulness consist not in the thing seen but in
the seeing? There came into my head as I asked myself this
the memory that a rural community is insatiably inquisitive.
Glancing through windows, peering over hedges, lurking to
look or listen : the rustic world described by Thomas Hardy,
for example, is prolific in such behaviour, which is regarded
as common form. In a village school one learns that certain
enterprises of this sort are 'rude', and that the village policeman may have something to say to children who thus peep
at unsuitable activities. Could something in this general area
be operative in Martha Uff's mind?

Perhaps I should add that I didn't carry my speculation
far. For one thing, it somehow failed to answer to my sense
of this particular girl. Mentally Martha was on the half-
witted side; and she was lumpish and sullen and awkward
and slatternly. But lurking in her I had felt the potentiality
for some sort of response to experience that would not be
despicable. There had been a quality in her voice, I remembered, distinguishable beneath her uncouth accent, that had
said something of the sort to me. I couldn't see her as
engaged, at least, in the baser sort of peeping.

Outside the house, I encountered Holroyd. He had the
appearance of having been minded to come and look for
me—and also of severity, as if he judged that I had been
neglecting my duties. He had himself, I knew, been up in
what was called the muniment room—where I had specifically obtained permission to make what researches I

pleased, but which I should have thought to be a little outside my friend's concern. This last was a persuasion in which I was to prove strikingly mistaken.

'I've had a very enjoyable walk,' I said blandly. 'I wish I'd been able to persuade you to accompany me.'

'You'll stop wishing anything of the kind, when you hear what I *have* been doing. Ho-ho, ho-ho!'

'Well?' I demanded—for I realised that it was a triumphant man who stood before me.

'That shipwreck, my dear fellow. I've found it. It was in 1832. The barque *Gloriana* out of Plymouth. Lost with all hands.'

5

'1832, and no survivors?' We faced each other in the library —to which Holroyd, a hand on my elbow, had impulsively led me. The Gothicising of Vailes had been carried into few of its interior features, but this was one of them. The room gave the effect of a chunk of Scott's Abbotsford (or, I suppose, Beckford's Fonthill) lurking like a foreign body in an alien organism. The books were less shelved than entombed, and there was nothing to sit on that looked more comfortable than a choir-stall. Senderhill's working quarters had been elsewhere—in a study combining modern convenience with Georgian elegance, but in that we had for some reason refrained from ensconcing ourselves.

'All hands, and all passengers too. In the Bay of Biscay.'

'Then that disposes of one idea that has passed through my mind.' I sat down gingerly on a settle of the kind on which lovers gaze into one another's eyes in Pre-Raphaelite canvases. 'It occurred to me that Lucius Senderhill might once have been in a shipwreck himself.'

'Ho-ho! An interesting conjecture! We should then have a staggering example of eidetic imagery.'

'What the devil is that?'

'The reviving of a past optical impression with hallucinatory clearness. But it won't wash.'

'Evidently not. My other conjecture has taken me definitely into the realm of the supernatural. Some ancestor of Senderhill's had perished at sea.'

'Ah, now you're in the target area. But I don't know what you mean by the supernatural. It has never seemed to me a very helpful term.'

'Then I promise not to use it again.' I couldn't help laughing at the largeness of Holroyd's dismissal of one of the master interests of his species. 'I know how sublimely a rationalist you are. Don't you even manage to take your friend O'Rourke and his prescient dice in your scientific stride? But tell me about the *Gloriana*, and how you've come on her.'

'Extremely simply. I've spent the morning with the printed memorials of the Senderhills. Naturally, there are family histories and biographies and memoirs enough. But a very brief rummage happened to turn up Bertrand Senderhill. Only a sentence or two, because he wasn't at all important. But something at least to the point. He was drowned at sea.'

'But is not an ancestor of our late friend?'

'Definitely not. He was a young unmarried man of no more than nineteen.'

'Was he brought up here at Vailes?'

'Yes, he was. His father—who was an Otho, which is a regular family name—was only the second son of the first Marquess. But he married a considerable heiress from the City, and for some reason he kept up, and lived at, Vailes, throughout the minority of the second Marquess. Bertrand was Lord Otho's eldest child, and he was sent to Eton and then to Christ Church. But it seems he soon decided he'd had enough of Oxford, and he told his father that he was clearing out. He said he wanted to travel. So he was packed off on the Grand Tour.'

'Was it still called that in 1832?'

'You're a most pedantic chap. Whatever it was called, off Bertrand went.'

'With a private tutor in the traditional style?'

'Apparently not. He said he was going to join Lord Somebody-or-other in Italy—a college friend who was already equipped in that way. Do you think that he was perhaps pulling a fast one on Mum and Dad? Ho-ho! You may be right.'

'But it was no laughing matter, since he was incontinently drowned?'

'Just that. The *Gloriana* went down.'

'I see.' I got up from the settle—which had been designed, I imagine, by William Morris, and creaked badly. 'And that's all?'

'It's all I know.' Holroyd, who had been prowling the library, came to a halt before a chimney-piece much encumbered with heraldic devices. 'The question is, did Lucius Senderhill know the story?'

'Surely he must. After his vision, or whatever it's to be called, he must have searched the family papers for records of shipwreck.'

'One would suppose so. Indeed, he might well have known of the young man's drowning already. But perhaps he never got round to it. What Tommy Hartsilver told us the other evening doesn't suggest that he did.'

'He *must* have—if you want a tolerably rational explanation of his experience.' I paused to work this out. 'Say that the story of Bertrand's drowning had come to him as a child, and enormously impressed him. Then he forgot about it—even repressed it, as I believe the expression is, because it was so terrifying. Then—after his calamitous love-affair and when he was in low spirits—it suddenly miraged up on him. He took a look at his blessed lake in moonlight, and suddenly he *saw* something.'

'It *sounds* like that.' Holroyd was staring at me doubtfully. 'I can't quite make it out, all the same. A hallucination of such a kind—suddenly a whole actual scene blotted out, and what' you might call a first-class spectacular taking its place : well, it needs some uncommonly potent psychic charge somewhere. You understand me? Some link between that drowned youth and our Lucius Senderhill—himself still a *young* Senderhill, remember. A congruity of circumstances— something like that.'

'You beckon me into deep waters. I suggest we discover what Mrs Uff is providing for lunch, and then take thought about the possibility of discovering anything else.'

'There *must* be something else.' Holroyd spoke with a sudden vehemence which surprised me. 'We go on rummaging until we find it.'

I have admitted that it was curiosity which really took me to Vailes. But my expectations had been those of an amateur historian; it had appeared to me possible that, while allaying Lord Melchester's unnecessary anxieties, I might take a look at some of the older papers preserved in the place for anything of interest they might contain; I certainly had no notion of being drawn into Holroyd's kind of thing. And I believe it was at this point—and when, to be precise, my friend again used that word 'rummage'—that I was conscious in myself of a reluctance to pursue at Vailes any further enquiry into the affairs, whether natural or preternatural, of the Senderhill family. I believe I even had an impulse to pack my bag and send for a cab.

That I was actually under the influence of what is called a presentiment is something I would be inclined to deny, although my mind is without conviction on the point as I now write. I had never been subject to anything of the kind, and I should have received with complete scepticism the suggestion that either that or any other uncanny experience would ever visit me. There must be a streak of superstition in me, all the same. The oppressive emptiness of the mansion—which we had touched on during our dinner with Hartsilver—was coming to bear on me more heavily, and I had taken something very near a dislike to that harmless, and indeed quietly beautiful, lake.

I also felt an uneasiness in the presence of Martha Uff (who had turned up to serve us, after a fashion, at lunch), and I am glad to recall now that this was at least not mingled with any sense of hostility. Nor was I antagonised by the impatience with which Holroyd marched me off to the muniment room after the meal. His pertinacity still amused and. even attracted me. Nevertheless I was some way from regretting my own conviction that no more light was going to be vouchsafed us on Lucius Senderhill's long-past hallucination. It was almost as if I had begun to share Mrs Uff's primitive conviction that there are matters not meant for man to know. The dangerousness of trafficking with the supernatural is an immemorial persuasion, and probably a healthy one. The ghost of Hamlet's father might indeed have been a goblin damn'd, and tempted him towards the flood as Horatio feared. Although I had never much considered the matter, I was at least aware of the traditional notion that such apparitions may do us injury.

But that *we* may injure *them* was something that had never come within the scope of my imagining.

PART TWO

I

A MUNIMENT ROOM, in the strict sense, was precisely what the gloomy chamber—deep in dust, trailing cobweb across hand or face as one moved, yielding tokens of the habitation of bats—was not. Title-deeds and the like had been removed long ago, and what remained was family lumber. But this family, of course, had for some centuries accumulated property and administered estates on a substantial scale; and it was in the main a mass of written evidences of the fact, no longer of interest to anyone, that was quietly mouldering here. In chests and cupboards and on open shelves were the letter-books, accounts, and inventories of stewards and agents, bailiffs and attorneys, head-keepers, huntsmen, chaplains, and other confidential personages. The records of forgotten law-suits, the pleadings of tenants, the cellar-books of butlers, the reports of governesses and tutors had been thrust here and there in careless heaps. And, with only a little less consideration, the letters and diaries and commonplace books even of numerous Sender-hills themselves had been tied in bundles and stacked wherever there was space. It was an entirely dismal and uninspiring spectacle.

'There may,' I said to Holroyd as we surveyed it, 'be matter at least of antiquarian, if not historical, interest buried in all that silt of paper and parchment. But I declare myself as abandoning any notion of hunting for it. No doubt it has been like this since the time of the third Marquess, who departed to greater grandeurs without giving a damn. But I'm surprised that nobody since has ordered any sort of tidy-up—Lucius in particular, who was something of a scholar.'

'It's a little daunting, I agree. In fact, the place is uncommonly mucky. I had a go yesterday, and I know.'

'Do you notice the scattering of feathers all over the floor? I believe that a whole race of owls has lived and died here.'

'I don't think so. Haven't you looked through that open door at the far end? There's real solid junk there, including a mass of abandoned bedding and pillows. The feathers are drifting through from them all the time. Which shows that there's at least a current of air. And that has kept things from mouldering too badly.'

'They can't moulder away too quickly for me.' I was surprised, as I spoke, by the completeness of this volte-face in myself. 'And going after anything by or about poor young Bertrand Senderhill is like looking for a needle in a haystack —or a pile of feather-beds.'

'I intend to have a shot at it, all the same. Of course, my dear fellow, if you prefer a quiet afternoon in the library, I'll join you for tea. You'll find a pile of not-too-old journals —*The Field,* I think, and *Country Life*—down there somewhere.'

'Very well, Holroyd.' I repressed my irritation. 'Let us rummage. But systematically, if rummaging is susceptible of that.'

It would fortunately be irrelevant to my narrative to attempt to convey the messy tedium of the succeeding three hours. In my office it is my habit to insist that every file of papers, even if taken directly from a safe, should be dusted before appearing on my desk. Here I was positively smothered in grime within twenty minutes.

Holroyd quickly professed to find occasion for taking a hopeful view of our quest. This was because, every now and then, we came upon bundles of personal papers which had evidently at some time been hastily examined and then put carelessly aside. Some of them bore a scrawled endorsement on an outer leaf or cover in what was undoubtedly the hand of that impatient and aspiring third Marquess who had (quite literally, in this context) shaken the dust of Vailes off his feet. *Grandmamma: pious rubbish* appeared on the cover of a substantial notebook into which some Senderhill lady had transcribed passages of particular edification encountered in her reading of eighteenth-century divines. *More from Noah's Ark . . . Poor Uncle Humphrey's dotages . . . Miscellaneous twaddlings not worth examining . . . Licentious versifying by Timothy S. but damned dull:* these were some of the spot judgements we came across. It scarcely seemed to me that all this afforded us much rational encouragement. Yet, however this may have been, my friend's sheer drive was rewarded. In a chest containing for the most part a mere litter of loose papers he came upon a commonplace-book, bound in finely-tooled vellum. Across this had been scribbled, with what struck me as even more than the third Marquess's usual brutality, *Some unlicked cub's romantick lucubrations.*

'I wonder!' Holroyd said, and handed the volume to me. 'Have a look.' As he glanced at me I was more than commonly conscious of the cold glitter in his light blue eyes—and I even asked myself (it is evidence of the atmosphere I was coming to feel around me) whether he owned an unconfessed clairvoyant power which was at this moment exercising itself.

'Very well,' I said, and opened the book.

On the inner cover there was a book-plate. It was a fancifully allegorical and not a regularly heraldic affair.

Against a background of mountains, fountains, and what appeared to be leaves swept before a gale, a lion which had just broken a massive chain was about to spring upon its prey—a prey not in any prosaic or realistic sense likely to prove succulent or rewarding, since it consisted of a skeleton somewhat rakishly sporting royal robes, a sceptre, and a crown. Beneath this inchoate insurgence appeared the surprisingly formal inscription : *The Honble. Bertrand Julian Fitzalan Senderhill Armig,* and beneath this again there had been added in ink : *Commensalis E.C.* But in another ink this last had been struck out, and there had been substituted some lines now so faded on the paper that they appeared only uncertainly as a fragment of verse in which *a world of woes* was made to rhyme with *tyrants and foes.* Then, in yet another ink, and in a handwriting rather more maturely formed, came : *AEdes Christi in Academia Oxoniensi.* And to this finally had been added :

> *Eheu fugaces, Postume, Postume,*
> *Labuntur anni.*
> > *Domus et placens*
> *Uxor.*

'Odes, two, fourteen,' I heard Holroyd murmuring in my ear. '*Eheu fugaces,* of course. "How soon hath time, the subtle thief of youth"—eh? Eton or St Paul's, Christ Church or Christ's : the lament comes to every grown schoolboy's lips. Ho-ho! But what about *domus et placens uxor?* Optative, one may say. We've been told young Bertrand didn't make it. He perished unmarried and at nineteen.'

My friend was excited. My own feelings I find it hard accurately to recall. But at least I *had* feelings. I am in no doubt about that, and it would have been humiliating had it not been so. An age and an order were compressed in the memorial before us—and it was none the less compelling for ending with a kind of cry. I recalled Holroyd's telling

me that morning, on the strength of what he had found
printed record of, that Bertrand Senderhill had 'soon decided
he'd had enough of Oxford'. But at Eton already one could
now guess that he had been a rebel, as his idol Shelley had
been before him. There could be no doubt about the
idolatry. It was there in the touchingly absurd book-plate.
It was there in the scrap about *woes* and *foes*. I had remembered the place in which that comes: a place in which a
hounded schoolboy dedicates himself to truth and justice and
freedom. Suddenly I knew that the youth whose drowning
had mysteriously risen up before Lord Lucius Senderhill in a
vision was alive in my mind—far more so than Lord Lucius
himself, whom I had known, and who had more than once
gravely shaken hands with me.

'Look at the other side,' Holroyd said.

I did as I was told. The fly-leaf bore an inscription in a
woman's hand: *To Bertrand Senderhill from his Mother
on his sixteenth Birthday, in the hope that it may be
employed for the furtherance of his private Devotions.*

'The poor lad was meant to compose prayers in it,' Holroyd said. 'And copy out bits from Tillotson and South.
We'll see how far he got with it.'

'But not in this beastly attic.' I looked at my watch. 'Mrs
Uff hasn't ventured to send Martha to disturb us, and we're
now past all chance of tea. We'd better go back to the
library, and examine your precious find at leisure. It's my
bet that what we'll find copied into it will be chunks of
Rousseau and Voltaire—and Godwin and Thelwall and
Tom Paine. The heady wine of revolution, as first bottled
for young Englishmen about a hundred and eighty years
ago.'

'Perhaps so. Well, come along.' But Holroyd hesitated,
glancing here and there around the disordered muniment
room. 'There's still the deuce of a lot to rummage through.

And coming on one "find", as you call it, doesn't mean there mayn't be others waiting for us.'

'My dear man, for pity's sake!'

'And next door, as well. Just come and take a look at it.' Hideously stirring up dust with his toes, and once or twice kicking aside heaven knows what residual Senderhill archives as he moved, my friend strode across the floor. I followed resignedly into the adjoining chamber. It was totally different in its dimensions, being no broader but enormously long. I observed with a sinking heart that it did in fact contain further receptacles in which papers and documents might lurk, although here nothing of the kind was simply lying around. For we were now in the presence of junk and lumber in a big way. At one time, I saw, a very large amount of Victorian furniture, bric-a-brac, ornaments, paintings, and peculiarly repellent sub-erotic marble statuary must have been introduced into Vailes, and later simply banished, with a grand disregard of expense, to these un-visited regions. There were upholstered objects of which the outer integument and confining webbing had rotted away, so that they were now all Laocoön-like writhings in rusty steel. Even more distressing were the piles of abandoned bedding that huddled in corners like sullied snow-drifts. It was from these, as Holroyd had remarked earlier, that the feathers came. Indeed, from one peculiarly voluminous mattress, precariously stuffed above a massive wardrobe by which I was standing, a feather now floated down to rest gently on my head. I brushed it hastily away.

'We'll find nothing here,' I said. 'Unless it's death by asphyxia as a result of this stuff lodging in our windpipes.'

'Perhaps another time.' Holroyd turned away reluctantly, and presently we made our way downstairs. 'By the way,' he said suddenly, 'I suppose the boy has written *something* in that book?'

'Yes, of course. Don't you remember?' And I tapped the

vellum volume, now tucked under my arm. ' "Some unlicked cub's romantick lucubrations".'

'Ho-ho! To be sure. Well, what are the first words? Just take a peep.'

We paused on the threshold of the library, and I obeyed this injunction.

'The first words,' I said, 'are *Perdita, Perdita, Perdita.*'

'Perdita?'

'Just that. Shakespeare's heroine, I suppose.'

'Wasn't there an actress—?'

'A very secondary Perdita: Perdita Robinson, who died before this young man was born. No, this is the true Perdita out of *The Winter's Tale.* And saluted thrice.'

'Well, I'm blessed.' Holroyd made his impulsive gesture of taking me by the arm. *'Avanti!'* he said, and pushed open the door of the library.

What he and I there read, with Bertrand Senderhill's vellum-bound commonplace-book on a table before us, I now proceed to transcribe.

2

Perdita Perdita Perdita

Lately turning over old family papers, I came upon the ledgers (as I suppose they are called) of a certain Bertrand Senderhill (a younger son's son such as I) turned loathsome usurer *regnante Carolo primo.* Above each daily record of extortion and rapacity my namesake has written *Jesu Jesu Jesu*—a pious ejaculation, as that superstitious age would have called this hideous abuse of the name of one whom I revere scarcely less than that of Plato, M. de V., P.B.S. himself!

But *Perdita Perdita Perdita* a second Bertrand can fitly

write. Loveliest girl! Do I not see embodied in thee every beautiful idealism of moral excellence?

1 September 1832

It is now some three years or more since my Mother gave me this book, fondly hoping that the follies and evils of priestcraft would fill its pages one day. Filial respect has restrained me from putting it to any more rational use till now. But now! Perdita, art thou not my religion, my light in the darkness of this age of tyranny and dungeons and chains—chains even riveted (Oh, worst oppression!) upon what ought to be the sovereign intellect of Man? Art thou not she who has come as a very redemption from the long, dark misery of a boyhood knowing only misunderstanding and calumny and several frightfully painful beatings? Oh, Perdita, Perdita, my joy!

I renew my resolution not to return to *that place*. My moral being suffers there. This of being beaten recalls the fact to me. When Wm Gladstone, my schoolfellow but no gentleman, being the son of a rich merchant in the North and a psalm-singing hypocrite to boot, was soundly drubbed in his rooms by the ruffian and drunken element in college for some act of low informing against men comporting themselves irreverently in chapel, did not I feel a *dark satisfaction*? I am entitled, indeed, to feel contempt for the obscurantist pietism of this upstart Liverpudlian pleb. But ought I not to deplore an assault upon his person, disagreeable although that be to me too? I will NOT go back to Christ Church with its boozings and barbarities thus rampant while Canons loll in monkish slumber in their stalls!

2 September

I regret that contemptuous word *pleb*. Are not the boast of heraldry, the pomp of power (Gray) anathema to me—I who recognise no other authority than the light of reason flashed upon an independent intellect (? Wm. Godwin)? Among the cottagers here is a family called Cowmeadow. Is it not an honourable, at least a pleasing, name—suggesting, as it does, the innocence of rural nature and of beneficent, non-carnivorous creatures? *And what of Stickleback?* Does not one think, as he utters it, of children, as yet unstained by the world, playing by some purling stream, or of the long happiness of gazing down into the depths of my own dear lake of Vailes? *Joan Stickleback.* My Perdita!

3 September

A letter from Jack Palliser. He is at Padua, his father having required him to make certain studies in the botanick gardens there with a view to improving horticulture on the family estates. It is but a dull place, but soon Jack hopes to be in Venice—*throned on her hundred isles!* He urges me to join him. With him, he says is only a *religious caterpillar* of a tutor, Dr Blowbody, whose expectations of later favour bring him well under Jack's thumb. Dear Jack, thou art the most loyal of friends, and yet a sad fellow to whom every woman is but a pair of legs to be parted. Thou knowest nothing, Jack, of the purity of the hearts' affections. A fig for thy Venetian courtesans! I would as soon obey a summons to the moon. Indeed, even were there no Perdita, could I ever bear to bid Vailes farewell?

> *Nescio qua natale solum dulcedine captos*
> *ducit et immemores non sinit esse sui.*
> *Some sweet compulsion haunts their native soil*
> *And holds them captive in its mystic toil.*

I do not English old Ovid very well. But 'tis better, Jack, than thou couldst do!

I rather please my fancy with this archaic style I have

lit upon. It something reminds me of the beginning of
Childe Harold's Pilgrimage.

5 September
I have spoken to her! I have touched her hand!

12 September
How fortunate that I am known to be studious, and supposed to be (like that humbug Gladstone) ambitious to take
a Double First! I have only to have books in my hand, and
wander away in this fair autumn weather, to be held
blameless even if I fail to present myself for dinner. My
father positively orders that, upon my return, chops and
claret are to be served to me in my study. And thus I have
a little space in which to *recover*.

And from what a whirl of passion—pure yet tumultuous!
From what an elevation of the soul and quickening of every
faculty! My darling is not learned—indeed, I see that steps
must be taken to teach her something more than her ABC
(and perhaps the *pianoforte,* the laws of pronunciation, and
a politer style of dancing than she has hitherto been
familiar with) if she is to take her place . . .

But what craven nonsense is this of one so sweetly read
in Nature's lore, whose singing is as the lark's, whose speech
is like a golden shower, and who moves like the waves of
the sea! Perdita, thou queen of curds and cream! I have
taught thee to call me Florizel. Wilt thou ever—oh,
trembling thought!—murmur to me of *a bank for love to
lie and play on*? I could almost wish that there were a
hearkening God, that I might thank him for the all of fire,
the little of earth, that is my love for my darling. Else where
might we already be?

I take my cockle-shell from the boathouse and scud or
scull down the lake. At its extremity I conceal the little craft
amid the reeds even as she leaves the cottage, her basket in

her hand. It so happens that the good Mrs Stickleback—mother, as she must be called, of my surely changeling princess—holds some rustic fame as a compounder of remedies of the herbal kind. She is happy that her daughter should wander the woods all day garnering the materials of her art. So into the forest we fade, hand in hand but without more intimate embrace. (Only once has she allowed me to kiss her, and that as a brother might a sister!) Sometimes, more daring, we walk on the lake's farther shore.

13 September

I said, with a boldness I scarcely felt, that I would take her to Mama. She has what Mama would call good principles. She is, in fact, a very religious girl—and for this simplicity in her I find I have so great a tenderness that I cannot utter what she would regard as an infidel word. Might not this piety avail with my mother? Perdita says not. Alas, she is undoubtedly right! Humble as her upbringing has been, she has an intellect as clear as mine. Strangely, too, she has something of that aristocratic spirit which I reprobate in myself—linked as it is to centuries of arrogance and oppression. I believe I am liberating my own conduct from it—as Mankind must do! Surrounded as we thus are by the cruel ordinances of Wealth and Privilege, it is exceedingly fortunate that I am myself so strongly armed in Natural Virtue. Otherwise might not this dear girl be betrayed by me? Ah, my Perdita, we shall not be sundered, though years may pass before we are united!

20 September

We are lovers.

21 September

I had thought there were no words for it. But there are, and they are my own poet's:

The Meteor to its far morass returned:
The beating of our veins one interval
Made still; and then I felt the blood that burned
Within her frame, mingle with mine, and fall
Around my heart like fire; and over all

A mist was spread, the sickness of a deep
And speechless swoon of joy, as might befall
Two disunited spirits when they leap
In union from this earth's obscure and fading sleep.
Was it one moment that confounded thus
All thought, all sense, all feeling, into one
Unutterable power . . . when we had gone
Into a wide and wild oblivion
Of tumult and of tenderness?

I am ashamed of the mawkish and exclamatory stuff earlier written in this book. We must be secret. I must plan. I am not of age. Perdita is older than I, but also a minor. To defeat those who would forbid us marriage I must scheme and tell lies—and take care they are not found out.

22 September

I have told my father about Wm Gladstone being thrashed in his rooms by drunken undergraduates. My father very shocked. I spoke of the low company one is constrained to keep upon at all venturing into the obscurer colleges. Of the ease of wenching, etc. and worse evils at Oxford. A day or two needed for this to sink in. Passion must not make me reckless. A change of plan must appear rational and unimpulsive. Say two weeks. *Festina lente.* Celerity should be contempered with cunctation, as Sir T. Browne has it.

23 September

By the greatest good fortune, a second letter from Jack

Palliser *expressly written to show my father*. The high standing of scholars, *virtuosi* etc. in good Italian society, so that
improving conversation possible even at a ball. Encouragement to proceed in the best Latin authors derived from
actual viewing of monuments of antiquity. Devotion to his
tutor Dr Blowbody, with whom he never fails to read for
several hours daily. Scope on the Continent for moderate
amours with no risk of scandal. Consequent likelihood of his
being perfectly content on return to England with whatever
matrimonial alliance may be proposed by his family. All
this and more, written as if unconstrainedly to a familiar
friend, I shall certainly take occasion to show my father. He
has always been pleased that Jack has been my intimate—
knowing more, one may say, about his lineage than his
morals. Jack a good fellow, although he knows no more of
love than a young he-goat or bull. I shall show my father
this letter when we are at dessert, this evening. I have
already read it to Perdita, and explained what an engine
we can make of it. She understands it perfectly, whereas it
might well be Greek to her. She *remains* Perdita, although
I have now got her out of the romances and know her for
the peasant girl she is—and with all the future difficulties
that lie in that. No more nonsense. That she is very clever
is not of her essence, and is therefore in a sense irrelevant to
our love. But it is—how shall I express it?—a piece of
uncommon good luck.

> *What are the kisses whose fire clasps*
>   *The failing heart in languishment, or limb*
> *Twined within limb? or the quick dying gasps*
>   *Of the life meeting, when the faint eyes swim*
> *Through tears of a wide mist boundless and dim,*
>   *In one caress? What is the strong control*
> *Which leads the heart that dizzy steep to climb . . . ?*

But no—not even more Shelley. For I am become a
practical man.

30 September
We have spent a night together in my boat on the lake.
The thwart was inconvenient—but what of that? Only there
must not be such another mad occasion, since detection
would now mar all. A short month ago, I would cheerfully have considered renouncing my whole modest patri-
mony for love. It would have seemed a killing of two birds
with the one stone : an action at once in the high romantic
manner and at the same time consonant with a fully philo-
sophic view of the evils incident to the acquisition of wealth
without toil. But now I am for more sober courses.

I recall my mother as once speaking to me of the hazard
to position and property which may be occasioned by rash
and impetuous attachment to a member of the other sex.
Perhaps it is something that she herself once escaped, since
the theme roused her to a surprising vehemence. But if I
paid no attention then, I do now. I cannot become a peasant, since I should be too poor a hand at it. And without
money and acknowledgement from my family, my Perdita's
lot would be hard in any other station of life. My parents
then, must be presented with *un fait accompli,* else they will
take such means as rank and power own to thwart our
union perhaps for ever. Equally, they must then have some
enforced interval for reflection, and one during which they
may hear well of my bride from persons they will acknowledge as of judgement.

Hence my plan for flight to Italy. There the bear-leader
Blowbody shall pronounce us man and wife—he shall do it
though honest Jack have to stand over him with a switch
the while. And provided it be within the dwelling, and in
the presence, of the English Resident in one or other of the
great cities, the validity of the contract will be beyond

question at law. And Jack shall certainly contrive that our eventual return to Vailes be by way of Fawn Court, and after our enjoying there the countenance of his father the Duke. How shall such sponsorship be resisted by *my* father, with his paltry courtesy title of Lord? Almost do I spy some merit in the vanities of aristocracy.

7 October

My parents are won over to the Italian scheme—happily just before any need to return to Oxford to keep there the Michaelmas Term. Servants and a covered waggon have been despatched to fetch my furniture, books, etc. from Christ Church, and I have written a proper letter to the somnolent Dean, thanking him for his civilities during my residence in the House. I am off to tell my darling the news.

8 October

Near disaster! Success having made me bold, or careless, I walked from the lake's end up the green ride to my darling's cottage, first hand in hand with her, and then with our arms entwined. Having soon to part, I could not refrain from drawing her within the shadow of a great beech and there embracing. We *stood* embracing, that is— but it was closely and passionately enough. And thus did her mother come upon us! The good woman seemed to be wandering the woods to gather herbs on her own account. Observing us, she gave a cry. The encounter was awkward, and I believe I handled it ill. Thus surprised, would it not have been best to confide in her—to trust my beloved's mother with at least the essential part of our secret? Surely I had but to convince her of the honourable character of my intentions to make her not wholly hostile to such a match for her daughter? But something in the woman's look made me hesitate. I reflected that it is not so strange a thing for a young man of my station to make free with a village girl—at least to the extent of a few imperious kisses —should he come upon her in a convenient privacy. Hateful as conjuring up such a picture was, I now instantly adopted it. Touching my Perdita's cheek lightly with a finger (as if whimsically to minimise what had plainly passed), I told her mother, laughing, that she had the prettiest daughter in the shire. And with that I sauntered off into the wood!

I was little pleased with myself. I could not bear to think of Perdita rebuked after some rough, rustic fashion. Still less could I contemplate without pain having seemed to treat her—however much it were a mere deceit in sudden exigency—as a common country wench to be idly kissed in frolic. And I continue extremely uneasy now. The mother—I judge from what seemed terror on her face—may fear that, should her child be judged as leading me astray, my father's displeasure may result in her husband's losing both his cottage and his employment. One hears of such abominable petty tyrannies often enough. If this merely keeps her silent, all may be well. But what if she thinks to forestall such a penalty by going to the bailiff with some warning, or even thrusting herself into the presence of my parents themselves? Nothing of the kind need be fatal, no doubt. I might carry it off with my father by a promise of circumspection together with the ghost of a gay look such as might appeal to him. Or he might even be prompted to hasten my departure!

Time is all-important now. *I* must effect that hastening by my own endeavours.

12 October

So far, there has been no sequel to the alarming *rencontre*. But it has made all approach to Perdita hazardous.

13 October

We have met—hastily and at a signal from me near the
cottage. Nothing has been said by her parents about her
mother's unlucky discovery. But her father, like her mother,
she reports as apprehensive and fearful. And suddenly there
is talk of sending her away—that she may look after some
bed-ridden aunt in a distant part of the country, and at the
same time relieve what is declared to be a straitened household of one mouth to feed. She is sure that this is but an
excuse to place us beyond one another's reach. If this threat
becomes more imminent, my best course will be to declare
myself to these simple people. I find myself wondering
whether they know *more* than the mother came upon : that
simple embrace, I mean, in the woods. Can they be aware
that their daughter has been—grotesque word, yet justified
in the world's regard!—*seduced* by me? This would
account for their extreme alarm. But speculation is idle,
and I must hasten my plans. With my father's approval, I
am now enquiring after some ship bound for Genoa. There
are sailings almost every day, it seems, from one or another
of the southern ports. But I must tread warily if the vital
part of my design is to prosper.

14 October

I have considered whether, during so long a passage,
Perdita might pass undetected as a youth. My younger
brother? A serving lad? The latter seems impossible, since in
her coming and going on my behalf she would be much
exposed to curiosity. Nor would the former serve unless we
had with us (as we shall not) confidential attendance of our
own and could thus keep ourselves close in our quarters.
Moreover such notions only come from reading idle
romances. My first, simplest, and boldest plan is the best.
It is fortunate that my father is proving liberal of his purse,

and that I have, besides, those few hundred guineas put by. Just before sailing, I shall announce to the ship's captain a change of plan whereby my wife travels with me. She shall drive up to the quay (suitably habited), and we shall be at sea before much thought can be given to the matter. That we are a runaway couple may soon be guessed at. But by then, and with money flowing, we are little likely to meet with any check or even impertinence. Fit conveyance to the port etc. I can manage—although I could wish I had to run my errands some fellow I could trust. My father, indeed, has been awkwardly of the same mind in this. It does not suit his notion of our consequence that I should join a Duke's son without a man or two about me. It is, I own, an almost impossibly awkward degree of singularity. But I have rounded this sharp corner with some address. Lew Custance, the huntsman's boy, whom fortunately I have had much about me these last two years, and whose lately broken leg is now mending, is to be shipped out after me as soon as he is serviceable.

15 October

The threat to banish Perdita to her distant aunt's is afoot again. But now, if all can be timed aright, I shall make this work for us! How to prevent instant alarm upon her disappearance has seemed an insoluble problem. But here, with good fortune, may be eight-and-forty hours granted us, which is twice the measure that we need.

A letter has happily come to my father from the Duke, and been shown to me. An old beef-witted Duke, and indifferently skilled in his orthography. But he expresses himself so amiably, and with a regard so high for sundry Senderhills living and dead, that my father has incontinently brought out another purse for me, and as a parting gift has presented me with his best gold repeater to boot.

16 October

It is the *Gloriana*—and from Plymouth in three days
time. I have lately been inclined to admit at least the
hypothesis that a Supreme Being may exist. Unfortunately
I cannot conceive Him as disposed to hearken to Bertrand
Senderhill. Were it so, I should to-night be on my knees for
the safety of my darling in what lies before us.

Vailes
Midnight

I open my casement upon a stormy sky and a great gale
blowing. Chariot us, oh wild West Wind!

3

'Well?' Holroyd asked. Having finished the last page of
the diary first, he had waited for me to catch up. 'What do
you say to that?'

'These violent delights have violent ends, and in their
triumph die.'

'Yes, indeed. A few days after the young man almost
brought himself to pray for his mistress's safety, both of
them were drowned. I've noticed before that Shakespeare
is your poet. Not Shelley.'

'Shelley? Those lines about the physical union of two
lovers are by him?'

'They're about Laon and Cythna in *The Revolt of Islam*.
Impressive, wouldn't you say? I doubt whether just *that*
was ever better recorded by poet. But what of this real-life
love-affair? Would you call that impressive too?'

'I don't know that we can judge. Perdita—Joan Stickleback—may have been a paragon, but we have only an
excited boy's word for it.'

'Yes—yet at least his experience seems to have been a

maturing one. Don't you notice? At the beginning of September he is an adolescent with his head full of nonsense. By the middle of October he is rash, no doubt, but quite unmistakably grown-up. Which, I suspect, says something for the quality of the relationship. The Reverend Doctor Blowbody never read from his Prayer Book over them. But I'm glad that they had been husband and wife, all the same. It's the cheerful point in a sad story.'

I saw no need to dispute my friend's judgement—which might equally have been delivered of Shakespeare's lovers in the play that had been running in my head. I knew nothing about Laon and Cythna, but Romeo and Juliet had always been very vivid to me. I wondered whether Bertrand Senderhill and his bride would now a little haunt me too.

'Isn't it strange,' I said presently, 'that after beginning a diary under stress of the affair he should simply have left it behind him?'

'Perhaps he had a presentiment of disaster, and wanted some record to remain.' Holroyd glanced at me quizzically. 'Ho-ho! You think I have precognitive experience on the brain. I dare say you are perfectly right. And as for this diary, young Bertrand had a great deal to think about—one must admire his bringing the thing off as he did—and as a consequence it simply got left behind.'

'In which case it would have been discovered and brought to his parents.'

'That's a probability. Yet it may have been otherwise. Imagine its being come upon by a servant with a fondness for the lad, or indeed for the family. Such a one might think it best simply to shove the thing out of sight. You and I—and such a servant, if he existed—may be literally the only persons in the world ever to have known those young people's secret.'

'That's perfectly true.' Suddenly, I didn't understand why, I felt uneasy. 'Do you know, Holroyd, I rather wish we *didn't?*' I paused, searching for some justification of this remark. 'Perhaps it's as if we were disturbing their shades.'

'Of course, we don't positively know that they *were* both on board the *Gloriana.*' Holroyd seemed too struck by this thought to attend to what I had said. 'Young Senderhill, yes. He undoubtedly went down with the ship. But might not there have been a hitch about the girl? She might have been caught by her parents. Or her heart may have failed her. Who knows?'

'In that case, Bertrand would surely not have sailed tamely for Italy himself.'

'He might have, in a kind of despair, if the girl had ditched him at the last.'

'But they weren't like that, either of them.'

'I believe that's true.' Holroyd said this soberly, and I realised that, like myself, he sensed a strong intensity of passion behind this long-past and disastrous runaway affair. But he rapidly reached for a robust note. 'Ho-ho! Would you say that it is perhaps Shelley who has sold us something?'

'Bother Shelley! I suppose it might still be possible to find out for certain whether the girl *was* on board the *Gloriana?*'

'I doubt it. She left home to go to an aunt, and of how she was actually conveyed to Plymouth it is almost inconceivable that any record can remain. And what would happen when she got there, with the barque all set to sail? The vessel's master, or his purser, would presently take money for her passage, no doubt. But that would simply be on board ship, and any note of the transaction would go down with her.'

'Perhaps something could be discovered about the Sticklebacks?'

'My dear chap, it's most unlikely. Consider how short as well as simple are the annals of the poor.'

'I doubt whether that quite meets the case. In any civilised society a missing girl is quite something.' I paused, perhaps to wonder why, since my own instinct was to avoid further investigation, I should be pressing these possibilities upon Holroyd. 'Surely the magistrates would have ordered some sort of inquiry as soon as the parents reported the thing.'

'If they ever did report it. They may have learnt the truth, or suspected it—the fact, I mean, of their daughter's having run away with the young gentleman from the big house. And so they may have kept mum out of sheer fright. Bertrand records, remember, that they were dead scared. And if it was known in the neighbourhood that the girl was to go off to a distant aunt for keeps, no one outside her own home would necessarily give her a thought ever again. No, no—whoever the Sticklebacks were, and wherever that cottage was, depend upon it, we shall learn no more about them.'

'At least there's no obscurity about the cottage. On the strength of what Bertrand records, I can take you to it, or to the ruins of it, tomorrow. Incidentally, it appears to be Martha's favourite haunt.'

'Martha?' It was quite blankly that Holroyd had repeated the name. He was staring absently at the vellum-bound book.

'Mrs Uff's apathetic daughter.'

'Yes, of course.' My friend's tone was inexpressive, but he raised his alarming eyes to mine in what I can only call a queer look.

We had been talking about the poet Shelley—which is one reason, no doubt, why, at this moment, the poet Keats came into my head. Or, rather, not Keats at all, but simply Keats's philosopher Apollonius in *Lamia*—a fellow, I thought, with a gaze just like Arthur Holroyd's.

4

On the following morning—and it was the day on which
I had planned to end my stay at Vailes—Holroyd displayed
no particular interest in being shown the one-time home (as
it assuredly was) of the Sticklebacks. We might take a stroll
there, he suggested, after lunch. Meanwhile, he proposed
a return to the muniment room, so-called, and its adjoining
attics. For this I had myself no further fancy, and I believe
I even found something curiously obsessive in his concern
with all that cobweb and dust. It was true that in Bertrand
Senderhill's diary he had come upon a document of considerable human interest—and of something more than that,
no doubt, if the shipwreck to which it was an unconscious
prelude had been unknown to Lucius Senderhill when his
hallucinatory experience of just such a disaster had occurred
to him when himself a young man and ill-fated lover. But
what more was there any likelihood that the family archives
would reveal?

At least I declined to companion Holroyd in his further
rummaging, with the consequence that I had another morning to spend as I pleased. And it was a gorgeous morning.
I ought, I think, to emphasise that. The previous day I have
described, I see, as 'bright and rather blowy', but this succeeding day seemed to belong more to a golden summer
than to an early spring. There wasn't a cloud in the sky.
This must appear improbable of any English day, but I
think it is literally true—and that the heaven so remained,
indeed, until dusk fell. At least I can say that what happened—anything that *did* happen—had clear sunlight as its
accompaniment.

It was shortly after breakfast that I set out to retrace the
steps of my previous exploration. The encounter with the
bicycling Mrs Uff had prevented me from rounding

the lake, and this time I was resolved to succeed. But first I walked down to the boathouse and peered inside. Perhaps I had taken it into my head that there might be a craft in which I could make a small water-expedition instead. And this certainly proved to be so, since I spied a dinghy in excellent order, and ready for launching, within. But lawyers have an exaggerated sense of decorum in such matters, and I may well have decided that it would be improper to make free with what must now be within the trusteeship of the Senderhill Settled Estates. Whether for this reason or another, I turned away and resumed my walk.

And once more it was, I suppose, a ruminative rather than an observant perambulation. On the previous day my mind had lingered on the complete unaccountability of Lucius Senderhill's experience; now, I constructed more or less to my own satisfaction a rational explanation of it, or at least an explanation in which nothing supernatural need be posited. If Hartsilver's recollection was accurate, and if Senderhill had dealt candidly with Hartsilver, the story of Bertrand Senderhill's drowning in 1832 was something of which Lucius Senderhill was completely ignorant. There was nothing impossible about this; young Bertrand had been a person of no note in his family's history; the scanty record of him which Holroyd had turned up might quite conceivably have escaped Lord Lucius. In fact, I told myself, it certainly had; and the same certainty was applicable to Bertrand's diary. For Lucius, having resolved to tell his friend the vicar of his long-past experience, could simply *not* have mingled his confidence with deliberate misstatement. To do so, I acknowledged, would have been totally out of character, and wholly pointless as well.

But it by no means followed that what Lucius did not know at the time of his apparitional experience, or again when he recounted that experience to Hartsilver so many years later, was something he had *never* known. I had

presented Holroyd with what seemed to me not a bad hypothesis here. The story of a kinsman's drowning, and even a
hint of that kinsman's love affair, might have come to
Lucius as a child—perhaps as a family legend of no great
consequence, lingering in the mind of some old nurse or
servant. It might have frightened him to such a degree that
he quickly repressed all memory of it. Such acts of mental
burial are said to be so common as scarcely to merit in-
clusion within the bounds of abnormal psychology. And the
buried 'trauma'—if that be the word—might later have
seized a favourable opportunity to reassert itself in the form
of that momentary illusion of tempest and shipwreck.

   This speculation of mine reeked, perhaps, of strangeness
and unlikelihood, but at least it didn't make large demands
upon the ghostly or magical. And having arrived at my
picture, I found that my interest in Lucius Senderhill and
his vision of a spectral barque was for the time being
exhausted. My mind turned to something more simply
human and a good deal more moving : the star-crossed love
of two young people who had called themselves Florizel and
Perdita. Once upon a time—yet in a certain definite year
which had seen, I could recall, the Reform Bill and the
death of Goethe—they had walked together where I was
walking now. They had made love in places round about
me, and also in a small boat out there on the lake. Their
love had been (I somehow told myself with confidence) all
that it should have been, and nothing that it should not.
Then they had got on a ship called the *Gloriana*, by which
time Perdita had conceivably been bearing Florizel's child.
And then, quite promptly, they had been drowned.

   I tried to imagine them. I tried to imagine them not in
their passion and hope, an exercise beyond the tether of a
middle-aged solicitor, but simply in their persons and clothing as they had walked or sailed here together during some
six weeks of early autumn weather long ago. Perdita, or

Joan Stickleback, I saw clearly enough, although perhaps anachronistically by several decades. Gainsborough's daughters went to my vision of her, and great ladies whose muslin gowns, following the Revolution which had swept so much away, were high and lightly girdled affairs combining rural simplicity with Arcadian elegance. But I also imported, I believe, a strong dash of Opie (I am fond of the English painters), thus preserving for Perdita something of what was presumably Joan's peasant type, and at the same time setting her in a strongly accented light and shade which lent a touch of the dramatic appropriate to her history.

This was a very idle occupation—but at least, as I say, I did seem to see the girl. Bertrand Senderhill was more elusive. Would a young aristocrat of a poetic and egalitarian turn of mind dress out of Bulwer-Lytton, or like Count D'Orsay? It seemed improbable. When at Vailes did Bertrand affect the country gentleman's sporting rig of buckskins tailored to an unnatural tightness—or did he walk abroad in almost equally constricting white duck trousers strapped under the instep? Was he soberly suited in the subfusc of his advancing century, without scope for extravagance except in the shape of an out-size cravat? I didn't know the answers.

And again I was at the end of the lake without having noticed the fact, and now I turned to survey it. This morning the still expanse was as blue as our earth seems to be when viewed from the heavens, and it was of course quite empty. I say 'of course' because I had seen nothing except wild-fowl on its surface yet; it looked as if nobody cared, or had permission, to fish in it; probably the dinghy I had spied in the boathouse was the only craft kept anywhere on its shore. Nor, apart from Mrs Uff, had I encountered anybody near it. In many places of the sort, even securely within the ring-fence of a private park, the surrounding rural inhabitants go prescriptively to and fro about their occasions.

There was no sign of this. The lake at Vailes was a secluded scene. It must have been additionally so more than a hundred years ago.

It was no part of my plan to revisit the ruined cottage. If I was to conduct Holroyd to it in the afternoon there was no point in a further reconnaissance now. But I did feel drawn—am I right in thinking rather mysteriously drawn? —into the surrounding beech-wood. The ground was dry beneath my feet; the undergrowth was in no way troublesome; I was presently pleasing myself with the thoroughly childish amusement of deliberately getting lost. And this was how I again came upon the ruined cottage, after all.

This time, however, it was from rising ground which lay behind it, and in which alone the slightest vestige of any former cultivation lingered. There had been an orchard here, and the remaining trees, although they could scarcely date back to the Sticklebacks' time, had certainly endured a barren old age in gnarled and lichened petrifaction. They stood like strange emanations of a rocky earth, writhing in muted and defeated gestures towards the sky. Beyond this the crumbled walls of the cottage showed square and straitened, as if here had been no more than a fold for some diminished race of sheep. Beyond that again was an abandoned well—perhaps of some depth still, since its mouth had been covered with a graceless sheet of galvanised iron on top of which had been piled for security a heap of earth and stones. I wondered whether children came to play in this place, and if so where lay the cottages in which they lived. On the farther side of the well, where once there might have been a vegetable and flower garden of some extent, a hawthorn thicket, with here and there a white poplar, had established itself like a marauding band poised for final incursion upon the last traces of human habitation. A single thorn, indeed, as if carrying an insolent

ultimatum, stood firmly planted within what must have
been the door of the dwelling.

I had become aware of all this before I became aware of
Martha Uff.

She had not been in my mind since I had bidden her
good morning at breakfast. Her reply, if respectful, had
been dull and ungracious; she presented me with a coffee-
cup swimming in its saucer; it was my impression that she
had even contrived to plant a thumb on the rasher of bacon
she placed before me a moment later. I told myself that
Mrs Uff did wrong thus to attempt to employ her daughter
at all; that she would do best to leave the child to whatever
withdrawn and dreaming life she led, and that breakfast
would be a more agreeable affair if she herself placed it
briskly before us at her kitchen table. And I don't suppose
that I recalled at this time my earlier impression (based, as I
have recorded, upon an imponderable quality in the girl's
voice) that there lurked in Martha some potentiality for a
less sluggish response to experience.

But at least she must have been unwontedly nippy thus
to get to the ruin before me—and to have been established
here, I somehow felt, for some little time. Because of the
configuration of the ghost-orchard in which I stood and the
hazel-copse beyond the ruin, I was in a position to see without being seen, and for some moments I watched Martha
at leisure. She had with her a basket which I supposed must
contain those articles of plain sewing, mentioned a little
defensively by her mother, which were one day to be so
useful in Africa. But she had set this down unopened, and
her only occupation seemed to be to gaze at the cottage, or
rather at the vacant air where the cottage had once stood.
For this purpose she had disposed herself on the stump of a
tree with a curious effect of what I can only call frontality
in relation to some proposed spectacle. She might have been,

so to speak, in the centre of the third row of the stalls—and awaiting with impatience the rise of the curtain. There was about her an intentness which can scarcely have been a matter of her expression, since I was too far away to distinguish that. But, however communicated, the quality was there. Keeping to my image of a theatre-goer (or cinema-patron), I can best express it by asserting how far she plainly was from that placid approach to the pleasures of dramatic entertainment which expresses itself in the contented opening of a box of chocolates.

Whether this thought was actually in my head at the time, I don't know. Certainly it cannot have harboured there for long. Only some seconds after I had become aware of this picture of Martha, it had vanished and another had taken its place. The girl had got to her feet—not in any such surprise or perturbation as to make her neglect to pick up her basket—and walked towards me. She was walking, that is to say, towards the ruin, and I, on higher ground beyond, was to be seen if she cared to see me. But her gaze, as she came to a halt again, was on something else. It was upon the single thorn-tree that I have described as growing immediately within the cottage's vanished door. Or it was upon the place (to be plainer) upon which that tree stood.

And now her expression *was* legible to me. I had never seen it on her face before. Instead of being apathetic it was grave. And something—perhaps a light parting of the lips—had oddly transformed Martha Uff. Almost, it was as if she were beautiful.

The direction of her gaze shifted, I thought, to near the well, and then to the spot where a garden gate might once have stood. Seconds passed, and she turned and walked slowly down the bridle-path towards the lake. There was nothing covert about her movements. She might simply

have known that the time had come to go and meet somebody : a somebody whom there was joy rather than mere
pleasure in encountering. So much, once more, a single
glimpse of her face told me.

I ought to have been delighted that the lumpish and
somewhat sullen Martha had a lover, and what appeared
to be an irradiating lover at that. This response, indeed, did
momentarily rise up in me. And then it was checked in a
curious way. I scarcely know how to describe this, or for
that matter a good deal that must follow.

Nor do I know (it occurs to me) what sort of impression
I have given of myself in this narrative so far. I may have
exhibited myself as being as dull as Martha herself, or
perhaps as being muddle-headed, credulous, and impulsive.
I just can't tell. But what I certainly have to record of
myself now is that I jumped to a conclusion. My satisfaction
in the thought of Martha Uff's attachment was checked by
the knowledge—it was the kind of knowledge that comes
suddenly in a dream—that it was an attachment to, or a
trafficking with, something not of this world. Martha's
kindled gaze was for a wraith or revenant.

I felt quite unsurprised by this. It represented simply an
unsatisfactory addition to my knowledge. A real-life lover
(such was my thought) would be an altogether better
proposition.

It will be apparent that my mental processes had taken
on a curious cast; they were those of a man in some
hypnoidal or hypnagogic state; I was seeing sense and nonsense as compatible with each other. And my impression
of time was also confused. I had supposed myself to have
walked past the ruined cottage and taken, at an oblique
angle, a few indecisive steps after the girl. Actually, I must
have followed her briskly and without any more thought of
concealment than she was showing on her own part. For

suddenly we were both standing, and standing close together, beside the lake.

Nothing had changed in the scene. The unbroken water
reflected the sky's clear blue, and among the trees at its
farther end one could glimpse enough of Vailes to recognise
a mansion of major consequence. To our left the bridle-path
continued along the western shore; to our right the lesser
path, now thrice my own chosen route, sometimes hugged
the bank and sometimes disappeared behind encroaching
thickets. The air was still. And not a sound met the ear.

I glanced at the girl beside me, and saw that she was
unaware of my presence. This wasn't natural, any more
than was the intentness with which her gaze was fixed upon
mere vacancy, or at least upon mere inanimate nature,
somewhere to our right. I felt powerfully impelled to recall
her to herself, and I spoke her name sharply. Without turning her head, she put out a hand to me. It was, I now
believe, a gesture to command silence. But at the time I
misinterpreted it—perhaps as an appeal for support, for
something that would draw her back from some perilous
verge. This is why I took her hand in mine, and held it
firmly through some succeeding moments.

It was in the first of these—and with an effect, I have
now to record, such as succeeds the flicking of a switch—
that I noticed my immediate surroundings as not quite
unaltered. Only a few yards from me there floated on the
verge of the lake a small empty boat. The bank here, perhaps a foot high, would have rendered laborious an attempt
to haul it to land. So the painter had been used to secure
it—but in a fashion casual or impatient enough. The rope
had simply been brought ashore and a sizable stone placed
on top of it. Nothing more was necessary on this windless
day.

I had scarcely known myself to be agitated until I
detected a sense of reassurance in this commonplace circum-

stance. I now looked farther afield, and saw that the prospect was not, after all, wholly untenanted. Some way up the
path on our right, and walking away from us, was a lad in
jeans and a nondescript sweater. He had emerged from the
trees, I supposed, and it wasn't unaccompanied. With him
was a barefoot girl who, in the classless fashion of the time,
showed no sign of being dressed in anything but a cotton
frock coming something less than half-way down her thighs.
This rural couple were chattering to each other gaily. I was
rather surprised that no sound of their talk reached me. But
what I did presently hear was a deep sigh from Martha.
There could be no doubt of what had occasioned it. The
pair of lovers in the near-distance had halted, turned to one
another, and passionately embraced.

I can recall that I wanted to laugh—to laugh at the
absurdities I had been imagining for the girl beside me.
Poor Martha was, after all, given to *voyeurism*—but in
relation not to the dead but the living, and in a fashion
surely romantic and innocent enough. She was projecting
her whole soul into the happiness of some more fortunate
village girl.

The lovers were walking on again, hand-in-hand and
with a movement, perhaps a mere swing of the arms or turn
of the head, which affected me suddenly and indescribably.
Am I absurd in calling it noble and splendid? It seemed to
declare that the sensuous, the sensual, moment which had
just passed was at once an all but extreme ecstasy and something of no account save as a symbol of an immeasurable
and supersensible thing. But the apprehension of this—of
the total *vitality* of the moment—was no sooner in my
mind, or somewhere else inside me, than I had to cope with
a new development in the small drama.

Another figure had appeared on the scene: a man who
had rounded a corner of the path the rustic lovers were
following, and who was now approaching them. It was

Hartsilver. I recognised him at once, and I should have identified at least his calling at a farther hundred yards' distance from the fact of his wearing the old-fashioned form of clerical head-gear known as a shovel hat. He and the lovers were within a few paces of each other. They met and passed.

Suddenly it was very cold—so cold that I glanced up at the heavens, expecting some preternatural change. But I was dazzled by a blazing sun, so that when I looked along the verge of the lake again I could see nothing at all. But I knew what I *had* seen. It had been the sight of a beneficed clergyman of the Church of England, in the midst of a rural solitude, almost brushing past two persons—whether parishioners or strangers—with no faintest acknowledgement of their existence. It was a small thing. But it was an impossibility, all the same.

I dropped Martha's hand, I believe to pass my own across my eyes. Then I looked again at the scene before me. The lovers had disappeared—was it, once more, among the trees?—and only Hartsilver remained visible. Something made me turn my glance to the spot, not ten yards away, where the little boat had been moored to the bank.

The little boat had vanished too.

PART THREE

I

'A wool-gathering old chap, Hartsilver,' Holroyd
said. 'And, in any case, he may have given them a nod you
didn't notice.'

'But I tell you I spoke to him!' The scepticism my friend
was deploying as we ate our lunch irritated me considerably.
'It was rather awkward, as a matter of fact.'

'Awkward?'

'It seems absurd. It was Hartsilver himself, after all, who
told us a good deal. But somehow I didn't want to explain
to him—or not straight away—what I'd *seen*. I simply
asked him if he was acquainted with the couple who had
walked past him three minutes before. He replied that nobody had walked past him. And he gave me an odd look.'

'Ho-ho! So it *is* socially embarrassing to have hob-nobbed
with ghosts. Which is a good reason for not believing in
them—or not in the full ghostly sense.' Holroyd reached
placidly for the cheese. 'And what about the girl—what did
she say?'

'Nothing. She just ran away—after not admitting to
seeing a thing.'

'No more she did, perhaps. You yourself may have been
the only percipient on the job.'

'Absolute nonsense!' My impatience mounted. 'What I
first saw was Martha *seeing* something. The impression of
that was overwhelming. Moreover, she was seeing something
that she had been waiting to see. And what I saw, I saw

only because I had happened to take her hand. It was like
an electric circuit closing. When I let go, the lovers
vanished.'

'And the boat as well.'

'Yes, the boat as well. No, thank you.' I had rather
crossly refused the cheese. It was as if the boat were being
exploited by Holroyd to make my tall story yet taller, and
from a professional investigator of psychical phenomena I
found this hard to take. 'Well, there they were,' I said, with
what must have been something like truculence. 'Bertrand
Senderhill and Joan Stickleback.'

'In modern dress.'

'Why not in modern dress? You can have Hamlet and
Ophelia in modern dress—or, for that matter, Othello and
Desdemona. So why not Florizel and Perdita?'

'Yes, yes.' To my increased annoyance, Holroyd contrived to intimate a sense that feeble jokes were to be
deprecated. 'Of course this girl—Martha—*would* see
modern dress. Any other sort must be virtually unknown
to her.'

'It isn't unknown to *me*. As a matter of fact, I was trying,
shortly before this thing happened, to imagine just how
these two young people would have been dressed in the
year 1832.'

'So at least they were in your head.'

'Of course they were in my head. And it's equally certain
that they are pretty constantly in yours. First Hartsilver's
account of Lucius Senderhill's hallucination, and then, hard
upon that, we come on the story of Florizel, Perdita, and
the *Gloriana* preserved in the lad's diary. It's a perfect
explosion of the uncanny under our noses, and we shall
neither of us think of much else for some time.'

'Ho-ho! And now you've had the lion's share of the
bang. By the way, about that boat—'

'It wasn't the dinghy from the boathouse. That hasn't

been in the water. I've looked. And real dinghies don't
vanish in a flash.'

'That's undeniable.' Holroyd was now busying himself
with a small coffee-percolator provided by Mrs Uff. Martha
had not put in an appearance at this meal. 'Don't suppose
me to deny that you and the girl between you have cooked
up something very pretty indeed.'

'Not pretty.' There was in my own voice a conviction
that surprised me. 'I mean, not *merely* pretty : *Swan Lake*
stuff, romantic idyll—that kind of thing. Think, Holroyd!
It has been going on for quite some time.'

'It?'

'This haunting of the spot where their love grew and was
consummated. Drain the lake, and it would still go on. Isn't
that—well, how one has to read the thing? There was once
so fierce and clear a flame, so deep and true a vibration,
that now, one has to suppose, it's for ever. *There* for ever—
in whatever other or further mode of existence I've had
my peep at.'

'My dear chap! You get *this* from—how shall I put it?—
that?'

'Not from what I *saw*. One can't see the quality of a
passion. But from what I *felt*—in the girl.'

'Perdita?'

'No, no. Martha. What it meant to her.' I paused on
this for a moment, I suppose soberly enough. 'Holroyd,' I
asked, 'can you produce a view, an interpretation, of this
mystery?'

'Only a very partial one. You have experienced what it's
not unreasonable you should experience : a hallucination
generated by things we've been hearing and reading about.
But, unless you're uncommonly unreliable, I give it to you
that Martha has experienced the same thing—even has
been in the habit of experiencing the same thing—without
any prompting knowledge at all. Unless, of course, Lucius

Senderhill *did* know Bertrand's story, and communicated it
to Martha at the time he took it into his head that she
might have psychic powers. If that's so—and it isn't wholly
unlikely—we might persuade the girl to tell us about it.
But the interesting possibility remains that something was
messengered to Martha before that something was known to
any living mind. Such phenomena are recorded from time
to time.'

'No doubt.' I found myself resenting Holroyd's prosaic
note. 'But it *is* always hallucination, and is most reasonably
explained as a basically telepathic affair? That's what you
mean by "messengered"?'

'Something like that.' Holroyd poured me out my coffee.
'At least I don't judge it helpful to suppose that there
actually was something *out there*—so many yards from
Martha and yourself, who saw it, and so many from Hartsilver, who did not. I don't mean more than that, you
know, by saying that I don't believe in ghosts.' Holroyd
drank his own coffee at a gulp, having splashed into it
sufficient cream to make this impatient act feasible. I saw
that it had been obtuse in me not to realise that he was in
a state of some excitement. 'And now,' he said, 'I suggest
a division of labour. For we have to discover what. more
we can.'

'Are we obliged to do that?' Although I had just been
demanding light from my friend, this straight proposition
made me strangely uncomfortable. Obscurely in my mind,
perhaps, was the thought that our activities—if we did
effectively contrive any—might result in some sort of laying
of ghosts or exorcising of demons. Until this very morning
it looked as if Florizel and Perdita had been, so to speak,
Martha Uff's exclusive property. Had they perhaps come
to represent something she would be the poorer for losing?
I didn't pretend I knew the answer. 'Are we obliged to do
that?' I reiterated.

'Certainly we are. Ho-ho! Are you thinking, my dear chap, that all charms fly at the mere touch of cold philosophy?' Holroyd glanced at me. 'Why ever do you look so startled?'

'Because it came into my head lately that you have a touch of Keats's Apollonius yourself—or might have. He gave a nasty look, you remember, and a whole fabric of beautiful illusions crumpled up and vanished.'

'I hope I don't deal in nasty looks.' I saw that I had been stupid, and that Holroyd was displeased. 'But I continue to pray for clear ones.' Perhaps seeing that I was chagrined, my friend produced his most robust laugh. 'You're the one,' he said, 'who has begun to gain that girl's confidence. Try to have a talk with her. And I'll have yet another go in those attics.'

'Surely you don't expect to find anything more there— relevant, I mean, to Bertrand Senderhill?'

'One can't tell till one has tried.' And Holroyd's gaze glinted on me in its most disturbing brilliance. 'So here goes.'

I found Mrs Uff—for I judged it necessary to do that— in her kitchen. Not that it *was* her kitchen. This was evident from the fact that there had plainly been moved into it, with an effect as of mere encampment, certain objects rather of ornament than utility, such as are appropriate, I suppose, to a housekeeper's room. Having a little lost my way in the abounding offices of Vailes, I penetrated to this only through a vast and antiquely comfortless servants' hall —never again, I told myself, to be haunted by so much as a knife-boy. Perhaps, indeed, numerous boys of roughly similar endowments and proclivities might soon be accommodated here, but they would be known as juvenile delinquents, and the original home of the Senderhills would be mysteriously denominated an approved school.

The kitchen had an ancient and enormous range, which

ought to have been scrapped long ago, but which had, instead, been expensively adapted to consume electricity. Opposite this was an answeringly enormous dresser, and on this Mrs Uff had disposed a line of framed photographs. One represented the façade of the Hôtel Continental as viewed from the Garden of the Tuileries, and presumably commemorated some early phase of Mrs Uff's employment as a lady's-maid. Others were group photographs of ranked domestics posed either in kitchen-gardens or before majestic porticos according to the whim of their employer; and in these I was sure that the career of Mrs Uff could have been traced from obscurity to eminence. But what was going to happen to her now? No doubt she had a little put by, and no doubt there would be some decent mention of her in Lucius Senderhill's will. But where would she go, and what would become of her daughter? I put these speculative questions aside in favour of something more practical.

'Mrs Uff, I wonder if I might speak to Martha?'

Mrs Uff, who was expertly trussing a fowl, had decorously set aside this employment as I entered the kitchen. She seemed, not unreasonably, a little startled at my request.

'Martha, sir! Has she done anything wrong?'

'Dear me, no—nothing of the kind.' I took this to be an honest reply, even although there have been times, no doubt, in which it was held highly blameworthy to hold sustained commerce with the dead. 'It is simply that I met her when out walking this morning, and that she seemed almost to run away from me. I want to make sure that I have not frightened or offended her in any way.'

'I'm sure I'm very much obliged to you, sir.' Mrs Uff produced these words distinguishably by way of gaining time, and she took a freshly appraising glance at me before going on. 'Would it have been beside the ruined cottage that you came up with her?'

'Yes, it was.'

'Martha is in the laundry, sir. That's at the end of the corridor.' Mrs Uff had given something like a resigned sigh. 'I told her I'd clear the lunch, while she got on with her own washing. I try to keep her nice about herself. You're certainly welcome to speak to her. She's quite taken to you, sir, if you'll pardon the familiarity. A proper gentleman, she called you last night. And there's not many she has that much favour for.'

This was an unexpected testimonial, although I don't think it took me with any marked increase of confidence into Martha's presence. She was standing before a robot-like machine which, having arrived at some crisis of the laundering process, was rocking and quivering in a frenzy of hopelessly shackled energy. The whole place seemed to shake under its efforts to break free. But Martha regarded it only with a kind of dull attentiveness, picking her nose the while. It would have been hard to imagine her as capable of vivid interest in anything.

'Good afternoon, Martha.' I had to raise my voice to contend with the throb and thump of the mechanism. 'Do you remember telling me this morning that you couldn't see anybody except ourselves beside the lake? That wasn't quite true, was it?'

'Mr Hartsilver—'e was there.' Martha got this out with an effort—but rapidly, as if hoping it would end the matter. She had turned round and backed against the washing-machine, plainly afraid that I was going to grab and shake her. The result of this was that the washing-machine shook her instead, and she thus presented the displeasing spectacle of a person trembling in abject terror. 'There was nobbut parson,' she said.

'I'm sure that's not quite right, Martha. Try to remember. Wasn't there a courting couple as well?'

Suddenly the washing-machine gave a final jerk and became immobile, and I saw that the girl really was shaking on her own account. But she was looking straight at me now, and in her gaze there showed something that might be a spark of defiance.

'You seen nothing!' she said violently. 'Why should yer? A foreigner, you are, with no call to. Why, *'e* couldn't 'is self—so why should you?'

'Mr Hartsilver?'

' 'is lordship. Talked to me about perhaps seeing great signs and wonders—like what parson talks on in pulpit—out on the lake one day. But, all the time, what could 'e *not* see? 'im! *'e* could see nobbut tip of 'is own nose.' Martha's voice had turned scornful. But now she checked herself abruptly, and was staring at me in dismay, as if dimly conscious of having betrayed something. 'I seen nothing,' she said sullenly.

'So you said, Martha, on the day I arrived. But isn't it other people who see nothing? Lord Lucius saw nothing. Did he ever tell you any story which might make you expect to see what you *do* see?'

' 'is lordship tell me things?' There was unmistakable incredulity in Martha's voice. '*Not* telling me was 'is line—not even about what great thing was going to 'appen-like on the lake.'

'I see. Well, now, Mr Hartsilver saw nothing this morning, even although the couple were almost touching him as they went past. He gave no sign. Wouldn't you have expected him at least to say good morning to them?'

'Foreigners they'd be. From beyond Lindop or Doddington, like enough. I don't take no account of such—nor would 'e.'

'You mean that when you say there was only Mr Hartsilver beside the lake this morning it's because you don't count the young man and girl, since they are just foreigners and not worth bothering about?' I hope I felt some compunction about seeking virtually to trap Martha in this way.

Looking back now, I can see that I was myself in a confused state of mind, neither wanting to press on nor able to
hold back. It must be remembered that, in this girl's company, something very surprising had befallen me only a few
hours before. 'But,' I continued, 'you do agree that they
were there? And that they've often been there before?'

'Nobody never seen nothing afore! What yer mean,
saying as you did?' Martha's strangely attractive voice—
condemned to hideous articulations part rustic and part
vulgarly urban—was now touched by desperation. 'What
yer mean coming to the 'ouse, if yer not police?'

'Martha, I'm not your enemy. And I'm as puzzled as
perhaps you are. Perhaps only a very few people do see—
well, what you and I were seeing this morning. Perhaps I
might not have done so myself, if we hadn't taken each
other's hands. You remember?'

Suddenly I saw that something was happening to Martha
Uff's face, and it was a moment before I realised that it was
at least nothing more dreadful than a storm of weeping that
had distorted it. I believe I made a movement towards her.
But she had flung herself face-down upon a long table—an
ironing-table, it must have been—and was sobbing con-
vulsively.

'They're mine, they're mine, they're mine!' she cried out.
'Yer not to take them from me. They're *mine*!'

And her violent weeping renewed itself.

2

'I've given her a kind of promise,' I said. 'That they
won't be taken away from her.'

It was an hour later, and I had joined Holroyd in the
muniment room. In the sunbeams streaming through its
dormer windows the dust was dancing madly—and

delusively too, since every mote of the grubby stuff had the gleam of fine gold.

'Taken away? Ho-ho!' For what was, I believe, the first time, my friend's robust laugh jarred on me. 'Does she still suppose you to be a policeman?'

'Whether she does or not, she feels her only cherished possession to be under threat.'

'I see.' Holroyd's voice was at once gentle. Although fanatically given to investigating whatever can be investigated, he is far from being an insensitive man. 'What's the poor girl doing now?'

'She's gone out of doors again, which is only sensible on an afternoon like this.' I had walked to a window—where I had to stand on tiptoe to see anything except the sky. 'And what about ourselves—shall we do that walk to the ruined cottage?'

'By all means—but just let me have another half-hour.' Holroyd was glancing round the already pervasively rifled archives of Vailes in a baffled and almost angry way. It was as if he knew in his bones—I found myself reflecting—that there was something still to find, and yet didn't know where to search further. 'I've been in *there*,' he said, as if reading my mind, and gestured towards the half-open door through which we had remarked the feathers come drifting. 'There's only the junk. I thought there might be documents, but I've drawn blank.' He turned back with a seeming effort to consider what I had been talking about. 'The girl's apparitions are safe enough,' he said.

'My apparitions too.'

'Yes, yes. But, in any case, they're not a commodity one can walk off with. You wouldn't want to take them home with you?'

'Heaven forbid!'

'It's just as well. Anything of the sort is most unusual. There are records of ghosts travelling round with people, but on the whole they stay put. Just as they do in popular lore. It's places, and not people that are haunted. By the way, what is Martha's view of the thing?'

'Her view?' The question took me by surprise. 'I don't know that the child is to be thought of as having speculated about it at all.'

'But she must at least have a notion as to what order of beings she goes spying on.'

'Holroyd, I honestly don't think we should speak of her as going spying. It's the wrong image. I know you feel that she in some sense creates these lovers for herself, and has been able momentarily to create them for me. Even so, she draws a kind of wonder and awe just from this trick of her own mind.' I paused. 'But there's another thing I must emphasise to you. I'm now virtually certain that she got no hint of Bertrand Senderhill and his mistress from anything Lucius Senderhill said to her. She really was—as we've conjectured—seeing these apparitions when there was no knowledge of their existence, let alone of their association, existent in any living mind.'

'She would have her niche in the history of science, poor girl, if we could really prove it to be so. But let me go back to my point. Does Martha believe that she sees living people, or does she believe that she sees ghosts? Even an almost half-witted girl must comprehend categories as simple as that.'

'I doubt whether she has asked herself the question. She knows that they are safe so long as nobody sees them except herself, and that my having seen them spells danger. It is very likely that there have been occasions upon which other people *ought* to have seen them, and didn't. But she might think of this as no more than a marvellous preservation of her secret. That's what they are : her secret. And her mind doesn't travel further.'

'It's our minds which have to do that!' There was such

a sharp and sudden passion in Holroyd's voice that I was greatly startled. 'Don't let anything in my manner, my dear chap, make you feel I don't find this affair staggering. Florizel and his Perdita are coming precious near, I admit, to vindicating themselves as honest-to-God phantasms of the dead. But perhaps there's a soft spot somewhere in the picture. A couple of days ago I'd have said there always is. And there must be something more to find out. I tell you there must!' My friend was silent for a moment—a moment in which I received a vivid impression of some extra-ordinary concentration of his will. 'Don't you agree?' he asked.

I don't know what reply I might have given to this appeal. For suddenly we were both distracted by a sound from the neighbouring attic chamber. It was a sound like a low sigh, and it was followed by a suspiration fainter still—as faint as the sound (if it is a sound) of falling snow. And through the doorway came a drift of feathers and dust.

That there was something unnerving in this moment is perhaps a persuasion which I now feel only as a kind of false memory. Certainly both Holroyd and I reacted in a commonplace way enough. We moved simultaneously to-wards the farther attic as if proposing to discover an eaves-dropper. I think I expected to find a woman—perhaps Mrs Uff. The sound might have been the stir or rustle of a woman's garments when incautiously moved. Yet not of *modern* garments. It is possible that this last thought was really in my head as I reached the door, and that I had a confused expectation of extending, as it were, my range of ghostly acquaintances. But the long, junk-filled room was untenanted, whether by the living or the dead. For a moment we were merely perplexed. And then—again simultaneously to both of us—the prosaic cause of the minute disturbance which had come to us was apparent.

I have mentioned the existence, in that farther attic, of

much abandoned bedding, in particular a bulky feather mattress perched high on a wardrobe and every now and then shedding or voiding a feather which floated down to join the general detritus on the floor. The rotten ticking (as I believe it is called) of this must have split open only a minute previously, with the result that a soft silt of feathers had been trickling to the floor. This, indeed, was still happening now. And, even as we stood there, we heard another and distinct, but again quite tiny, sound. It might be described as a well-cushioned *plop*. Something other than feathers had tumbled from the disintegrating mattress. It lay before our eyes, but with more feathers doing their best to bury it. It was an envelope of moderate size, yellowed and blotched with age, and it had fallen face downwards, so that what we were looking at was a wax seal. This showed like a drop of congealed blood on a jaundiced skin.

Without apparent hesitation, Holroyd had stepped forward and picked the thing up. He turned it over, to reveal some lines of writing in a browned and faded ink.

'*To the Right Rev. the Bishop of Bath and Wells,*' he read aloud, '*from the Lady Otho Senderhill. To be delivered under seal upon the writer's death.*'

'How uncommonly odd!' It was in natural astonishment that I stared at this undelivered missive. 'Have you any notion who Lady Otho Senderhill was?'

'Certainly. She was Bertrand Senderhill's mother.'

There have been, I believe, more than seventy Bishops of Bath and Wells, and there is certainly one at the present day. To him, it seemed to me, Lady Otho Senderhill's letter ought to be considered as addressed, since in default of a more specifically denominated ecclesiastic we could only assume that it was for the holder of the office rather than for an individual that it was intended. But Holroyd, not surprisingly, told me roundly that this was legalistic non-

sense; that we were both at Vailes under a general charter
to sift and enquire, and that it was thus within our province
to scrutinise any document coming our way. *This* document
had come our way in a fashion queer enough. But that didn't
affect our duty to have a look at it.

I have no doubt that my friend was right, and that my
contrary proposition arose from a mounting extreme reluctance to do any more enquiring at all. Since this feeling was
rationally indefensible, I was in no good position to argue.
And I saw at once that Holroyd saw no need to do other
than briefly humour me. Again he was probably right. We
were to pocket Lady Otho's letter, take our walk to the
ruined cottage as proposed; and discuss on the way the
propriety of breaking that—to me—curiously ominous seal.

On the terrace before the house we ran into Mrs Uff.
She was immobile by the lichened balustrade, and gazing
over the lake in so apparent a state of anxiety that for an
extravagant instant I wondered whether she was fearful that
Martha had done herself some mischief. And it was under
this prompting that I spoke.

'Are you looking for your daughter, Mrs Uff? She has
simply gone for one of her walks, I think. In fact, I saw her
set off just after my conversation with her.'

'Oh, sir—was she disturbed in her mind? I thought I
heard a weeping fit. She does have them terrible at times.'

'I am afraid that I did upset her a little, although I only
wanted to give her help. But she was fairly composed when
she left me. I had promised to do my best about something.'

'As I've told you, sir, Martha is a very secret child.' Mrs
Uff looked fixedly first at myself and then at Holroyd. 'But
not deceitful. I would not call Martha that.'

'They can certainly be two very different things, Mrs
Uff.'

'I've been thinking at times that she has taken up with
some worthless lad from the village who means no good by

her, and that that is why she hides her goings and comings from me. Do you think, sir, it might be that?'

'No, I don't.' I hesitated for a moment. 'I don't believe Martha has any encounters of that sort.'

'Then, sir, might it be—?' But Mrs Uff fell silent, aware of some fear too unformulated for expression. 'If either of you gentlemen were to see her, would you beg her to come home? I—I have things for her to do.'

'We shall certainly keep an eye open for her.' Holroyd produced this in a kindly fashion enough, but it was obvious to me that he was impatient for us to go on our way. 'But she'll take no harm on a beautiful afternoon like this.'

There was no doubt about the afternoon. We moved on through it as if it belonged to some Golden Age. And it was, I believe, the full sunshine in which the scene was bathed that put a fresh theme in my head.

'Ghosts, Holroyd—or, if you prefer it, phantasms of the dead: do they often look quite remarkably like flesh and blood?'

'Lord, yes! The other sort—bleached and semi-transparent and floating round crumbled tombs at midnight—turn out to be in a small minority when one starts counting up. Nothing surprising in that. We are constantly seeing perfectly real-looking people inside our heads—and it's there that you have the raw material for all those tricks of projection.'

'And tricks of projection, as you call them, can happen in sunlight just like this?'

'Certainly they can. And there may be nothing uncanny about them except that, so to speak, they snap on and then snap off again. But they needn't even do that. The apparitions may simply board a bus and be carried away at a completely sublunary thirty miles an hour.'

As had happened once or twice before, I didn't know

whether to be reassured or irritated by Holroyd's determined rationalism. If I understood him aright, he believed
that the human mind is liable to perceive as external phenomena what are in fact no more than its own inner imagin-
ings. This seemed to me probable enough. He also believed
that human minds may contrive with one another channels
of communication of an extra-sensory order, not yet understood by science, and that these channels can flow, as it
were, very oddly in time as well as space. Beyond this, he
seemed completely sceptical. Except, I supposed, that he
kept an open mind about O'Rourke and his labours with
those dice.

'I gathered from you,' I said, 'that Bertrand's father,
Lord Otho Senderhill, was the second son of the first
Marquess—and that he married what you called a consider-
able heiress from the City.'

'Certainly. The young lady's name was Lydia Cake-
bread.'

'So Lydia became Lady Otho Senderhill, and in the
fullness of time proposed this posthumous communication'
—and I tapped the pocket in which I was carrying our
discovery—'to the Bishop of Bath and Wells. How the
deuce do you think it got into that bed?'

'I imagine it to be the bed the lady died in. She had
concealed the letter in some sort of slit or fold in it. She
was anxious that its very existence should be unsuspected
until she was actually dying. Wouldn't that be it? She was
going to produce it, and speed it on its way, when she was
in articulo mortis. Only she left it too late.'

'Why should she propose so melodramatic a thing? And
why this particular bishop? Vailes can't be in the diocese—'

'An Evangelical bishop, don't you think? Formerly the
spiritual adviser of the Cakebreads, whom I do know to
have been excessively pious. The implication is clear. The
letter was designed as a kind of deathbed confession. Theo-

logically, the notion was perhaps a trifle irregular. But psychologically it was sound enough. Lydia Senderhill— Lady Otho—was easing her conscience, without any chance of awkward consequences on this side of the grave. Or on the other either, if the bishop did his stuff.'

'Do you mean'—I believe I was disconcerted for a moment by my companion's firm irreverence—'that what we are now in possession of is some kind of guilty secret?'

'Almost certainly it is. Ho-ho! What a gorgeous afternoon.'

'Yes, indeed—and Martha Uff is somewhere wandering round in it. Incidentally, I don't think we gave her mother any undertaking positively to hunt for her, and I suggest we ought not to do anything which might look like that. The child must not feel harried. Wouldn't you agree?'

'Most certainly.' Holroyd appeared surprised. 'But we're up to nothing of the kind.'

'Not consciously. But she may well have made her way to the ruined cottage again, since it's her favourite haunt— and the place where something uncommonly odd happens to her.'

'And to some of her acquaintance as well.' Holroyd gave me a cheerful sideways grin. 'But by all means let us explore the place cautiously, and withdraw for the time being if Martha proves to be in possession.'

I accepted this reasonable suggestion, and as a consequence our approach to the derelict dwelling was by much the same route as I had followed that morning. We paused, just as I had done, where the fruitless orchard still made its despairing gestures to the sky. For a moment there seemed something unfamiliar in the scene before us, and then I realised that all that had changed was the position of the sun. A deep shadow had disappeared from before the abandoned well, and new shadows from the encroaching thorn-trees probed with lengthening fingers the small quadrangular spaces which had once sheltered the Stickle-backs and all their worldly goods. Immediately beyond the tangled space where a garden had once been, and cutting the whole composition in two with the crude effectiveness of poster-art, lay the single broad shadow of a beech. And beyond that again, but on a tree-stump a good deal farther away than before, sat Martha Uff.

I became aware that Holroyd had sat down too, and with something of the celerity of a Boy Scout going to earth during a tracking game. His perch was a fallen tree-trunk comfortably upholstered with moss, and when he silently patted a space beside him I obediently joined him. Martha, I saw, remained just visible, and the consciousness that I was thus beginning to re-enact my peeping role of earlier in the day made me feel markedly uncomfortable. My companion, however, appeared not much concerned with the girl, so that my discomfort was mingled with irritation that a distinguished investigator of psychical phenomena should treat so casually the very situation that had brought me so astounding an experience only a few hours before.

'Well,' Holroyd said a little impatiently, 'out with it, my dear chap. Let's know what the lady found to say to the bishop.'

'As you please.' I took Lady Otho Senderhill's letter from my pocket. 'But ought we to read it just here? Isn't our talk going to disturb Martha?'

'Not unless we lose our tempers and shout at each other.'

'I suppose that's so.' I had measured the distance between Martha and ourselves. 'But, Holroyd, don't you realise what she's about? She's confidently waiting again for—'

'Yes, yes—and you think I ought to be absorbed in the spectacle. But that part of the pattern is clear enough, is it not? Anyway, I promise to be adequately interested in anything that presently turns up. And we can have a better look at her now, if you like.' To my surprise Holroyd produced a small pair of field-glasses from his pocket, and gave a few seconds to training them upon the girl. 'You'll be glad to see,' he said, 'that she appears to be in a composed frame of mind.' And he handed me the instrument. Martha's form, and then her features, leapt at me startlingly as I focused it. She was just as she had been that morning. The only difference was that, this time, her expression was more clearly revealed to me. I saw the identical grave expectation. The poor child might have been a bride on the threshold of her happiness.

'I'll bet you a bob I know how it begins,' I heard Holroyd say encouragingly.

'How what begins?' For a moment it was almost as if I had to recall myself to my friend's presence. 'Oh, the letter.' And I took the thing from my pocket. 'It will begin "My dear Lord Bishop".'

'Not formal enough for a dying confession. It will be just "My Lord".'

3

My Lord,

I beg you to excuse what must seem discourteously abrupt in this letter. You have heard of my illness; there is now no hope for me; my weakness makes it an effort to put pen to paper; there is the further difficulty that I wish to conceal what I do from those who are in almost constant attendance upon me.

You were for long—until your present elevation took you to a distant part of the country—my spiritual adviser, and you have remained my trusted friend. Did you ever guess, I wonder, that the confession of something momentous at least to myself often trembled on my lips?

It is not, thank God—and as it might be with many

women of apparently unblemished reputation that I know —a confession of *adultery*. It is a confession that I have borne an illegitimate child. Do not condemn me harshly until you have heard me out. *The secret is my dear husband's too.*

We met in Baden—a resort much frequented by my father. His wealth, as you know, had been acquired in trade, and it was in such watering-places that he found a first ready means of entry into good society. There was much of which he could not approve in such places, since both he and my mother, together with all their kinsfolk, were of the strictest religious principles. Social advancement, however, was almost equally dear to him!

Otho and I met in the gardens of the Kursaal. Later— and how grave a folly!—we used to make small clandestine expeditions amid the gentle Baden hills. Yet our love prospered, and eventually a formal alliance was approved by both Otho's parents and mine. How happy was I in the prospect of a lifetime with my lover! And how happy was my father that this same lover was the Marquess of Melchester's grandson!

The fell hand of war separated us, for Otho had suddenly to join his regiment in Spain. At the same time—but this was a blessing in disguise—such was the incivility of the Corsican tyrant that English persons even of quality were incommoded in many places of sojourn throughout the continent. My father judged it prudent to withdraw for a time to a more obscure resort. We had scarcely reached this refuge when I discovered myself to be with child.

Otho, meanwhile, had been taken prisoner, and we learnt that it must be many months before he should be released on parole. Yet correspondence was possible, and he and my father agreed on a plan.

It would have been unnecessary had *my* family been Senderhills. Our aristocracy did not at that time take much account of what would be judged the venal fault of a pre-nuptial mischance. But my own Aunt Dinah was another matter. As you will recall, my father's fortune, although considerable, was engaged to my brothers, and it was only the great wealth which was to come to me from this relative that had prompted the Marquess to sanction the proposed marriage. My Aunt Dinah was a spinster of the most exact piety. A breath of what had happened would seal the well-springs of her benevolence for ever.

You can imagine—my dear and reverend friend!—what had to be contrived. My daughter's birth was of a like guilty secrecy to that which had attended her conception. Bavarian foster-parents in respectable circumstances were to receive her. Yet this plan my *maternal fondness* forbade. The child was returned to England, and placed with persons of humbler station (since nothing else could safely be contrived) on one of the more remote Senderhill estates. And with that my troubles ended (*worldly* troubles, that is to say; of others, this repentant missive is a witness). Otho was released with unexpected expedition, and our marriage immediately followed. My dear son Bertrand (whose unhappy and untimely death at sea I must ever regard as a *heavenly judgement* executed upon me) was born but one year to the very day after his *innocent but untimely* sister.

My dear Lord Bishop, my confession is over. The chronicle is closed. I shall have been brought to another *judgement* ere this reaches you. Pray for my soul, dear Bishop, in your heart. Protestant theology, I am told, forbids that you should do so publicly.

Your Lordship's obedient daughter in God,
LYDIA SENDERHILL.

Post scriptum. You may wonder what happened to the child. Many years ago now, I was startled to learn that Otho had nonchalantly moved the foster-parents (and our daughter with them) to employment and a cottage on the

Vailes estate itself. Otho himself has been quite without concern or curiosity over what he calls 'the wrong-side-of-the-blanket one'. Yet she was only, I have been used to tell him, 'the wrong-side-of-the-altar one'. And I myself dared only to see the child; never to speak to her. She emigrated to the colonies with a lover, it seems, very much about the time of poor Bertrand's death. But I have never had particulars. The foster-parents have been strangely evasive. Their name—an absurd name—is Stickleback!

L. S.

4

I had read this extraordinary confession aloud. Not un-naturally, there was a silence between Holroyd and myself when I had finished it.

'One sees them,' Holroyd said.

'Them?'

'Otho Senderhill and his Lydia in Baden-Baden. Wander-ing the little rough-paved streets, or flirting in the grounds of the *Conversationshaus*. But would that have been there in the Napoleonic period? The countryside can't have changed much. Those little timber-and-plaster villages peeping out from a tangle of plum-trees.'

'My dear man!' I was astonished at my friend's falling into this evasive chatter, although I faintly knew it was a consequence of his being much disturbed. 'You realise what this letter tells us?'

'Yes, yes—but at least they lived long ago.'

'Otho and Lydia?'

'Florizel and Perdita. They were *really* Laon and Cythna —all the time.'

'What the devil do you mean by that?'

'Shelley's lovers were brother and sister—at least in his

first shot at the poem. Curious that Bertrand should have copied from its supreme moment into his book.'

'You mean Bertrand may have *known*?'

'No, no. But if this affair confirms us in anything, it's surely in the knowledge that human minds, living and dead, communicate with one another in remarkably devious ways. Do you know Kipling's story called *Wireless*? It's not about Shelley. But it's about Keats.'

'Confound Kipling.' I paused for a moment. 'No wonder those wretched Sticklebacks were upset. But they kept mum, and at least Bertrand and his mistress never *knew*. Indeed, the Sticklebacks must have been the only two human beings who *did* know. All knowledge of the truth—the full truth—perished with them. Until we opened *this*'—I tapped the letter—'and put our own small two-and-two together.'

'That's the probability, unless the Sticklebacks had a confessional urge too. Perhaps—' Holroyd broke off. 'Hullo! That girl has vanished.'

'Vanished?' Not unnaturally, I had for the moment quite forgotten Martha Uff.

'Not in any supernatural fashion.' Holroyd's brilliant eyes flashed at me alarmingly. 'She must just have walked away—following her dream.'

'Last time, it became my dream too.'

'Yes, indeed.' Holroyd was suddenly grave. 'Don't think I have no sense of the strangeness of all this.'

I made no reply. I was less concerned with Holroyd's state of mind than with my own. Several times since coming to Vailes I had felt, not wholly without cause, uneasy enough. But that had been, so to speak, in my head. My sensation now was scarcely cerebral at all. Rather it was visceral: an obscure dismay and dread deep in my body, like a premonitory symptom of depressive sickness. It was in an effort to get rid of this that I did presently speak.

'Holroyd—Martha couldn't have heard us? She couldn't

have heard me reading *this*?' And again I tapped the yellowing paper and faded brown ink of Lady Otho Senderhill's letter to the Bishop of Bath and Wells.

'Not unless she's endowed with a most remarkable hyperaesthesia of the auditory faculty. Otherwise, she could have heard nothing short of a shout. Not that some other form of rapport—' Suddenly Holroyd stopped in the middle of his jargon. 'Listen!' he said.

The injunction was needless, for I had already heard the sound. Nor was it again repeated after some faint echo had done with it amid the beech-woods. It had come from the direction of the lake: a single and despairing cry.

We were running—two elderly and agitated men—down the long green ride that led from the ruined cottage to the water. It was my thought—shocking yet prosaic enough—that we should find Martha as they had found Ophelia: drowned while incapable of her own distress. Martha, however, was still on dry land.

She, too, was running—frantically by the margin of that small, tranquil flood. But, even as we first glimpsed her, she stopped, and flung out her arms strangely in an imploring gesture to empty air. She turned and ran again; stopped; the gesture was repeated in the direction contrary to the first. And this time she sank down upon her knees.

It was thus that we came up with her: a distraught child, her face bathed in streaming tears. I scarcely expected that she would so much as see us. But she did, and our presence brought her to her feet. She faced us, and spoke.

'You've taken them from me!' she cried. 'And now I know as wot they'll come no more.'

I looked beyond her to the unmoving and empty water of the lake. It shone still a heavenly blue. The early evening was indeed one of extraordinary beauty. There was not another soul or living thing in sight. There were only our three selves, required to make what we could of the impassive face of external Nature.

'Listen, Martha!' I cried. 'You must try to understand. They are only—'

The child was running again. I had broken off at the sight of her freshly contorted face. Now that was invisible to me. For she had turned, and it was straight for the lake that she ran. This was in itself no crisis, since the water could not have been for some way deep enough to allow of her doing any mischief to herself. But my thoughts were confused, and I felt that I must stop her at once, must hold her until some sort of calm words were possible. So I too ran, and it was only at the verge that I seized her hand. We both halted—so abruptly that I almost stumbled over a sizable stone at my feet. I glanced quickly down at this, and saw that it lay on top of a short length of rope. And suddenly it was very, very cold.

The little boat was there. I could have put out my disengaged hand and touched its prow. But my gaze rested on it only for a moment, and then I looked beyond; looked to where, that morning, I had seen two lovers hand in hand. The young man in the jeans and sweater was there again now. Only whereas my morning's experience had been lucid and rational, about this one there was something fantasmal and dreamlike. He was walking slowly away from me, but some breach in the laws of optics permitted me to view his face. I saw it with an extraordinary clarity, as if through an instrument more refined than the one in Holroyd's pocket now. The young man was very handsome and very pale. And over his features lay an expression of numb horror so unnerving that I could not bear it. I looked to the other side of the lake.

The girl was there. She too was retreating, and her face too I could nevertheless see—or rather I could see the two hands in which she carried it buried. For seconds these two

figures—planted solidly on earth despite the strangeness of
my vision of them—walked slowly on; sundered by the long
vista of water that led to Vailes. Then something seemed
to happen to the girl. It was something that made me
wonder whether my grip on Martha's hand had slackened.
But it was not so; I held it as firmly as before. I looked
again at Perdita, and knew that she was fading on my
sight. I looked at Florizel. He was there still, but something
was happening to his clothes, to his body—for through and
beyond them I saw some further thing : thorn or bramble
or hazel-bush it may have been. A moment later and he
was there no longer—nor his mistress on the other bank.
Yet for some heart-beats in each place something lingered :
shadows faintly human like those traces called *pentimenti*
in old pictures, where the artist has repented of some
botched creation and expunged on his canvas all but the
shade of a shade.

'You saw them again?' Holroyd had joined me, and it was
as if some spell were broken by his voice.

'Yes.' I put my arm round the weeping child at my side.
'But Martha is right. They'll come no more.'

The Men

I T W A S 5 P.M. and the dons were packing up to go
home. Or so the Jarvie phrased it to himself as, glancing
through a window which commanded the main gate of the
college, he saw yet another middle-aged man strapping a
pile of books to the antique 'carrier' of his bicycle. The
time was coming, the Jarvie thought, when at this hour
of the day he would be the only senior member left in the
place.

He was universally known as the Jarvie, and as 'Jarvie'
he was almost invariably addressed. This was because, in a
closed society, 'Strathalan-Jerviswoode' becomes tedious to
articulate, and because he had gained his Fellowship long
before the use of Christian names was the practice in Oxford
common rooms, whether senior or junior. So 'the Jarvie' he
became—upon the information, some averred, of a contemporary who had known him to have been so nicknamed
at Winchester. At one subsequent period, indeed, a few
venturesome persons—who had all become 'Charles' and
'Theodore' and the like to each other, and who possessed
that just distaste for the exceptional or anomalous which
distinguishes the academic mind—tried calling the Jarvie
'Vivian'. The Jarvie had thereupon let it be known that,
although he would not dream of questioning his colleagues'
taste, it remained his own feeling that this completely
familiar form of address ought to be employed only by those
who were his intimates.

'Intimates' was a good Jarvie word, and the Jarvie did
actually know a number of persons who could be so
denominated. There were even a couple of them resident

in Oxford, whom he dined or went to dine with regularly. The others—stringy old men with drooping moustaches like discoloured tusks—were understood to be in general the proprietors of extensive though totally barren estates in North Britain. These did actually call the Jarvie 'Vivian'. They were perhaps a little surprised to hear their ancient friend call his professional associates at High Table 'Theodore' or 'Charles'. But the Jarvie would have thought it poor form not to concur—at least this way on—with his younger colleagues' conventions. It was true that, if one of them chanced to have initials susceptible of enunciation as a word, the Jarvie would ingeniously cheat by himself producing a kind of nickname out of them. There was a man called William Oldfield Gifford, an inorganic chemist of obscure origin, whom the Jarvie habitually addressed as 'Wog'. Late at night, when he had drunk too much brandy and become a shade quarrelsome, he would try to insist on other people calling Gifford 'Wog' too. On the other hand, were anyone outside the college to asperse Gifford in the Jarvie's hearing—on the score, say, of his accent or his finger-nails—the Jarvie would turn on an icy aristocratic contempt that simply froze further words on the speaker's lips. College loyalty was a first principle with the Jarvie.

It came under strain from time to time—as now, for example, as he watched the homing habits of married dons at five o'clock. He might soon be the only grown-up left in the place, he repeated to himself sadly as he turned away from the window to pace the worn Aubusson carpet which he had been let bring up with him when entering the college as a freshman more than half a century before. Not, he told himself quickly, that the men were not to be thought of as grown-up. Or at least spoken of, and to, as grown-up. One of the newfangled things that most annoyed him was the tendency of college tutors to refer to the men as 'boys'. It wasn't even an Americanism, although it sounded like one.

And as with all changes in verbal habit it was significant of something, although he wasn't quite sure of what.

The Jarvie's thoughts turned to making up his fire, and then to tea. Nowadays, his mind seldom proceeded very far in an analytical way.

He was accustomed to have tea served at half-past four, which was late enough considering that dinner was at half-past seven. But commonly he left the silver kettle undisturbed above its small flame until nearly five before setting about the actual business of infusion. His actions then, although he scarcely knew it, were exactly those of his mother long ago. He warmed each cup, or more commonly his solitary cup, with a little of the hot water, and a single drop of this he transferred in turn to each required saucer. This consulted the convenience of his guests, if there were any, by decreasing the liability of the cups (which like the carpet and the tea equipage came from Jerviswoode) to slither on the saucers. Or that was the theory.

Nobody having dropped in, he made tea now. There was a covered dish which revealed on inspection a sizeable pile of crumpets. The Jarvie, although he had expected nothing else and would have been put out by innovation, frowned at the buttery objects, put back the cover, and picked up a small tomato sandwich. As he did so, there came a knock at the door.

The Jarvie was not misled. This was the knock of a person who proposes to enter whether bidden so to do or not—but only in virtue of holding a station so lowly that he, or she, can be ignored if need be. It was, in fact, Mrs Crumble. And Mrs Crumble, seeing that the Jarvie was alone, wished him good evening.

'Ah, Mrs Crumble, I'm not quite finished, I'm afraid.' The Jarvie spoke particularly pleasantly to Mrs Crumble, for the reason that he didn't greatly approve of her, or rather of her presence in his rooms. Mrs Crumble was simply Crumble's wife, and it was, after all, Crumble whom the Jarvie employed. The Jarvie was the only don in college thus to have a private servant in fee; indeed, such a state of affairs must almost have vanished out of mind in the university as a whole. It was an extravagance, without a doubt; there were probably those who regarded it as an eccentricity. But then the Jarvie had had Crumble for a very long time—for much longer, certainly, than Crumble had had Mrs Crumble.

Mrs Crumble, however, was a respectable woman, and had probably been in good service before attaining with Crumble to her present connubial felicity. (The Jarvie was given to such phrases, at least in interior monologue, since he was no lover of women.) Perhaps it was sensible of Crumble to keep his wife in some degree in good service still, at least to the extent of appointing her his deputy from time to time. It would be unreasonable, the Jarvie felt, to object to the woman's making his bed, or even setting out or taking away the tea things. It was for this last purpose, he supposed, that she had presented herself now.

But he quickly realised that this could not be so. Mrs Crumble knew perfectly well that his tea-hour might not begin till five, and she was too well trained to appear only ten minutes thereafter for the purpose of 'clearing him up'. There must be another explanation, and in a moment he came to it. When he had made up his fire there hadn't been enough coal for the job. The probability of this had been in the mind of Crumble where he was somewhere enjoying his afternoon ease. And now Mrs Crumble was here to take his empty coal-scuttle, carry it down two flights of stairs, and then bring it up again laden.

It would by no means do. (This, as with most of the Jarvie's imperatives, was his mother again. She had been a very odd sort of woman, who had insisted that only men-servants should carry heavy burdens about the castle. Even unmarried women guests—of whom her husband had been rather fond—had to abide by the rule: dressed or undressed, their peat and their bath-water would be brought in by the footmen or not at all.) So here was a sudden crisis, of a magnitude such as the Jarvie had not had to face for weeks. He found he didn't want to say to Mrs Crumble, 'That's something I insist your husband should do, so put the scuttle down'. Thus to rebuke Crumble as it were *via* Mrs Crumble came to him obscurely as an improper intrusion on the mysterious, the utterly mysterious, marital bond. The woman wasn't going to go scampering and staggering round with the damned scuttle, all the same. Awaiting inspiration, the Jarvie temporised. He conversed.

'An excellent tea, Mrs Crumble. But nobody has come in to share it with me. Most of the men are in training, no doubt. Torpids, you know. And what they now call Cuppers, eh? And there are new notions about training, it seems. One of the men was talking to me about it the other day. Carbohydrates are in disfavour. And by carbohydrates are meant, it appears, crumpets and muffins. Great nonsense—eh, Mrs Crumble?'

'Yes, indeed, sir. I never did know a gentleman the worse for a crumpet to his tea.' Mrs Crumble paused, and then decided that it was permissible, even incumbent upon her, to venture further speech. 'As Crumble says, sir, there's never harm in a little of what you fancy. If you know how to get hold of it, he says.'

'Does he, indeed.' Mrs Crumble, the Jarvie reflected, must have been, at least for a time, a little of what Crumble fancied. 'But my talk with Mr Bellringer—the man I speak of is called Bellringer, and is apparently President of the J.C.R.—has suggested something to me. I think of giving breakfasts again. Formerly, all the tutors gave breakfasts. They were completely *sans façon*. One could even go along

in one's dressing-gown, which is how one normally break-
fasted in one's rooms.' The Jarvie had hesitated; he was
uncertain about its being proper to mention an article of
half-toilet when *tête à tête* with a female. 'But now they
all have to go into hall. Or rather they don't. They simply
lie in bed. I deprecate that.'

'The old ways did mean a lot of service, sir.' Mrs
Crumble, although uneasy in face of this protracted chat,
said what it was relevant to say. 'All those trays up all those
staircases. Crumble remembers his early days at that, sir—
as a college scout, that is, before he had the good fortune
to be taken into private service. It required what strength
a man had, sir.'

'Perfectly true, my good woman. Perfectly true, Mrs
Crumble.' The Jarvie had swiftly corrected himself in the
interest of proper accommodation with the conventions of
the later twentieth century. He observed Mrs Crumble to be
edging towards the coal-scuttle, and realised that he had
not yet decided on a plan of action. 'But if I begin giving
breakfasts again it will at least be no burden on the college.
We are an independent concern, are we not? And the point
is that we could have steaks. Rowing men should certainly
have steaks. And some of the reading men look to me as if
they would be none the worse of red meat. You must have
remarked it.'

'Well, sir, I don't know that I much notice the gentlemen.
It's not as if Crumble and me was on a staircase.' Mrs
Crumble adduced this consideration with a just consciousness of a certain social remove. For the Jarvie's quarters did
constitute very much an independent domain, and on the
strength of this the Crumbles took satisfaction in keeping
themselves to themselves. Crumble's intimates (as the Jarvie
might have called them) were understood to consist only
of the head porter and the senior-common-room butler.
'And not so many of the gentlemen come and go in your

own rooms, sir, as Crumble says he has memory of. It's a change in them as comes into residence, Crumble says. The new sort of gentlemen being less at ease, he says, in a gentleman's society.'

'Nothing of the sort. Your husband doesn't know what he's talking about.' The Jarvie had spoken so brusquely to this idiotic crawling woman that he felt some amends must be made. He honestly believed that he had been brought up to be undeviatingly courteous to servants. 'But it's true that our life in college is not quite what it was. Something of the sort was in my mind not an hour ago. No doubt rightly, family commitments occupy a great part of my colleagues' time. What has become, I ask myself, of the most important hours in an Oxford college? The two or three hours before midnight, that is, and sometimes an hour or two after that. In my time as Dean, I used to gate the ablest men quite regularly. On trumped up charges, if necessary.' As he produced this implausible reminiscence, the Jarvie gave a surprisingly savage little laugh. 'And then they would go round paying calls. For that matter, a man might invite one to drop in the very evening after one had gated him. And one would have real talk. There was a serious interest in philosophy in Oxford in those days.' The Jarvie checked himself, conscious that it was a little odd to be talking to Mrs Crumble like this. And once more he frowned at the untouched crumpets, decently invisible beneath their cover. 'And now, Mrs Crumble, I think you can take away the tea.'

'Yes, sir. But first I'll just fill your coal-scuttle.'

'Thank you, no.'

'Oh, it's no trouble at all, sir.'

'I didn't say it was. But put that thing down.' The Jarvie was now so annoyed with Mrs Crumble that he spoke very gently indeed, with the paradoxical result that Mrs Crumble dropped the scuttle as abruptly as if she had been bawled at.

'And please ask Crumble to come up the moment he reaches college. He must go over to common room for a bottle of brandy It is likely that some of the men will be coming in for music later. Good evening, Mrs Crumble.'

As soon as the woman had gone away, the Jarvie moodily turned on one of the electric heaters with which the bursar had insisted on providing him. The contraption purred officiously, much like Mrs Crumble calling attention to the assiduity with which she performed her offices. He found himself pacing restlessly about his large, lofty, rather murkily commodious room. It was full of the battered and worm-eaten but impressive objects which a younger son will contrive to carry away from a great house. On the walls, between the books, were eighteenth-century copies of seventeenth-century portraits. Most of the men supposed these to be of college worthies, but they were Jerviswoodes and Crawfords and Grahams, including that James Graham, Marquess of Montrose, who (as the Jarvie might have reminded some particularly favoured man) had written 'My dear and only Love'.

> *. . . But if thou wilt be constant then,*
> *And faithful of thy word,*
> *I'll make thee glorious by my pen,*
> *And famous by my sword.*
> *I'll serve thee in such noble ways*
> *Was never heard before:*
> *I'll crown and deck thee all with bays,*
> *And love thee evermore.*

The Jarvie, whom one would not have suspected of harbouring in memory much amatory verse, repeated the stanza silently to himself as he stood before the portrait. Then he moved back to the window.

Moist autumn dusk was seeping into the quad, nosing

out for a start only retired corners and the already cavernous
mouths of staircases; elsewhere it was not yet an assured
objective presence, so that the Jarvie fleetingly wondered if
his sense had clouded, his vision taken some swift
treacherous jump towards growing dim. But nothing of the
sort. He saw very well, and heard too. From quite far away
he could hear clearly now—for he had thrown up the lower
sash on an impulse—the shouts and laughter of the Provost's
young children, romping in their high-walled garden after
tea. Then, from near at hand, came a burst of laughter
much louder than this.

He looked down. Two young men, back from squash,
were passing beneath his windows. Foreshortened as they
were, their naked legs appeared to issue directly from
beneath a superincumbent voluminousness of scarves and
sweaters. The laughter had sprung simultaneously from each,
as if only the most intuitive impulse had prompted it. And
now they stopped before an archway before taking their
several paths. Unconsciously they shifted from poised foot
to foot, their bodies swaying like saplings. They half-circled
each other, and their rackets took small token swipes in air.
They had enjoyed their game and were talking nonchalantly
and gaily, acknowledging a faint casual reluctance to part.

The Jarvie listened—like a high-born maiden, he told
himself humorously, in a palace-tower. He listened inno-
cently, since it was so little anything like private communication that was going on. The words came up to him clearly,
yet conveyed nothing at all. Perhaps he lacked some key
to them. Or perhaps it was not really the particular remarks
of particular young men that he was listening to.

There was an impatient shout from an invisible source.
One of the squash-players bellowed a cheerful and rude
reply, regardless of disturbing the calm of more studious
persons on nearby staircases; then he turned from his companion and went with long strides at a slow double across

the quad. Meleager, the Jarvie said to himself, Meleager at the chase. The second young man had disappeared beneath the archway, and the quad was silent again. It was suddenly very silent, and also a little melancholy. The Jarvie was about to close the window, but first he looked at his watch. It was within a minute of six o'clock, and he waited for the bells.

They would come with the delicate disregard for brute synchronism for which Oxford bells are famous. The first were both small and far away, so that one would hear only notes on the verge of silence, as at the start of the New World Symphony. (The music to which the Jarvie was always ready to entertain the men tended to be of a sort much in esteem forty years before.) Then there would be medium-sized bells quite close at hand, and then small bells again in the middle distance. Next there would be a *mélange* of many bells all over the place, and finally—far away again, but loudest of the lot—the great Christ Church bell.

So the Jarvie paused, and not in vain. But what he heard was not what he had awaited; it was the sudden clangour of first one and then a second ambulance—or was it a fire-engine?—clamouring for way through some traffic-jammed street beyond the college. These bells rang demoniacally, and behind them the siren of a police-car added ululation to uproar. Neither spire nor tower nor belfry had a chance. The Christ Church bell alone asserted itself, and that only on its concluding boom.

He closed the window. He hoped that a life had been saved, or at least property preserved. But the urgent alarm had been like a tocsin. It had seemed to speak to him disturbingly of a world outside the college walls which was sudden, violent, and unexpected: no world of his.

2

But within the walls, also, there was one world that was alien to him. He would refer to it—without facetiousness and merely in the antique phraseology which he found natural—as the praeposital lodging. When Goldengrove, a bachelor and his oldest friend, had been Provost the Jarvie had taken on the role (as it used to amuse him to say) of Provost's lady; he had done this to the extent, at least, of constantly lending Goldengrove a hand at entertaining the men. Goldengrove had been properly interested in the men. When they had departed (with the trustworthy correctness of former days) from the praeposital library in which whisky had signalled the conclusion of the entertainment the two friends would linger over the fire till midnight, happily gossiping about this man and that. Young Howard was tipped for a First in Greats. Somerset was the split image of his grandfather. The rather awkward Open Scholar from Huddersfield was a delightful lad, but that grandson of old Berryman's, having got into Pop at Eton, showed no sign of any ability to get out of it. And you only had to glance at the shoulders of that quiet Rhodes Scholar from Harvard to know that the college was going to go head of the river.

Oh, golden nights with Tony Goldengrove! The Jarvie's eyes—for he was an old man—would grow moist as he thought of them.

Not that he bore the new order in the Lodging any ill-will. It was only after that injudicious third brandy in common room that he had murmured to one of the droopy-moustached Scottish lairds that over there the Lion and the Lizard now kept the Courts where Jamshyd gloried and drank deep—or as deep as is proper in the Head of a House entertaining freshmen. Nor would he have ventured so trite a quotation but for the inviting fact that Finch, the new

Provost, wore his hair in a fashion consciously leonine, and that Mrs Finch, though doubtless a charming woman, was, with her dartingly protrusive tongue, most damnably *like* a lizard.

Mrs Finch was very conscious of the Jarvie as the late Provost's friend, and as therefore peculiarly associated with a departed order. It would have been inaccurate and unfair to say that, because of this, she set out to be gracious to him. More troublesomely, she was determined to be friendly. In the past the Jarvie had been accustomed to give in his rooms each term a single luncheon party to which ladies were invited. In the way of hospitality returned, these somewhat formal occasions had served to balance as many incursions into general society as politeness constrained him to adventure upon. The system would have brought the Finches in contact with the Jerviswoode silver ('Strike agayne' was the motto on the spoons and forks) once a year, and the Jarvie to fiddling with Mrs Finch's pretentious Venetian finger-bowls not much oftener than that. But Mrs Finch let it be known at once that these exiguous and equipoised exchanges would by no means do; that she was going to rely upon the Jarvie a great deal; and that her absolute gratitude would go out to him if he accepted as many of her invitations as he could. The Jarvie, Mrs Finch said, stood for all that was most important in the continuing life of the college (she abounded in phrases of this kind) and above all would be invaluable to her in her efforts to get to know the undergraduates. It was universally recognised that the Jarvie had an unrivalled understanding of young men.

The Jarvie's first exposure to all this cost him a sleepless night. But Crumble had hardly brought in his early morning tea before it came to him that Mrs Finch must be obeyed. Or obeyed more often than not. He would respond to, say, three summonses out of five. Her lights might be dim, but it was honestly according to them that she was making an effort to be a Provost's wife. He didn't at all see himself in the character of what was now called a P.R.O.—private relations and not public relations were what he judged as important in civilised behaviour—but it was his duty to back the woman up even if he was to be treated in her drawing-room as a minor institution. He had also to remember that, being now a mere Emeritus Fellow, he continued to reside in college only by favour of the Provost himself. It would scarcely be sensible to offend the Finches.

Nothing of this was in the Jarvie's head as, having closed his window on the defeated bells, he turned and walked back to his fireplace. He had remembered that the Eroica Symphony was to be broadcast that evening, and at a time which would enable him to spend a quietly convivial hour in common room before coming back to hear it. But no sooner had he registered his satisfaction over this than his glance chanced to fall upon a square of pasteboard on the mantelpiece. It was one of Mrs Finch's too-frequent dinner invitations, and it was for this very evening. He had inexplicably forgotten about it. Being unread in the psychopathology of everyday life, the Jarvie found this unaccountable as well as tiresome. There was nothing to be done but submit. It was all the more vexatious in that there was such a probability that men would be coming in for the music. The Jarvie went over to his desk, took a piece of scrap-paper (for most of his habits evinced the Jerviswoode frugality), and wrote:

> *Third on Third at 9.30*
> *Go in and turn on*
> *Back not long after 10*
> *V. S-J.*

The Jarvie laughed barkingly at this, recognising in it the

authentic Jarvie flavour. He would pin the invitation up on his unsported oak before presenting himself in Mrs Finch's drawing-room.

An hour later, having admonished Crumble in the matter of the coal and transferred himself into the dinner-jacket laid out by his chastened factotum, the Jarvie emerged into the dark quadrangles—quiet, deserted, and almost unlit at this hour when few people were not in Hall. From five to seven the men had been reading their texts or writing their essays, each in the roomy solitude of his set (although the college's New Building, indeed, consisted of bed-sitters : atrocities brought into being by the pressure of external forces incomprehensible to the Jarvie). Or perhaps some of them had been talking—for that is all-important too—in small groups of intimates sharing a bottle of sherry. And now all the life of the college (as Mrs Finch would say) had been drawn together for the common meal. The Jarvie counted the flight of time chiefly in terms of the diminishing number of these sacramental occasions that could lie ahead of him. It was the fact of missing one of them, rather than the mere boredom almost certainly impending in the Lodging, that irked him as he cautiously skirted the invisible ancient grass.

Caution was necessary because the flagstones beneath his feet were cracked, uneven, and in places slippery. Moreover, although it was debatable whether the Jarvie was yet to be described as failing, there was undeniably the hint of an old man's totter in his walk. It was as if in each setting down of a foot there lurked a minute element of deliberation. At this moment his head was registering a motion which did not in fact exist, that of a gently rolling deck beneath his tread. But physical disabilities can bring odd compensations. Entering the main quad, and thus having the long line of lighted Hall windows at some remove on his

right hand, the Jarvie seemed suddenly to be in the presence
of a great ship, a great liner, sailing by. Behind it was a sky
powdered with stars.

Whither, though, was it voyaging? The question was
sufficiently puzzling to occupy the Jarvie until the Provost's
front-door lay obliquely before him. It was beneath the
clear light shining from it, indeed, that he found himself
almost on a collision course with a running undergraduate.
Or not really almost, since the Jarvie had scarcely needed
to modify his careful stride. So it was hardly incumbent
upon the young man to check his flying speed, turn round,
and apologise. Yet this the young man did. The Jarvie's
satisfaction in a show of decent manners increased when he
saw that here was Miles Honeybeare, one of the nicest of
the second-year men.

'Jarvie! I'm so sorry.' The men addressed the Jarvie either
thus or as 'Sir', and it was generally felt that about fifty-
fifty was what the old fellow liked. 'I oughtn't to have been
going at such a lick.' The friendliness of Honeybeare's
smile was delightful; it had a warmth that was somehow set
off by the bleak light beating down on him. Honeybeare's
features were soft and dusky, and above them, and sometimes across them, tossed a tumble of long dark hair. 'Are
you going to dine with the Provost, sir?'

'Yes, Miles. It happens from time to time.' The Jarvie
felt that between Miles Honeybeare and himself there
flashed a glance of discreet and merry understanding. 'But
—do you know?—I'd clean forgotten about it. And they're
doing the Eroica on the Third Programme.'

'Oh, too bad, Jarvie.' Although Honeybeare had been
in such a tearing hurry a minute before, no flicker of
impatience appeared in him now. He might have been one
of those squash-players—it came to the Jarvie with a stab
of pleasure—idly pleased to prolong his chatter with his
fellow.

'But would you care to hear it, Miles? It's at half-past nine. Do go in if you'd like to. One or two other men may be there, and I suppose Crumble won't have forgotten something to drink. With luck I'll be back by ten.'

'It's most frightfully kind of you, sir.' Honeybeare was the sort of young man who could say such things without seeming faintly to sound a false note. 'But I've got my essay, as a matter of fact. That's why I'm going over the way to get a bun at the Stag. You save about half an hour by cutting Hall. As it is, I'm afraid I'll have to work till two or three. My tutor's given me a subject on which I'm quite criminally ignorant.'

'Ah well, another time.' Through long habituation, the Jarvie was able to approve these studious professions without quite believing in them. Nowadays, he knew, many of the men actually formed acquaintanceships in the ladies' colleges, took girls out to meals in restaurants, and even— within permitted hours—entertained them in college rooms. The Jarvie did not conceal from himself that he regretted these changed ways. They took something away from the place, away from a surely magical three or four years set beyond the rumour of the common world. Yet he did not tell himself that it would be better were such contacts postponed until the men went down. Certain misfortunes and even disasters, well known to his generation, were obviated by this particular sort of maturation coming earlier. The Jarvie wasn't a fool. It is scarcely possible for a Fellow of an Oxford college to be that. But he was of a simple mind. And this simplicity certainly showed no sign of attenuating itself upon the approaches of old age.

'Then you'd better cut along,' he said now. As he spoke he turned upon Miles Honeybeare the particular regard with which (although he would never have conceived of it in this way) he had for long been accustomed to captivate young men. The conventional word for what was most

obvious in this look would have been 'quizzical'. It was
appraising, and the issue of the appraisal appeared to be
a faintly amused yet friendly scepticism. At the same time
something in his expression—or it may even have been the
slightest of conceivable movements of the head—remotely
signalled the passing of a test. And if the Jarvie thus
approved you it wasn't because you were good-looking, or
clever, or in some way a charmer, or notably well-bred.
These things might be ponderable counters with him. But
what he had essentially concluded about you was that you
would be all right in an open boat, or in any similar
exigency in which what may be called manhood is rather
to the point. The Jarvie got away with this (for it can be
considered in that light) because he managed it in a fashion
so reassuringly remote from, say, the shameing explicitness
of a sermon in a school chapel. There had just flickered
between you and him the existence of a code which would
utterly violate itself by utterance. It was something too
momentary to be embarrassing.

Miles Honeybeare seemed unembarrassed now, and even
indisposed to accept the injunction to cut along. Instead,
he threw back his head—which was his way of getting his
hair out of his eyes—and offered the Jarvie something uncommonly like a *quid pro quo* in the way of reticent
approval.

'It must be rather fun,' Honeybeare said—and he had
exactly the tone, approved by the Jarvie, which balances
deference to seniority against the perfect unconstraint which
should subsist between gentlemen—'It must be rather fun to
live in college as you do, Jarvie. It's like the eighteenth
century. We all envy you enormously. I even envy you
Crumble.'

'Envy me Crumble?' The Jarvie was amused. 'Why, the
fellow's a rascal. I believe he beats his wife.'

'At least he's not always exclusively occupied with other

people's shoes and tea-pots, like the other college scouts. But perhaps he's not a scout at all? He doesn't seem to take up with them. They all go to the Leather Bottle, you know. But Crumble doesn't.'

'He's my own man.' The Jarvie was careful not to speak shortly. Young men are extremely sensitive to rebuke, and Honeybeare when he went away might become conscious of having spoken a shade out of turn. 'And quite often I have Mrs C. on my hands as well.' The Jarvie gave his short barking laugh as he said this. 'They certainly don't mingle with the college servants.'

'So you're a little world apart, sir. A kind of *piccolo mondo antico*.'

'No doubt, Miles, no doubt.' The Jarvie was delighted that here was a man who knew his Fogazzaro (a writer much admired by the Jarvie's mother), and who could exploit the fact in delicate mockery. 'But now I must get into the Lodging. A *palazzo moderno* nowadays, eh? And I'm a traveller from an antique land.'

'Good luck, sir.' Honeybeare had laughed, but not too heartily. He was certainly among the most engaging of the second-year men. 'And may I drop in one evening—perhaps with a friend or two?'

'Any evening you like—and turn on the wireless, or make free with the record-player, if I haven't got back. On Tuesdays and Fridays that's not before eleven.' The Jarvie delivered his familiar formula with the brusquerie proper to it. 'And now, Miles, get off to your abominable bun.'

And Miles Honeybeare got off, achieving his previous pace with the rapidity of acceleration beloved by advertisers of sports-cars. Yet it had not been before, ever so fleetingly and in taking his leave, he had given the Jarvie yet another appraising glance. It was almost as if, like the boy (not the man) in Browning's poem, he had been stung by the splendour of a sudden thought.

3

Although it was with the young that the Jarvie was supposed to constitute Mrs Finch's special support, the dinner-
party turned out to be entirely a dons' affair. But this was
as he had expected, and he addressed himself to conscientious conversation with his colleagues'—strictly, his
former colleagues'—wives. In many ways he was out of
things, and it was the women, somehow, who chiefly made
him aware of the fact. Perhaps merely because they didn't
understand his position, they seemed perpetually to be
referring to matters he didn't yet know about and they
had no business to know about at all. Dons oughtn't to chatter about the confidential affairs of a college to their wives.
But there was no doubt they did.

'I am so distressed about Larry Thimble,' Mrs Purchase
said to him. It was before they went in to dinner, and Mrs
Purchase, who was quite young, was uncertainly waving a
glass of sherry halfway between her own nose and his, so
that he found himself wondering in horror whether she
drank. 'We are *all* so distressed. It seems such a shame.'

'Thimble?' the Jarvie repeated, and tried not to seem
upset. Larry Thimble was a particularly nice man. If some
misfortune had befallen him it was intolerable that this
woman, who was not even the wife of Thimble's tutor,
should be running round chattering about it while he himself
was still in ignorance.

'But haven't you heard? The Drug Squad again. They
pounce, you know—and the result is that some rather harmless boy vanishes from Oxford. Of course one realises it's a
problem, and that the police have a terribly hard job. But
Charles says they work in too much with the University,
and that the colleges get by-passed. And I did so like Larry.
He was perfectly brilliant—didn't you think, Jarvie?—in

that last OUDS production. He came to one of my parties afterwards.'

'That was delightful of him.' The Jarvie, when provoked, could produce this kind of dry remark. He thought poorly of imbecile women who hunted undergraduate celebrities, and he was disturbed by what Mrs Purchase had said about colleges being by-passed. He hadn't quite followed, but he did know that he always had been and always would be very much a college man. Here seemed another instance of the fact that the University had to be kept an eye on. And he recalled—rather oddly, as he managed to break away from this tiresome lady—his momentary sensation earlier that evening as he heard the ambulance or fire-engine go past. Beyond the curtilage of the college, without a doubt, lay a world he made less and less of.

At dinner he found himself placed on Mrs Finch's right. Although not particularly gratified by this tribute to his seniority, he felt it saved him, or half-saved him, from worse things. He must by this time be said to know the Provost's wife rather well, and this couldn't be said of Mrs Purchase or of three or four even younger females scattered round the table. And at least Mrs Finch, unlike those nervous juniors, wouldn't wait to have conversation made to her; she was a vehement woman, and the Jarvie judged that her vehemence would see him comfortably through until the point, a good deal later on in the meal, at which he would have to turn to the woman on his other side.

This expectation was not belied. Mrs Finch had much to say, and it was only occasionally that she signalled— actually by a curious click of the tongue which was like a sophisticated phonograph telling itself and others that here was the end of a record—any request for more than a confirmatory murmur from her interlocutor. Mrs Finch had not heard about Larry Thimble, or if she had he was

not within her sphere of interest. It was not for Mrs Finch
to have been impressed by a twenty-year-old who had given
an athletic and tremendously audible performance as King
Lear. Mrs Finch's stamping-ground was less the college
than the University, and less the University than all the
other universities of the United Kingdom. There was nothing parochial about her. She was said to have taken it into
her head that her husband should go away and become a
Vice-Chancellor somewhere—a move not very positively to
be regarded as promotion except in Mrs Finch's own mind
—and she abounded in more or less statistical information
about Essex and Sussex and Warwick and Keele.

The Jarvie knew very little about these institutions. He
supposed that they were to be spoken of with respect, but
left to go about their own affairs. Mrs Finch appeared to
have arranged them, along with more places of the same
sort than he had at all known to exist, in a kind of league
table. And chiefly in point of Student Power.

The Jarvie had given some thought, although not perhaps
notably consecutive or analytical thought, to this phenomenon—one which had declared itself only in his senescence
and which there was every reason to suppose would accompany him into dotage. It was true that he had no great
grip of its terminology. A teach in and a sit in, a free university and an anti-university, young people of Maoist or
Trotskyist persuasion, Revolutionary Socialists, placards
about the N.L.F., pin-ups (as they had to be called) of a
handsome bearded character called Che Guevara, chantings
in the street of mysterious vocables such as *Ho-Ho-Ho:*
these formed a mere compost in the Jarvie's mind. But
from springs very deep in his nature there rose in him the
persuasion—logically quite indefensible, as laughing and
affectionate colleagues would point out—that there is not
merely a special pathos, but also a special merit, in being in
one's nonage. When things had happened in Paris he had

sat in front of his television set like a child, merely and simply hoping that the police would lose and the students win. And this was really because the police were older than the students. When the college's tutor in French, a severe scholar for whom he had a great regard, had passionately declared that these students were profaning Latin civilisation, the Jarvie was much too bewildered to be angry. And when American professorial guests, sitting over dessert in common room, discoursed of recent happenings at Berkeley or Columbia, the Jarvie either jumped up to get them brandy, or put on his turn as a frigid aristocrat strayed within the groves of academe, according as to whether these rather serious and solemn persons were for or against the young.

Not that the Jarvie was not uneasy about the whole thing. He became more uneasy, simply listening to Mrs Finch now.

'Order or disorder: which do we want?' As Mrs Finch put this bald choice she looked challengingly at the Jarvie, but without producing her gramophonic click. And she at once made additionally clear the rhetorical character of her question by adding briskly 'It's as simple as that. Disorder spells death to the academic life.'

'I rather think that in the mediaeval universities—' The Jarvie broke off without completing his remark. The often turbulent character of the institutions to which he had been going to refer was no doubt a historical irrelevance, whereas Mrs Finch had obviously studied the whole contemporary problem. It would be civil to listen to her. 'I suppose it differs a good deal from place to place,' he offered placatingly and vaguely. 'And has made very little impact here.'

'Quite the contrary. Oxford is sinking into indiscipline. Disorder is becoming the order of the day. We can't afford it.'

'A Board School can't afford it.' It was with some astonishment that the Jarvie heard himself snap out this. 'But if we can't assimilate a good deal of disorder here, there's not much good to be said of us.'

There was a small silence, and the Jarvie realised that again he had been irrelevant. There had been the men who, in the middle of the night, had turned the J.C.R. of a rival college into a rural landscape : turfed all over, with a purling brook, and at dawn resounding to the song of black-birds. There had been the men who, also in the small hours, had rounded up the cattle in Christ Church Meadow and firmly padlocked them within the precincts of Merton. There had been the men who had hired a hippopotamus— But all that, although certainly disorderly, was not the disorder that Mrs Finch had in mind. The Jarvie under-stood this. And now she was talking about the O.R.S.S. He had no notion of what the O.R.S.S. was, except that he glimmeringly supposed that the R stood for 'Revolution-ary'. Bewildered, he took refuge in his icy note.

'I find nothing much wrong with the tone of the college,' he said.

But Mrs Finch had turned to the man on her left. Her conscience was clear. She had done her best with old Mr Strathalan-Jerviswoode, that rather pathetic relic of the Goldengrove era.

It was better when the women had withdrawn, and the men for a brief but blessed interval had clumped together at the Provost's end of the table. These were, for the most part, the college tutors who had hurried off at five o'clock. They had returned, accompanied by their wives, a couple of hours later. In the interval, the Jarvie supposed, they had read a chapter of *Redgauntlet* or *David Copperfield* to their children, and performed other duties—replenishing coal buckets, exercising dogs, overseeing home-work—incident to the married state. But here they were, and the Jarvie, although with a glance always carefully cool and ironical, surveyed them with secret admiration and affection. Not even anywhere else in Oxford, he told himself, would one find such a concentration of ability. The scientists (he supposed) were mostly Fellows of the Royal Society and the humanists were mostly Fellows of the British Academy— not quite the same thing, perhaps, but obviously a most respectable citadel of learning. They printed papers in professional periodicals, published books which they presented to the college library, bobbed up on television screens, and proliferated in shilling weeklies. The Jarvie, who had never in his life done any one of these things, judged them to be without parallel in the kingdom. At times, it is true, he judged them in other regards and to a different effect. Some, for example, were so innocent in matters of deportment taught in the nursery as to be positively perplexing until one recalled that they had probably never *had* a nursery, and were thus not in a position to know better. Others were intellectually aggressive at unseasonable times, or had weird personal idiosyncrasies such as having their suits made without waistcoats or associating insomnia with port and even madeira. But at least not one of them was a bore. Being for long habituated—thanks to the collegiate structure of the University—to the society mainly of people in disciplines quite remote from their own, they had almost wholly learnt to eschew shoppy talk. But larger academic issues were proper enough, and it was these that were being canvassed now.

Student Power, it seemed, owned a substantial existence outside the untutored fancy of Mrs Finch. It was around, and there was some hazard of its getting in the way of such more or less sensible purposes as Oxford had hitherto been able to retain for itself in a modern world. It was therefore worth enquiring into, getting to the roots of, steering use-

fully back—since there was a great deal of energy in it—
into the mainstream of university life.

Listening more or less in silence to this talk, the Jarvie
found the uneasiness generated in him by Mrs Finch to be
abating. He had lost the habit of following undergraduate
journalism, since its topics had become progressively unfamiliar, and the writing seemed mostly to be done by
men who were not quite his sort of men. Nor, as it happened, had he chanced to stumble in the streets upon the
species of near-riot known as a demo. Only a few days
before, indeed, on walking down the Broad, he had been
mildly astonished to find the entire front of Balliol—up to
the height which could be reached by one young man
standing on the shoulders of another—covered with white
chalk *graffiti*. But it was a habit, he recalled, for which
there was respectable, or at least interesting, classical precedent. He had once read in a learned journal (in the days
when he still read the learned journals) a paper which had
explored in some detail the fondness of the citizens of Pom-
peii for this form of self-expression. On the walls of Balliol
most of the slogans had been incomprehensible to him, and
a few had struck him as quite funny. For example, there
had been *Egg-heads of the world unite: you have nothing
to lose but your yolks*. It seemed a passable pun. Some were
in the form of newspaper headlines: *More dons abuse
undergraduates*. (The Jarvie was back in his rooms before
his eyes had suddenly rounded upon a full view of that one.)
If the entire exhibition had a little disconcerted him, he had
reminded himself that chalk, unlike paint, is a harmless
stuff; and that the whole affair might be construed as a
species of sympathetic identification with students less
happily circumstanced than in England.

'I have the most unbounded faith in the young,' a man
called Judlip was saying. Judlip was not a don, but an old
member of the college and now a prominent Q.C., whom

some streak of piety brought up to stay with the Provost from time to time. 'There they are,' Judlip said, '—long hair, filthy clothes, brawling with the police, waving seditious placards, and every now and then up before the beaks. Deuced perplexed beaks, too, not at all knowing what to do with the offensive young idiots so as not to make martyrs of them. But what happens? A couple of years pass. And there they are : umbrellas, bowler hats, bristles hogged short, and *Yes Sir* and *No Sir* the moment you speak to them. Splendid fellows, really. You just have to be patient and give them a chance.' Judlip paused, and appeared favourably impressed by the silence greeting this speech. 'They come back on an even keel,' he corroborated himself authoritatively. 'Common sense prevails.'

Charles Purchase, husband of the woman whose party had been graced by the now rusticated Larry Thimble, was the only person to respond to this. But as his response took the form merely of a sharp, contemptuous laugh, the conversation received no impetus from it. Finch, in consequence, showed some signs of intending to rise and lead the way back to his wife's drawing-room. The Jarvie found that he didn't want this; having heard as much as he had about a state of affairs which had been passing him by, he was anxious to hear more. Nothing rational on the subject was to be expected from the women upstairs. But Finch himself might have something to say. Although a wretched enough epigone in the succession to Tony Goldengrove, the man wasn't without brains.

But as these thoughts went through the Jarvie's head his glance unfortunately travelled over his other companions and lighted on Gifford—William Oldfield Gifford. A man can be silent without being dim—the Jarvie himself had been fairly silent—but to be both is offensive. Or at least it could be offensive to one Jarvie—the Jarvie who (obscurely in the interest of the honour of the college) could grow arrogantly intolerant after that third glass. If a man couldn't talk like a gentleman over his wine, at least he could look like one! It was in this insufferable character (which so fortunately was only occasionally irruptive in him) that he addressed Gifford now.

'Wog,' he called out, 'have you been at all offering us your attention? Have you anything to say for yourself?'

Gifford had certainly fallen into an abstraction, and seemingly a sombre one. He was having difficulty in keeping his cigar alight (which was another thing always likely to irritate the Jarvie), and now it did a panicky wobble between his lips. The two youngest men present, who happened not yet to have become much aware of the old man except as a legendary and reclusive presence about the quads, exchanged startled glances. But Gifford, whose dimness was a matter of the social surface, and whose abstraction stemmed from certain personal circumstances which the Jarvie ought to have remembered, contrived adequately to respond to challenge.

'I'd assess the whole problem,' he said, 'as having approximately the same dimensions as the Suffragette problem sixty years ago.' Gifford paused. 'Which,' he added with a sudden flare of what wasn't charity, 'you must so clearly remember, Strathalan-Jerviswoode.'

'Of course I do.' What the Jarvie did suddenly and over-whelmingly remember was his mother's attitude to the dis-natured creatures called Suffragettes. And this in turn called up in him other and earlier memories so vividly (a mental habit growing on him of late) that for a moment all this talk of Student Power and the like seemed shadowy and insubstantial. He brought himself back to it doggedly, never-theless. 'You mean these rowdy young men want the franchise?'

'Not exactly. I understand they're getting that in their teens, and entirely without shouting. It's in an altogether wider context, I think, that they want to assert their majority. They believe they're grown up.'

'So they are.'

'Nothing of the kind. That's a mere sentimental convention.' For the first time in a number of years' acquaintanceship with the Jarvie, Gifford appeared to have nerved himself to counter-attack. 'And least of all does it hold of your public-school boys. They've scarcely dipped a toe as yet in anything that can be called an adult world. Still, even with them, the signs and portents are there. You've noticed how undergraduates have largely given up kicking balls about, or whacking them with cricket bats and tennis rackets, or flogging those expensive boats up and down the river?' Gifford now looked round his colleagues as a group. 'They've taken to this marching, and sitting in, and defamatory scribbling instead.'

'Not here, Wog,' the Jarvie said stiffly. 'On the contrary, the college is likely to be sending an Eight to Henley.'

'All that carries on in a vestigial way, I agree. But the real drive is elsewhere. On second thoughts, I doubt whether the Suffragettes offer an adequate analogy. Probably we ought to go back to the Chartists.'

'Or the Luddites.' It was Charles Purchase who broke in with this. He was a young tutor and still not very sure of himself, a condition inclining him to alternate between long silences and vehemence. 'Don't kid yourselves that these lads and lasses want to get on committees and councils and governing bodies, or reform syllabuses, or have lasses and lads in their rooms all round the clock, or legalise pot. Nothing of the kind. They see this place as a machine that must be destroyed—precisely like loonie Ludd among the stocking frames in that Leicestershire village. So let's face it. We live in this city amid a mob of ten thousand artificially retarded children. And an increasing number of them are turning systematically hostile, destructive, and bloody-minded. We may find the whole place a shambles any day.'

A brief silence was produced by these extravagant re-marks. The Provost made a movement once more as if to rise, and again checked himself. To his credit (the Jarvie, who was perceptive in such matters, realised), it had struck him that an abrupt adjournment at this moment might carry a suggestion of rebuke. Finch was a tactful and composing man. In the end—it was necessary to admit—he would make a very tolerable Provost.

'My dear Charles,' Finch said easily, 'I'm at least glad to hear they're not out to legalise pot. And—do you know? —I believe that brings up a point of some significance. All this political, or quasi-political, activity may be dangerous. I don't minimise it. Throughout the world today, students are a class that has gained a small measure of privilege and fails to see its way to much more. The whetted appetite has always been the prelude to revolution—as you, as a histo-rian, know. Still, action in a political sphere—even very rowdy action—has a certain wholesomeness about it. A common purpose is inherently more respectable than a hunt after private satisfactions. One would rather have one's son pushing down the railings and breaking the windows—rioting, if you like, in Grosvenor Square—than joining in some nasty little sexual orgy in a back street, or making lonely experiments with LSD in an attic.'

Nobody had anything to say to this. The Jarvie, indeed, was about to snap out something like, 'One would still rather he did neither.' But a single very sufficient thought restrained him. Finch had a son, albeit quite a small one. He had not. He had only, from time to time, the solace— or was it the illusion?—of acquaintance ripening into friend-ship with one or another of the men. And certain current young men were in his mind now. As he left the Provost's dining-room he managed to glance quickly at his watch. The prospects didn't look good for a civil get-away by ten.

He very nearly made it, all the same, so that the clocks had not yet chimed the quarter-hour when he climbed the staircase to his rooms. The scrawled invitation was on the door as he had left it, and he took it down. The fire was burning brightly, the radiogram was open, the drinks were waiting, from the wall the Marquess of Montrose looked down with an air of having been perfectly willing to act as interim host.

There had not, however, been any visitors.

4

Gifford was the last man to leave the Lodging. Finch had detained him. Finch had remembered (what the Jarvie had not) that it was now more than a year since Gifford's wife had been put away. She had gone off her head, poor woman, and in some fashion admitting only a slim chance of cure. The house to which Gifford proposed to walk back in North Oxford would be an empty house. So Finch had detained Gifford for a few final minutes in his well-warmed hall. Some other sort of warmth, a suggested warmth of personal regard, was what Finch had it in mind to intimate. He was full of good intentions.

The two men had stood in awkward silence for some moments, all the same. The Provost was not by temperament well-equipped to ope the sacred source of sympathetic tears, or even to achieve the remote approximation to such a thing that would alone be decorous in the present circumstances. Nor was Gifford, perhaps, a man very ready to respond to anything of the kind.

Fortunately it was at least possible to exchange a few words on college affairs. Gifford had lately been induced to take on a small office of the kind that involves keeping confidential minutes, or issuing notices, or corresponding with headmasters, or signing forms for young men. What had been designed was additional employment of an unexacting kind which might help to keep his mind from private troubles. This appeared to have worked well; he showed signs of moving into college affairs. Hitherto he had been the sort of scientist whose work centred in some remote laboratory, and who came into college only to do his necessary teaching there, or to dine no more frequently than the proprieties of the place required. (It was this scanting of social obligation, the Provost reflected, which had made the Jarvie take an ill-will to him; and the Jarvie's tendency to bait Wog had rendered Wog's appearances all the more infrequent, so that there was a kind of vicious circle between them.) But nowadays Gifford was a little more in evidence again, and prepared to occupy himself, almost to a point of portentousness, with whatever of college policy or concern turned up.

'About Strathalan-Jerviswoode,' Gifford said suddenly, as he was reaching for his coat. 'Is he still doing any teaching for us?'

'Yes, I believe so. I believe anybody with a fancy for doing Greek verses goes to him. It can't amount to much. But it no doubt helps him to feel that he's doing something definite while still staying on with us.'

'Still? Is there any term to it? Any understanding in the matter?'

'There's nothing of the kind.' The Provost was conscious of refraining both from a frown and from edging towards his own front-door. It was unfortunately true, he was thinking, that Wog was a colleague in whose presence one's more genial impulses were reduced to making heavy going. Wog had started in on something that was no business of his. 'The Jarvie is a strength to us,' Finch was prompted to add, rather in the accents of his wife, 'in a variety of ways.'

'I suppose, Provost, he's quite *safe*?'

'Of course he's quite safe.' Finch was now too annoyed to make any pretence of being at sea before this question. 'Anyone who can tell chalk from cheese must know that.'

'He must have been an excellent moral tutor in his time, having the interest—the double interest—in young men that he has. And I have no doubt whatever about his continued keen concern for their welfare. What you say, however, greatly relieves my mind.' Gifford paused. 'Does anybody know his age?'

'His age? Well, we know when he retired, and he must have been sixty-seven at that time. But I imagine you can look him up in *Who's Who* tomorrow.'

'Yes, yes. I would merely remind you, Provost, that senescence can be very treacherous. It would be unfortunate if we were to find ourselves landed with a scandal. Even in middle life, terrible things can happen to . . . to the human mind.' Gifford was discernibly trembling, and Finch realised with sudden shock that the man was staring into his own domestic abyss. 'Our defences are so slender! And in old age, if painfully achieved inhibitions lose their grip—'

'I don't see any danger, William.' Finch did his best to speak at once gently and firmly. 'There are facts of character as well as facts of mind. And in this case I must put my money on character. The Jarvie remains here on my invitation. So it must be regarded as my show.'

'I beg your pardon, Provost. I can see you are inclined to charge me with a morbid view. I can see I have spoken sadly out of turn.' Gifford's hand was on the door-knob. 'A most delightful dinner,' he said mechanically. 'Good night.' And he was gone.

There was a malign as well as a suffering streak in the man, Finch told himself with an attempt at impatience. Or if that was too harsh, it was at least true that in Gifford's attitude to the Jarvie an unacknowledged personal factor was at work. For years the Jarvie had made something of a butt of Wog—an activity very little to his credit. And Wog, without perhaps clearly knowing it, had an impulse to retaliate. In directing the imagination of disaster upon the old man, he was doing something not wholly remote from fashioning a wax image of him and sticking pins in it.

Instead of going upstairs at once, Finch crossed the hall, switched on the lights in his study, and stood for some moments in front of a dying fire. (Just here, although he didn't think of it, the Jarvie and Provost Goldengrove had been accustomed to sit, exchanging favourable opinions about sundry young men.) Finch was well aware that the Jarvie entertained no very high opinion of him. And there was a number of reasons why he himself should have no outstanding regard for the Jarvie. The man had spent a long life in the college without, so far as Finch knew, ever having made the slightest contribution to learning. That was all right in its way; indeed, it was the regular old-fashioned thing. Yet, of course, the Jarvie *was* a liability. Finch, who had been inwardly cursing Gifford for his fussing, equally cursed himself for imperfect candour. He ought not to have snubbed Gifford. It had been scarcely honest.

The Provost walked over to his desk, produced a bunch of keys, and unlocked a drawer. A brief rummage produced a letter which was already pretty familiar to him. But he read it again now.

My dear Provost,

I am in some doubt about writing this letter, and please treat it as of the 'no reply' order if you choose. It is *about* a letter. The fact is that towards the end of the vac—only a couple of days before going up again, indeed—Alastair got talking about the Jarvie, who seems to have been very kind to him. As you know, the Jarvie was my own tutor, and is moreover some sort of remote kinsman, so it is of course wholly pleasing that he should a little take up Alastair. But then Alastair produced this letter. In justice to my boy I must say that he did so, it seemed to me, only in a spirit of the most kindly amusement. He says that, in vacations, the Jarvie is known to do quite a lot of such writing. And it is a follow-up of a certain amount of similar talking that he does with junior members of the college.

It is absolutely clear to me that what the Jarvie is concerned with is what he conceives to be the moral—and physical!—welfare of these young men. There is (curiously, perhaps) nothing whatever in his letter to Alastair, any more than there is in this talking I speak of, about the hazards of homosexuality. Alastair says everybody is confident he has never heard of such a thing! But the old chap is convinced that these young men are bound to have their sexual initiation in brothels (in which I suspect him to be, whether happily or unhappily, somewhat behind the times: Alastair has certainly been sleeping with the daughter of more than one of my neighbours—and I scarcely expect you to rusticate him because I tell you so). So the Jarvie writes confidentially on the virtues of potassium permanganate and God knows what.

So far, so funny—or touching. But—to be frank—he is injudiciously *curious* about these young men's lives. He wants to *know*. (As a consequence of this, I gather from Alastair, they have been, with a wholly unconscious cruelty, tending to steer clear of him. How bloody life is!) Moreover his letter to Alastair is couched in terms of what might be called injudicious warmth.

By this I mean, of course, that if he writes many letters of the kind some of them may go to quite simple lads, and hence conceivably into the hands of parents who are out-

siders. At Eton in my grandfather's times there was a beak
called Billy Johnson. He was a most honourable and moral
man, but he did in holidays write that kind of letter. There
was a row, with the angry parent of some colleger badger-
ing the Head Man, and poor Billy Johnson was bewildered,
appalled, and abased. He fled the place forthwith, buried
himself in a cottage somewhere in the New Forest, and
devoted the rest of his days to teaching young women Greek.
Incidentally, he hastily changed his name to William Johnson Cory, and under it is familiar to poetry-lovers in Golden
Treasuries and the like.

Well, as you can see, this letter is strictly for information.
It is most kind of the college to invite me to the next
Gaudy, and it has been sad to have to decline. I shall be
back in my wretched Government House by that date, alas!

Yours sincerely,
CLAVERHOUSE

It was an impeccable letter, yet it irked Finch anew as he
reread it. Wondering whether this feeling had percolated
into his reply, he rummaged in the drawer once more, and
found the draft which he had later fair-copied with his own
hand.

Dear Lord Claverhouse,

I am grateful to you for writing. Alastair (who continues
to hold his place with us) will not be astray in a matter of
this kind. He is an intelligent and well-balanced boy.

We shall keep our fingers crossed about Billy Johnson. A
parent less effortlessly urbane than yourself might well turn
up on us! Our next Gaudy, I am told, will be on the
same date (not day) next year. Is it too much to hope that
you might make a jotting of this fact now?

Yours sincerely,
JOHN FINCH, Provost

It hadn't been exactly cordial, Finch told himself. Perhaps it betrayed the hand of one whose own youth had belonged with what Claverhouse called 'quite simple lads'. But it had been all right. Certainly it had been discreet.

Having read through this correspondence, the Provost was prompted to crumple it up and toss it on the fire. But the fire looked too far gone very certainly to consume even a few sheets of writing paper, and in any case it might be as well to keep the record intact. So he locked it up again, turned off the lights, and went upstairs to bed.

'I was afraid you'd had to go back to work,' his wife said. She was brushing her hair preparatory to disposing of it in an orderly way for the night. 'Your secretarial assistance is quite inadequate. It wouldn't happen in a larger place.'

'I suppose not. But I didn't really have work to do. I had a final chat with William Gifford—Wog, as the Jarvie still persists in calling him. And then, as a matter of fact, I had another look at that tiresome letter from Lord Claverhouse.'

'He hasn't written to you again, has he?' Putting down her hair-brush, Mrs Finch looked sharply at her husband.

'No, no. He will have gone back to govern his blackamoors—if they are blackamoors any longer—by now.' Finch extricated himself from his dinner-jacket, which was growing a little too tight for him. 'Anthea, is it your impression that the Jarvie really makes a nuisance of himself—a well-intentioned nuisance—to the undergraduates?'

'Hardly at all.' Mrs Finch perceived that this was an occasion upon which reassurance was the marital duty required of her. 'He is really too much on the shelf for that. Talking to him at dinner was positively difficult, simply because he is so much at sea in contemporary Oxford.'

'That wouldn't necessarily preclude—'

'Not in itself. But he belongs so much to the past that the young people can't be bothered with him.'

'I see.' Finch was still doubtful. 'But hasn't it been your line that it's precisely *with* the young people—'

'One tries to keep him cheerful. It would be sad if he went into a depression, as the old so often do. He would have to be got away. Of course he must have plenty of money, and could afford one of those expensive private places. But it wouldn't look well.'

'It wouldn't *be* well, either.' Finch gloomily got out of his trousers. 'It's this suggestion of plying people with questions that I don't like. Of course he isn't going to corrupt anybody. But that sort of curiosity can't, at least, be called wholesome. It's part of the set-up of the *voyeur*.'

'Whatever it is, I assure you that the poor man is ceasing to have scope for it.'

'But he entertains a great deal, doesn't he? Sometimes groups of undergraduates, and sometimes just one man for a long talk? He's told me so scores of times—and precisely by way of justifying his continuing with us. Why, he makes a joke about his bill for muffins or crumpets or something.'

'It scarcely happens any more. The men feel they've *had* the Jarvie. He's had his day with previous generations, no doubt. But now they're fading him out.'

'I didn't know.' Finch found himself not caring for this image of his wife's. 'Do you mean,' he demanded, 'that there's a kind of boycott?'

'Oh, no—nothing like that. I'm sure everybody continues to be very nice to him. But they just don't much go along.'

'He sits there over his uneaten teas?' Finch was honestly and decently upset. 'That's rather awful, I must say.'

'It's inevitable.' Mrs Finch, who was now in bed, had the air of one closing a book. 'And perhaps it's just as well.'

5

It was again 5 p.m., and again the dons were packing up to go home. A very young don was hurrying across the quad carrying a shopping-basket stuffed with packets of breakfast cereal and bottles of detergent. Charles Purchase was going through the bicycle-ritual in the lodge; the books had to be stowed in a basket on the handle-bars because the area over the rear wheel was occupied by a contraption for ferrying an infant. A third man, obviously in a state of impatience, was talking to Purchase in a perfunctory way; his wife must be late in picking him up (the Jarvie told himself) because she was queueing for some other infant's orange-juice in a clinic.

The Jarvie barked sharply at this spectacle, and turned away from the window.

'Miles,' he said, 'ring the bell and we'll ask Crumble for more crumpets. Alastair, be a good chap and take over that teapot. If you're wondering whose portrait that is, Roderick, I'll give you a hint. He's a kinsman of mine and a kinsman of Alastair's as well. And he wrote better verse in English than I ever did in Greek.'

'Is he Robert Burns, sir?' someone asked with feigned innocence.

'He's the Ettrick Shepherd,' Miles Honeybeare said. 'Or perhaps he's the good Lord Clifford. Love had he found in huts where poor men lie. How much more edifying if the poor men had been truthful.'

The room seemed full of youths. But this was because they were so long-limbed and sprawled so happily about. Actually there were only half a dozen of them. It was merely a matter of things being as they had always been, and yet the Jarvie experienced, as he glanced around him, a fleeting sense of contrast with a state of affairs in the immediate past. The first weeks of term had been quieter : that was it. Perhaps it had so happened that most of the men with whom he had formed some acquaintance lately had been reading hard for examinations. There were examinations at odd times of the year nowadays. But now—and there were still four weeks of the term to go—life had turned lively again. Through the Jarvie's mind flitted a recollection of an idea he'd had for giving breakfasts. He wondered what could have put such an old-world notion in his head.

The door opened, and Crumble brought in more food. The Jarvie noted cheerfully that it wasn't crumpets. Things were going so well that the crumpets had run out, but the resourceful Crumble was producing what looked like Gentleman's Relish spread on hot-buttered toast. Mrs Crumble appeared to have been withdrawn from all attendance upon her husband's employer. Perhaps Crumble (although the Jarvie couldn't actually recall this of him) took positive pleasure in waiting upon a company of animated young men, or even in the contemplation of the Jarvie *tête à tête* with a single young man further on in the evening. He often seemed to be around quite late, and for no more substantial purpose than making up the fire or emptying ash-trays. He was particularly assiduous in emptying ash-trays. He had once or twice respectfully asked a question or two about one or another of the men, and seemed gratified to know that Mr Davoch was a son of Lord Claverhouse and that Mr Honeybeare's mother was a woman of great wealth. The fellow was a snob, the Jarvie told himself—and certainly a rascal into the bargain. But it was quite proper that he should take an interest in his master's friends.

> '*My dear and only love, I pray*
> *This noble world of thee,*
> *Be govern'd by no other sway*
> *But purest monarchy . . .*'

The urgent declamatory voice thus suddenly sounding startled the Jarvie, and for a moment he was outraged that anybody should begin shouting in his own room the poem sacred to his own boyhood. Then he realised that it was not by just anybody that the words were flung at whoever would listen. It was by Alastair Davoch, who had a better right to them, after all, than almost any other man in Britain. The Jarvie's indignation turned to an intense and mysterious pleasure.

> *'Like Alexander I will reign,*
> *And I will reign alone,*
> *My thought shall evermore disdain*
> *A rival on my throne.*
> *He either fears his fate too much,*
> *Or his deserts are small,*
> *That puts it not unto the touch,*
> *To win or lose it all . . .'*

At this point a couple of the men, to whom it didn't occur to connect the verses with the portrait on the wall, robustly shouted Alastair down. For some moments nobody was paying attention to the Jarvie, so that he had leisure to wonder whether it could possibly be true that he was inclined to have favourites among them. He supposed not, since anything of the kind would be opposed to certain principles of conduct which he had found it necessary to work out for himself long ago. Moreover, it was in a manner true that the men were too fluid, too protean indeed, to be laid hold upon with any sort of possessiveness. Adult though they were in one sense, in another (although he would not have admitted this to Wog) they were still hard at work growing up, so that you could almost say it was impossible to know the same man two terms running. Alastair Davoch himself had surely changed. Had he become more like his father? No, it wasn't that. On the con-

trary, he had become more like some fanatic ancestor; he
was craggier, paler, with a new glitter in his eye—and surely
he was moodier as well.

But something of the sort seemed true of several. Perhaps
the restlessness one heard of, the obscure malaise about which
the Finch woman talked such nonsense, had its effect even
on nice people like these. Certainly they were inclined to
present themselves already somewhat pronouncedly in one
frame of mind or another. And then, as they sat perhaps
through a long evening in the Jarvie's big shadowy smoke-
filled room, this would intensify itself further, so that they
would end up either deeply dreamy or splendidly vehement
much according as to how they had arrived. Moreover, they
owned a curious power of absorption in a drastically
restricted environment. People listening to the Jarvie's music,
for example, would be quite untroubled by others arguing
fiercely within a yard of them.

Miles Honeybeare was listening to music now. He had
put the overture to *Coriolan* on the record-player and was
hunched over it, as if unaware of the hubbub occasioned by
Alastair's declaiming certain verses by a Marquess of Montrose. Not, the Jarvie reflected, that much really escaped
Miles. There was something of what they called an organisa-
tion-man in Miles, as if what was happening in his neighbourhood was happening because he had himself arranged it
that way.

Judging thus of Miles, the Jarvie experienced one of those
sudden questionings, those elusive beckoning lucidities, by
which he was visited from time to time. Why was this particular man quite frequently in his mind? Honeybeare
wasn't, like Alastair Davoch, straight out of the Jarvie's
own stable. It was possible to say that he needed a hair-cut,
or even to suppose that he wore his hair as he did because of
the manner in which its darkness so strikingly shadowed the
already sufficiently dusky softness of his skin. And his mouth

—one's glance gravitated to his mouth—was too full, too
much in perpetual minutest movement, to be the mouth of
a man one would choose for that open boat.

Considering these facts, the Jarvie concluded that he had
been mistaken in supposing that Miles Honeybeare enjoyed
any disproportionate share of his attention. Miles was of
course a clean-run lad, and well-bred in spite of all that
money—even in spite of his unfortunate theatrical manner
with his outlandish cigarettes. But they all had an odd taste
in cigarettes, things damnably bad for their health. When
he knew this lot even better, the Jarvie told himself, he
would venture to do something about that. He was known
to be a man of means. With Christmas approaching, there
would be nothing against his taking them into Friburg and
Treyer's and buying them each a straight-grain pipe. The
expense would be enormous, he told himself happily. And
the innocent vanity of youth was enormous too.

The Jarvie's sudden sharp bark—it could never be said of
him that he chuckled—surprised those of his guests who
were any longer disposed to pay attention to him.

'A rescue operation,' Arthur Wimbush said. Wimbush
was the very junior don who bought detergents and corn-
flakes. 'There's no accounting for young men. Charles tells
us that we live surrounded by thousands of bloody-minded
and ingrate louts, solely concerned with asserting their
divine and youthful right to order everything precisely as
they please. And look at what we suddenly find. A bunch
of them behaving in a thoroughly nice way.'

'You interest and encourage us,' the Provost said. 'But
what are you talking about, Arthur? Explain.'

'Sorry. I'm talking about a subject of perennial interest—
the Jarvie. And about the rather decent behaviour some of
the undergraduates can produce. The puzzle is where it
comes from. It isn't Christianity, since that's something they

know nothing about. It's not that our young savages are noble savages, since the nobility of savages is a fiction. Is it the famous Decent Thing, as inculcated in our public schools? I just wouldn't know.'

'What you know or don't know is chiefly interesting to yourself.' Charles Purchase spoke robustly, and tapped out his pipe. 'Unless you have facts to communicate, we'd better go home to bed.'

It was late, and only a handful of dons were left in the smoking-room. Occasionally, when this is so and nobody unreliable is present, colleagues get talked about with some freedom. It's not quite proper, but it happens from time to time.

'Who are these nice young men?' Finch asked. 'Ought they to receive a college prize? It might be reasonable, if niceness among undergraduates is as uncommon as you seem to think.'

'I deprecate light-hearted talk about Strathalan-Jerviswoode.' It was Gifford who said this. He could seldom bring himself to refer to his elderly colleague as the Jarvie. 'It's a savage life in a place like this—growing old alone. There's a sense of being at bay about it.'

There was an uncomfortable silence, as often happened when Wog made gloomy remarks.

'But we *don't* grow old in the place,' Purchase said. 'Or not really old. The college turns us out in our mid-sixties. And no doubt we're all going to be at bay somewhere in the end, unless we have the good fortune to be hit by a bus. But it won't be here.'

'An exception has been made in the case of Strathalan-Jerviswoode. I doubt whether it has been wise.'

'I must be getting back to the Lodging.' The Provost had stood up sufficiently abruptly to make it clear he had heard Wog on this theme once too often. 'But first, Arthur, I want to know about the rescue operation.'

'It's quite simple. You know, Provost, about the Jarvie's tea-parties, and musical evenings, and conferences *tête-à-tête* on the dangers young manhood has to face? It all belongs with Noah's ark, and the little brutes have simply been ceasing to play. One can't terribly blame them, for the matter of that. But there the Jarvie has been. He dines, of course—although you might call it in a ritual rather than a social way. But over there he leads an almost insulated life. None of us goes near him—'

'He resents anything of the kind,' Gifford said.

'That's true. But the result is that his rooms might be a hundred miles away. That villainous manservant of his could cut the old boy's throat at any time, and it might be days before any of us knew about it. The boys have been his life-line. But increasingly over the last year or so, the boys have been ditching him.'

'So you've said, and it isn't exactly news to me. Anthea's been aware of it.' Finch spoke impatiently—and with a careful avoidance of pride in the firmness of his wife's grip upon the life of the college. 'She manages to coax him out from time to time.'

'Mrs Finch is absolutely splendid, of course.' Arthur Wimbush was pouring himself a final glass of Marc as he produced this decent tribute. 'But all his days, I gather, the Jarvie has been playing this role. Let me be your father and so forth. And since it can't be played as monologue, the poor old chap has become rather stuck. But now some of the young men have got together and mounted this rescue service. They go to tea, and all the rest of it.'

'In shifts?' the Provost asked.

'I don't know as to that. I hardly think it's organised quite to that extent. There aren't all that many of them involved.'

'Do you happen to know who has got it going?'

'A lad called Honeybeare, I think. And perhaps a crony of his called Davoch.'

'Most interesting.' If the Provost was surprised, he didn't show it. Nor did he judge it expedient to divulge that this same young Davoch had, in a sense, sneaked on the Jarvie to his tiresome father Lord Claverhouse during the course of the previous vacation. 'And one is delighted to hear of some civilised feelings being around.'

'Honeybeare and Davoch?' From near the door, where he had been picking up his gown preparatory to departure, Charles Purchase repeated the names on an interrogative note. 'They were friends of that lad Thimble—Larry Thimble—who got sent down. Mary made rather a pet of Thimble. She cultivates theatre boys at present, and this Larry was an uncommonly personable specimen. He brought in those other two to drinks more than once.'

'And why,' Gifford asked, 'was Thimble sent down?'

'Drugs, of course. Fornication won't do it for you now, you know—any more than being contumacious to the Proctors or offending the religious sensibilities of the citizens by hanging chamber-pots on the Martyrs' Memorial.'

'Changed days, Wog.' Wimbush broke in with this over his drained glass. 'Not like your stirring life and times, eh?'

This badinage, if kindly meant, was not kindly received. Gifford walked from the room without a word. And the Provost, with an expressive glance at his younger colleagues, departed by another door.

'Always crying woe, that chap Gifford.' Wimbush was wandering round the smoking-room, switching off lights and radiators. 'Tongue hanging out for disaster.'

'He's had some filthy luck.'

'Yes, I know. But a sado-masochistic type, if you ask me. Do you think he really believes that the Jarvie—'

'To hell with what he believes,' Purchase said irritably. 'Good night.'

'All right—good night. But I say! About that rescue service—'

'Your term for it.'

'Yes, I know. And I suppose one oughtn't to give things names. They get about. Still, it *is* a rescue service. So do you think they're clever enough to conceal the fact?'

'The Davoch-Honeybeare lot have decent manners and so forth. I shouldn't think they'll suddenly betray a patronising attitude to the Jarvie. Do you suppose he'd be unbearably humiliated if he realised they were doing a kind of boy-scouting good deed?'

'I don't know. I hardly ever run across the old man, except for a bit of table-talk. But, in any case, there doesn't seem much future for him over there. This lot of young philanthropists will depart, and no further lot will succeed. And as you and I are not nineteen, slim, fair-complexioned, and eager to be warned against the snares of a carnal world, it's not much use our taking on the job ourselves.'

'No it isn't. And so to bed.'

6

'I say, Jarvie, shall I open another window? They've been making a bit of a fug in here. Pretty warm, too.'

'Yes, Miles—please do. It's this odd kind of tobacco which seems so fashionable at the moment. Shockingly expensive, I don't doubt. In my time it was Russian cigarettes that were all the go. *Café au lait* in colour, and with rather a nice smell. But there were also some affairs in dead black, with gold tips. Vulgar enough for the stage. I'm sorry Crumble has taken away the tea.'

'Oh, I'm not paying a call, sir. Not properly dressed for that.'

This seemed true. Miles Honeybeare was wearing an

enormous sweater, quite a lot of mud, and not much else. He was carrying a lacrosse stick. As with the black cigarettes —the Jarvie found himself rather strangely reflecting—a certain effect of theatre was involved. But then many of the men had a great sense of style. They wore their obtrusively patched and stained and frayed jeans with a casual and positively aristocratic elegance. And it was satisfactory that Miles played lacrosse. He hadn't known that Miles played any game at all. He must turn out and watch Miles one afternoon. It would be nice to see Miles running.

'I just wondered, sir, if I might come in this evening and hear *Idomeneo*—if you're thinking of turning it on, that is.'

'Yes, of course.' The Jarvie was delighted. 'But wait a minute!' He moved carefully over to the mantelpiece, upon which he kept his engagements somewhat uncertainly recorded on cards and scraps of paper. 'Yes, Miles, here's a great bore. I've got my dining club. It's meeting in Magdalen. Happens just once a term. One of the few things that take me out of college, nowadays. I've been a member for over forty years, so I like to keep it up.'

'How very jolly, Jarvie. Have all the other members belonged for more than forty years too?' Apparently forgetting that he hadn't come to stop, Miles Honeybeare tumbled on to a sofa, mud and all. Firelight flickered on the fine gold hair running up his shins.

'Nothing of the kind.' The Jarvie liked this ability to be cheeky without being impertinent. 'There's always a bit of a young entry. Just get yourself made a don, Miles, and I'll have them elect you at once.'

'It's an attractive proposition, and I'll think it over. But I'm sorry you won't hear *Idomeneo*.'

'At least *you* can. Just drop in, and turn it on. It's Crumble's half-day, so you'll have the place to yourself—unless that nice man Roderick Dundark is fit enough to come. He usually turns up for Mozart.'

'Fit enough? Is there something wrong with Roderick?'

Like Alastair Davoch and the Jarvie himself, Roderick Dundark was a Scot. Unlike these two, he was hazy about even his great-grandparents. His father was a dentist, his home was in Glasgow, and the Jarvie, who highly approved of the college's accepting a certain number of youths of humble origin, had taken a great fancy to him.

'It's confidential, in a way. Men don't like its getting round that they've put on a bit of a turn, eh? But I can rely on your discretion, Miles?'

'I've got lots, Jarvie. So I think you can.' Miles was now looking at the Jarvie with what an objective observer of their relationship might have described as an uncustomary genuineness of attention. 'Has Roderick gone sick?'

'I suppose it may be called that. You know how reluctant I am, Miles, to discuss intimate matters with you men.'

'Yes, of course.' There was no hint of irony in Miles's voice. 'You don't think Roderick has been going with women?' This weird phrase of the Jarvie's—'going with women'—had long ago become part of the mythology of the college. On a wall in Miles's own rooms hung a lithograph by Toulouse-Lautrec with the query *Going with women?* pencilled neatly in the margin. But again no faintest trace of mockery had attended Miles's use of it now.

'It *might* be that.' The Jarvie looked gravely doubtful. 'Sleepless nights, eh? Fact is, he dropped off—and on that very sofa you're sitting on at this moment.'

'Went to sleep?'

'Yesterday, after tea. He was sitting there smoking—and in what you might call rather a dreamy way. I'd put something on the gramophone, so we weren't talking much. And Roderick fell asleep. Nothing very remarkable in that. Only I couldn't wake him up again when I thought it was time to do so. Fortunately Crumble came in.'

'Crumble?' There was something almost sharp in Miles Honeybeare's voice.

'The man's a rascal, of course.' It was one of the Jarvie's conceivably upper-class vagaries that he never ceased to take satisfaction in the presumed scoundrelism of his attendant. 'But resourceful, all the same. We got Roderick more or less on his feet. Something funny about his eyes, though.'

'So what happened?'

'Oh, Crumble got him back to his rooms, and tucked him up. No fuss of any sort. Would you describe yourself as one of Roderick's intimates, Miles?'

'I know him pretty well.'

'It just occurs to me that you might have a word with him. You know how reluctant I am to tread on delicate ground myself.'

'I have heard you say so, sir.'

'It's just possible'—the Jarvie had lowered his voice— 'that he may be masturbating excessively. Don't you think?'

'I can't say I *have* thought.' For a moment Miles Honeybeare's eyes had really rounded in honest wonder on the Jarvie. 'But it's an idea no doubt.'

'There's a great deal of pious rubbish talked about self-abuse. By the parsons, chiefly.' There was a vein of stiff anti-clericalism in the Jarvie. 'Endless damage done in private schools by telling boys they'll go insane, and so on. Still, μηδὲν ἄγαυ, eh? Loses its point when overdone.'

'Yes, of course.' Honeybeare would have been obtuse had he supposed the Jarvie consciously to have touched a note of levity. 'Whatever the situation is, I'll try to look into it.'

'Capital! Roderick Dundark is an extremely nice man, but he hasn't had the advantages you and I are so ashamed of.' This time, the Jarvie *was* being amusing. Most suitable men had heard, in contexts of similarly slender relevance, this particular crack. 'And perhaps you'll let me know.'

'Yes, of course.' Miles Honeybeare scrambled to his feet, removed a patch of mud from a naked thigh, and considerately tossed it into the fire. 'I'll tell you anything I can.'

It takes very little longer to change into evening clothes unassisted than it does when supported by a valet. But the Jarvie had forgotten this, and in Crumble's absence had begun the operation earlier than need be. So he found himself with time on his hands, and decided to make his way across the city on foot to Magdalen. When he went out at night nowadays—which, as he had told Honeybeare, was very seldom—it had become his habit to take a cab. So this walk was virtually a novelty.

Almost at once, he felt his surroundings to be alien and bewildering. There were too many people he couldn't conceive himself as talking to, and too many shops he couldn't imagine entering. Quite small things disconcerted him: the sudden appearance in an unexpected place of a lighted window with the surely rather engaging legend *Dear Friend's Restaurant;* a street-vendor selling clockwork toys that tumbled on the pavement in the London manner; the fact that there seemed to be a vogue among young men—could they be undergraduates?—for going about in their mothers' fur coats. He passed one of the women's colleges. A number of men were hanging about outside it, and every now and then a girl would run out, throw herself into the arms of one of them, and embrace with a passion—or at least sustained motility—which the Jarvie judged improper in a public street. Nor did there probably exist any reason why these escorts should not have called for their ladies within the decent privacies of the college, since the dons in such places were widely acknowledged to be sensible women. The spectacle, the Jarvie told himself, represented an upward percolation from the customs of the folk. It was just thus that the outdoor men and the farm lads would have waited, beyond the moat at Jerviswoode, for his mother's innumerable maidservants to scurry out to them. Only there would have been more decency and gentleness at Jerviswoode. The gallants would have had to coax their mistresses into some deeper shade, pay them the tribute of murmured semi-articulate speech, before anything quite like that jigging began.

The Jarvie quickened his pace, frowning. He was very deeply displeased.

And he had muddled the date of his dining club. Fortunately, he had not penetrated so far into Magdalen as to embarrass an unprepared host. A porter in the lodge, asked by an old gentleman in a dinner-jacket as to where Dr Furness was receiving his guests, had respectfully touched on the possibility that Dr Furness was expecting them tomorrow. The truth of this had flashed upon the Jarvie at once. Sharply enjoining upon the porter a maximum of reticence, he had withdrawn precipitately to that indeterminate territory where Oxford's famous High Street transforms itself into Oxford's equally famous Magdalen Bridge. It was cold, and had begun to rain.

The hour was too late to get into Hall. It was the evening of the week upon which neither Crumble nor his spouse could be summoned at short notice without tyranny. The Jarvie had no opinion of himself as one who, in a crisis, has the power to turn to upon pots and pans. He could indeed boil an egg, but there is a crucial gap between that and making an omelet. The Jarvie walked approximately eighty yards towards Carfax, and entered the hospitable portals of the Eastgate Hotel. More than fifty years before, he had eaten a sequence of hurried but satisfactory luncheons here between writing morning and afternoon papers in the Final Honour School of *Literae Humaniores*. It was probable that they still turned on a decent meal.

This they did. But although he didn't feel at all odd in his solitude and his dinner-jacket (since with aged Wykemists certain sorts of unselfconsciousness are absolute), there wasn't all that to linger on. And this was why he got back to his college rooms at an odd betwixt-and-between sort of hour.

Mounting his worm-eaten but reassuringly massive staircase, he recognised with pleasure the strains of *Idomeneo, re di Creta*. The man to whom inscrutable Nature denies the path to fatherhood is at least spared the risk of having to sacrifice a son to Poseidon. But the Jarvie would gladly have taken the risk. He would have liked a son, were a son not the gift of something as inconceivable as a wife. It was why he had spent his life in this place, with other men's sons around him.

From his sitting-room, where the music was, there came the sound of voices as well. Miles Honeybeare must have been joined by somebody else. It was odd, perhaps, that they should be talking while the opera went on. And was there not something odd, too, about the way the voices were behaving? This question only brushed the Jarvie's mind. For there was a light under his bedroom door—perhaps he had left it on when changing—and noticing it put into his head a notion which he didn't quite clearly formulate. A dinner-jacket is a dreary garment, whereas in his bedroom hung a smoking-jacket in faded rose-coloured velvet of which he was rather fond. He would first go into his bedroom and change jackets. That he would be doing this for Miles was the element in his project that he didn't quite let crystallise in his mind. So he opened his bedroom door—but only to stop dead on the threshold. There was a girl lying on the bed, curled up on top of the coverlet. She was asleep. And she had almost nothing on.

The Jarvie was very angry. Other emotions might follow,

but he felt nothing but simple anger now. As a consequence of this, he had no disposition to be deflected from action by the indecent exiguity of the girl's attire. He marched over to her, seized her by the shoulder, and gave her a good shake.

'Wake up,' he said. 'Wake up, dress yourself, and be so good as to leave these rooms at once.'

It was a rousing injunction. But, at least for some moments, it simply didn't arouse. The Jarvie had a queer sense of being back with Roderick Dundark—and when the girl did open her eyes and stare at him this impression was for some reason enhanced. But now his attention was recalled to the other room. The music had been turned off abruptly, and this made the voices more audible. Two men were talking. One was Miles and the other was Crumble. The voices were angry, and suddenly one of them— Crumble's—rang out very loud. It was as if the man had lost control of himself.

'Twenty bloody quid!' Crumble was saying. 'Are you kidding? It's a cool hundred from you, young man, and plenty from the others as well.'

The Jarvie had never heard a speech like this, and he didn't take in quite all of it. But he no longer had any disposition to bother his head about the little slut on his bed. She could go to the devil without any assistance from him. He made for his sitting-room in strides recaptured from twenty years' back, and flung open the door.

Miles Honeybeare, too, wasn't very completely dressed. But he didn't, somehow, look like a lover awkwardly detected in his pleasures. He looked much more like a small boy at a prep school who has been caught out in some nocturnal prank. And, the Jarvie told himself, at a damned bad prep school, where discipline is lammed into the children with a cane. The distressing fact had to be faced that Miles was putting up a poor show. He was extremely scared.

It annoyed the Jarvie that Miles, even if badly caught out, should be unable to hold his own with a servant. But at least the job could be done for him. It had better be done in as few words as possible.

'Miles,' the Jarvie said, 'is my man attempting to extort money from you?'

Miles, looking even more scared than before, just managed to nod his head dumbly.

'Speak up, please. Is Crumble trying to blackmail you?'

'Yes.'

'Crumble, you are dismissed. It would be improper that I should give you any money in lieu of notice. And you are to leave at once. If you have any property in my rooms, it must be collected by messenger. You will not again be admitted within the bounds of the college. I am only sorry for your wife, who is a decent woman enough. You may go.'

'*You'll* bloody well pay too, you old bastard,' Crumble said. 'Or you'll bloody well suffer too. And no mistake. I can still have this kid student of yours gaoled, for a start.'

The Jarvie's reaction to this was unexpected and resourceful. He turned and walked back into his bedroom. The young woman was now dressed, and in the act of making for the door. The Jarvie did no more than take a further good look at her. Then he returned to the other room.

'Crumble,' he said. 'you're a fool. The girl is twenty, if she's a day. It is true that you have it in your power to embarrass Mr Honeybeare in his relations both with his parents and with the college authorities. But nothing more. On the other hand, were a prosecution for blackmail to be brought against you, I am not a witness who would be disbelieved. Only let me hear of you opening your mouth about this wretched affair to a living soul, and I make you an absolute promise of a stiff term of imprisonment. Clear out.'

And Crumble cleared out. He did so in a cowed manner

but with muttered threats and imprecations, like a villain in melodrama who has suddenly been reduced to wholesome impotence. Miles Honeybeare, however, didn't appear to view his exit in this light.

'I say!' Miles said. 'I don't think you ought to have done that. I expect I could have found him some money.'

'Don't be silly.' The Jarvie, although he was looking at Miles Honeybeare more coldly than he had perhaps ever looked at a young man before, was careful to keep anything like disapprobation out of his voice. 'You have broken certain college rules, I suppose, but you certainly haven't broken the law. Therefore—'

'I . . . I didn't even have her, as a matter of fact. You see, when one's on a—well, when one's in rather a funny state—'

'Miles, I have no wish to discuss these details.' The Jarvie was shocked that the young man should have said 'I didn't even have her' instead of 'we didn't even make love', for he was quite as faithful to what he conceived to be the idiom of his class as to its *mores*. 'As you know, I never comment on *affaires* before marriage, except on strictly practical lines. But I do resent your behaving as you have done in my rooms. It has been an abuse of hospitality such as I wouldn't expect.'

'I'm sorry.' Miles Honeybeare wasn't so perturbed as not to get in this apology swiftly and adroitly.

'Thank you. We need not think of that again. As for Crumble, he is of course a rascal. I've always known he was a rascal. But put him out of your head. He is not going to risk trouble simply for the pleasure of indicting an undergraduate of . . . of ineffectual fornication.'

As he said this, the Jarvie produced, unexpectedly, his famous short bark of laughter. But Miles didn't seem at all relieved.

'Look, Jarvie, you don't understand! I ought to have

taken fright, after hearing about Roderick.' Miles didn't pause to let the Jarvie make anything of this remark. 'It's the hell of a mess! As things are now, they pounce simply on the strength of a single anonymous tip off. If once—'

'You're talking nonsense. I don't know how undergraduates can imagine such things. Neither the Provost nor the Dean would dream of giving countenance to anonymous letters. And now, Miles, you had better go to bed. And perhaps next term will be time enough for us to meet again.'

'Good night, sir—and thank you.' If Miles Honeybeare looked a little like one despairing in the face of obstinate incomprehension, he yet got this out creditably enough. And as he moved towards the door, the Jarvie laid a hand fleetingly on his shoulder.

The Jarvie, who seldom so much as shook hands with a man after their first meeting, hadn't permitted himself so extravagant a gesture for years.

7

It was a week later, and thus not long before the end of term, that the Jarvie went for an afternoon stroll along the tow-path. A good deal of more or less inexpert rowing was going on, for Torpids were as yet far off, and the freshmen were mostly at the stage of being promoted from constant tubbing to seeing what they could make of one another when shoved into an eight. The spectacle of freeborn Britons comporting themselves like galley-slaves at the command of bicycling coaches in enormous Leander scarves always pleased and amused the Jarvie, and the rhythm of the young bodies driving through from the stretcher, tugging back the oar to the expanded chest, feathering with a strong flexure of the wrists, thrusting apart their knees as they came forward for the next stroke, he judged a sight which the elders of Sparta themselves might envy.

Not that the Jarvie stared. He lacked the rowing man's expert eye which alone would have rendered seemly anything of the sort. Moreover, he had to give care to his step, just as he had to do in a quad at night. He moved forward using his walking-stick with precision, and one would have supposed him to be just one more elderly don (which he was) sunk in some wholly learned abstraction (which he was not). The Jarvie was thinking about the men, and in particular about his handling of Miles Honeybeare when that nasty business had so suddenly blown up. He was also giving thought to quite practical affairs. The departure of Crumble, the departure even of Mrs Crumble, had produced inconvenience, only imperfectly resolved by his having managed to arrange with the bursar for the temporary part-time services of a college scout. But Crumble had been a good riddance, all the same. The Jarvie smiled to himself as he thought of the scoundrel's vain threats as he shuffled away.

But the men, almost literally, had shuffled away too. He had surely been right in telling Miles to make himself scarce until next term, when time would have eased the constraint such a miserable *rencontre* had been bound to generate. But he hadn't meant to tell Miles to take his friends with him. Yet this seemed to have happened. Nobody had been near the Jarvie for days. The members of Miles's set whom he had encountered around the college had appeared alarmed and shifty; one or two of them had even walked past him with their eyes on the ground or the heavens, which was the most ill-mannered conduct of which a man could, in the Jarvie's view, be convicted. It looked as if Miles, far from keeping his mouth shut about his bad behaviour, had vindictively set going a kind of boycott.

But that was nonsense. The Jarvie, pausing before the

architectural monstrosity of the O.U.B.C., gazed across the Isis and towards its Green Bank in an introspection so deep as to make him oblivious even of the labouring torsos in a Balliol boat just jerking by. He realised that he knew one clear fact about Miles Honeybeare. Miles organised people. Miles had organised him, the Jarvie, during this current term.

He turned and walked on. He would go as far as Long Bridges. And he would face up to a fact which he had been cravenly dodging. He was an outmoded old person, and the young life in which he was interested was not interested in him. For weeks those crumpets had departed untouched! And then Miles had organised something : a kind of Good Deed of the Day.

A cold wind blew up the river. And as there was plenty of water going down (the Jarvie tried to fix his mind on oarsmanship) choppy conditions were making it not too simple for the crews. Miles had set going a free-and-easy frequentation of the Jarvie's rooms, but only because he had spotted the promise of their retired and isolated character. Having gained the run of them with his guileless friends, he could intermittently, during their owner's regular absences, use them for his more private purposes—in fact for 'having' (revolting phrase) his Paphian girls. And his exposure (a grim pun lurked in the word) having somehow leaked out, his associates had made a guilty withdrawal in his wake.

Having arrived thus so near to, yet far from, the truth of his situation, the Jarvie turned round and at a slow pace directed his steps back to college.

His rooms had the convenience of being (as he sometimes expressed it to the men) amphisbaenic in character. On one side they faced into a quadrangle, and on the other outward upon a secluded thoroughfare called St Botolph's Lane. There was nothing out of the common in this. But as well as having windows upon the lane, he had a staircase and outer doorway giving on that quarter as well, and in fact *27 St Botolph's Lane* was a valid address for him if he cared to use it. Technically, there was even some doubt whether his tenement was to be regarded as part of the college proper, or rather as an instance of what, in the learned language of the place, were known as *aedes annexae*. The point seemed without significance, but the actual topography involved made possible the perplexing appearance which now greeted him as he approached the college.

He seldom used the front door on the lane, preferring to come and go by the main gate of the college. Nowadays he found the staircase from the quad easier on his legs, and moreover he enjoyed having a word with the porter in his lodge. So the St Botolph's door often remained unopened for a month on end. But it was open now. And not only was this so. From the shadowed area within a pair of eyes were regarding him fixedly as he approached. They were oddly near the ground, and he was just conjecturing the presence of an impertinent child when the eyes thrust themselves forward by some inches and he saw that they belonged to a large dog. In considerable indignation, and raising his walking-stick in a conventionally threatening manner, he advanced with the intention of driving the intrusive creature away. The dog vanished with an abruptness suggesting a summons or a tug from within. And, again from within, the door was firmly shut.

The Jarvie was astonished. He also found himself agitated. For two or three years he had been aware of a liability to something of the sort upon quite trivial occasions, and he had marked the thing down as one of the hazards of old age. Here was another instance. A small untoward circumstance had presented itself, and he was foolishly perturbed.

But now another strange fact appeared. Whoever had shut the door more or less in his face had let its lock operate as well. It so happened that the Jarvie was without a key. Whether he wanted to or not, he must go round the other way. He did so, and found that the further petty outrage, whatever its occasion, had in fact steadied him. He held his accustomed conversation with the porter, an elderly man like himself, who had known many of the men's fathers. Then he went briskly on, refraining even from his customary pause on the half-landing where the wretched Crumble had had his pantry. So he was a little breathless when he entered his sitting-room.

There were two dogs. One of them, which he judged to be his late acquaintance, was sitting on its haunches and with its tongue out—stupidly goggling at the portrait of James Graham, Fifth Earl and First Marquess of Montrose. The second—more sagaciously, as was presently to appear —was snuffling and pawing at the shelves containing the Jarvie's handsomely bound, if not very frequently consulted, run of the *Journal of Hellenic Studies*. There were also two men, of respectable appearance. As the Jarvie came into the room they had exchanged glances, in the manner of competent professional persons when confronted with a situation some shades trickier than usual.

'What the devil,' the Jarvie asked, 'is the meaning of this?'

'Mr Strathalan-Jerviswoode?' One of the men had stepped forward. 'I am a police officer, sir, and here is my warrant-card.'

'Does it entitle you'—the Jarvie glanced stonily at the object exhibited to him—'to come barging into my rooms with those damned dogs?'

'No, sir, in itself it does not. But here is a further warrant. It has been issued by a magistrate, and authorises a named officer, myself, to enter and search these premises under provisions contained in the Dangerous Drugs Act 1965. And that, sir, is what we are doing now.'

'I see. And who has told you that you are likely to find drugs here?'

'That, Mr Strathalan-Jerviswoode, I am not at liberty to say. But it is public knowledge that the police are sometimes constrained to act upon information—'

'Anonymously received.' A sharp bark of laughter from the Jarvie appeared to startle the contemplative dog. 'Then you had better continue your rummaging. But could you prevent that second dog from slavering over my books? Norden's *Die Antike Kunstprosa* is a volume of which I happen to be fond.'

Even as the Jarvie spoke, however, the second policeman had pulled away the dog, removed Norden from the shelf, and peered into the space thus revealed.

'Good for Tinker!' he exclaimed. 'He's sniffed out another lot here, all right.'

'I knew the old man wasn't safe,' Gifford said. He spoke as one in decent distress, as he probably believed himself to be. 'Provost, you must recall that I gave you warning.'

'My dear William, nothing has happened that either you or any of the rest of us had the faintest prevision of. This is a bolt from the blue.' Finch was pacing his study restlessly. 'I am bound to say I feel some notice ought to have been given me by the police of what was proposed. To enter the college—'

'Not quite the college, Provost. 27 St Botolph's Lane. That mitigates the disastrousness of the precedent. Perhaps we may also be able to exploit it in toning down the scandal. It may be maintained that this has *not* happened within the curtilage of the college.'

'Fiddle-faddle!' This very brusque retort was an index of Finch's dismay. Not unreasonably, it offended Gifford.

'He will have to go, you know,' Gifford said. 'Purchase, don't you agree?'

Charles Purchase—who, although young, held a college office requiring him to be present at this emergency discussion—made no reply. He liked the Jarvie, although the Jarvie had plainly been a tiresome sort of tyrant in his time. He didn't like 'Wog' Gifford a bit. He was resolved to keep silent until he had these irrelevant considerations under control.

'To go?' The Provost distinguishably feigned an astonishment he didn't feel. 'You don't suppose he's done anything discreditable himself, do you? These young blackguards have simply fooled him in the most conscienceless way.'

'Smoked the stuff under his nose,' Gifford said. '*Literally* under his nose. And cached it in his room. And one of them actually used the place to lure a young woman into this pernicious habit, seemingly with the object of achieving a virtually criminal seduction. All out of a hare-brained notion that they had ingeniously found the most inviolate spot in Oxford for their wickedness.'

'Which was certainly pretty daft,' Purchase said gloomily. 'They'd have been more secure in a score of places. I suppose they thought it dare-devil, fantasticated, amusing. I call it perverse and bloody-minded.'

'It was absurd. But so far gone in senility is the unfortunate—'

'Exactly!' The Provost pounced on this. 'The Jarvie hadn't a glimmer of the truth. That's my point.'

'I doubt whether it would be the beak's point,' Purchase said. 'The position could be a damned dodgy one. If your premises have been used for this purpose, you may be held culpable in law, even if you knew nothing about it. It's as simple as that. In addition to which, if one didn't know the Jarvie, his unawareness would strain credulity. It's a mess.'

'*Drug orgies held in Oxford tutor's rooms.*' Gifford produced this much as if he were actually reading from a newspaper. 'I must not disguise my belief, Finch, that this will prove your first big test as our Provost. You have my sympathy.' Gifford paused, and appeared to feel that something further had to be said. 'And support, I need scarcely add.'

'Thank you very much.' Restlessly pacing again, Finch swung round on his colleagues. 'Do you realise how Oxford means everything to the man?'

'Not really Oxford,' Purchase said. 'Not an Oxford that any objective observer would recognise today. Only an Oxford inside his own head.'

'And hasn't that always been the only kind of Oxford worth bothering about, Charles?' The Provost, as he rather surprisingly asked this, sat down heavily at his desk. 'But you know very well what I mean. No family, no close relations—even precious few of what he calls intimates. And no maintained interest in the scholarship of his subject either, so far as I know. Just what he believes to be the spirit of this place. So don't let us mistake or minimise the issue. There might be a chance—' The Provost paused as his butler came into the room. 'Yes, Brown?'

'By hand and for immediate delivery, sir.' With due solemnity (for the whole college had at least some dim apprehension of crisis) the man presented a letter on a salver and withdrew.

'It's from the Jarvie.' The Provost had glanced at the envelope, and now he hesitated before opening it. 'Well,' he said, 'we'd better see.' There was a full minute's silence while he read. 'Gentlemen,' he said with formality, 'Mr Strathalan-Jerviswoode writes to inform me that he resigns his Fellowship.'

'Resigns his Fellowship!' There was at once incredulity and lively indignation in Gifford's voice. 'Why, his Fellowship determined years ago! He has nothing to resign except . . . except some sort of status as a lodger. He is the mere tenant of a set of rooms.'

'I suppose that is so.' The Provost stared at Gifford. 'But in great distress of spirit such a formal slip or misconception is natural enough. I think I can receive and transmit the Jarvie's resignation as it comes.'

'Perfectly absurd! How can the Governing Body of the college affect to receive and accept the resignation of a person who has nothing to resign? As one of its senior members, I must—'

'And now,' the Provost said with unusual firmness, 'if you will both excuse me, I must write to the Jarvie at once.'

So Charles Purchase and Gifford left the praeposital lodging together.

'A bad business,' Gifford said. 'A thoroughly bad business. I deplore it very much.'

'Yes, indeed.'

'Where shall we be heading for, Purchase, with a Provost who is prepared to play fast and loose with the proper forms?'

'Oh God, Wog!' Charles Purchase said. 'Oh God! Oh Montreal!' he said, obscurely and rather rudely. And he walked away.

Cucumber Sandwiches

'I'VE DISCOVERED,' Charles Shand said suddenly, 'that Corderoy had an illegitimate son.'

It was a small night. Most of the men dining had gone off after Hall, leaving only half-a-dozen to move into common room for dessert. And since Shand had addressed nobody in particular, it became incumbent upon everybody to listen to him. Two independent conversations were broken off, and the result was a silence. Shand's announcement was, no doubt, an arresting one, since Walter Corderoy had been the last of the great Victorian novelists. But the only person present who had much interest in literary matters was Hilliard, a brooding and withdrawn mathematician who seldom spoke. He felt it civil to speak now.

'And you are interested?' he asked. 'It's significant? At least such investigations are fashionable. I've read a book claiming that Thomas Hardy had an illegitimate son. Incidentally, I suppose Corderoy was of much the same generation.'

'He was ten years younger.'

'Remote enough to have become fair game for biographical curiosity. Are *you* going to write a book, Charles?'

'Of course not. But the question of writing *something* is another matter. Briefly, of course. Say a letter to *The Times Literary Supplement* or a note in *The Review of English Studies*.'

'Is there really an affair called *The Review of English Studies*?' a young physicist called Coverdale asked. People teased Charles Shand from time to time. But not very much. Shand could occasionally be felt a shade obtuse, or at least as not quite aware of what was developing in front of him. And this could make a joke turn awkward, which was something nobody liked. At the moment, Shand was un-heeding.

'But there's a question of taste,' he said, 'which is also a question of policy. One of Corderoy's children is still alive.'

'Not the illegitimate one?' Rupert Fenton asked with interest. Fenton was the college's Law Tutor. 'You might have to watch your step over that.'

'No, no. He died—one might say suddenly—a long time ago. It's a daughter, Lavinia, who married a landowner called Verity and has been a widow for many years. She probably knows nothing about her illegitimate half-brother. She mightn't like it, at all. And she'd have reason.'

'You're going to take tea with her,' Fenton asked, 'and let her know?'

'Perhaps something like that.' Shand spoke with caution, as if he really had something sizable on his mind. 'I've met her on a number of occasions. She controls all Corderoy's copyrights and papers. One could scarcely continue to work on him if one fell out of favour with her. And she inclines to be cagey about family matters.'

'What a very odd world you inhabit, Charles!' Coverdale said cheerfully. He paused to push a decanter of port down the table. 'And why is she cagey? Are there other family skeletons as well?'

'Hardly that.' Shand paused again, and from somewhere across Oxford a big bell began to tumble its dumb nocturnal syllables into the room. 'Mrs Verity's attitude is something inherited from Corderoy himself. And his own reticence wasn't, I imagine, a matter of protecting any settled irregularity of conduct. It sprang originally from his grand-father's having been somebody's butler. The Victorians were very sensitive about that sort of thing.'

'Dickens,' Hilliard said. 'But if the old lady possesses valuable papers and so forth, why risk upsetting her with this quite trivial discovery?'

'It isn't quite trivial. That's the point.'

'Less trivial than grandpapa being a butler?' Coverdale threw this out challengingly as he reached for the madeira. 'It all sounds pretty average backstairs nonsense to me.'

'The ancestral butler first popped his whiskers out of his pantry less than a dozen years ago.' Shand, constitutionally an earnest man, sometimes made a grab at this lightness of air. 'Corderoy himself had been dead for twenty years. The family was upset, all the same.'

'Upset, I suppose,' Fenton said, 'at being detected in having long concealed a circumstance not in any decent sense dishonourable. We are a queer race. But I haven't discovered why the unearthing of the love-child has any great interest.'

'It's because he wasn't quite nobody.' Shand hesitated, as if afraid of telling his story in the wrong way. 'Of course he didn't call himself Corderoy—'

'He should have called himself FitzCorderoy,' Coverdale said. 'It would have served the snobbish old scribbier right.'

'But he didn't.' Shand had flushed with annoyance. 'He called himself Mainprize, which was the name of his mother. It has been my clue in getting at the truth, as a matter of fact. Just how, I may tell you later.'

'Mainprize,' Fenton said, and stared at the tip of his cigar.

'I suppose,' Coverdale asked, 'that this Miss Mainprize wasn't of the same class to which the Corderoys had so happily attained?'

'She was a servant-girl.'

'She would be. But doesn't that lighten the scandal, according to the ghastly morals of these people? And I really don't see why your precious Mrs Verity should be all that upset now.'

'There are two reasons—and the first of them is ugly and the second horrible. Martha Mainprize was a kitchen-maid, or the like, in Walter Corderoy's house, and he got her with child within a couple of months of his marriage. We needn't suppose he was a blackguard. Say the girl had caught his eye, and that by chance one day—' Shand broke off. 'He would have enjoyed the poor benefit of a bewilder-ing minute. And be feeling ashamed of himself a quarter of an hour later.'

The common-room door had opened. They were bringing in the coffee, and in the pause this produced people seemed to rearrange their thoughts.

'I do see,' Coverdale said in more subdued tones than he had used before, 'that it was a bit steep, with his young bride in the house. The kind of nastiness that might lead to something.'

'It led to a baby.'

'I don't think I was meaning that. If this daughter of Corderoy's, Mrs Verity, has never heard the story—and I gather you can't be quite certain of that—there's no reason why she should like it a bit. In fact, Charles, you ought to keep the lid on it till she's dead. As she's the daughter of an eminent Victorian she must be even older than you are, after all.'

'Lavinia Verity is seventy-seven.' Shand glanced with conscientious humour at Coverdale. 'And if you care to look me up you can check that I'm fifty-three.'

'We haven't had the second reason why Mrs Verity should be upset,' Fenton said. 'The horrible one. Not that I believe I need it myself. The penny has dropped. There aren't all that many Mainprizes.' He turned to Shand. 'This bastard son was called William Mainprize?'

'Yes, and I see you know about him.'

'Most people did, at one time. And it would have been round about 1910?'

'1911. William Mainprize, the famous novelist's illegitimate son, was hanged in Winchester Gaol for a peculiarly revolting series of murders.'

The great Christ Church bell had stopped booming, and there was silence alike in common room and in the still autumn night outside. Coverdale was the first to speak.

'Hard cheese on Corderoy, I must say. First a butler for a grandfather, and then a murderer for a natural son. Good God, Charles!'—Coverdale was suddenly excited—'what you're proposing is an absolute outrage. Here's this old woman, Mrs Verity, tottering and teetering on the brink of the grave, probably with her long-dead father's literary eminence as her only comfort and stay—and along you propose to come, drink a cup of China tea, nibble a genteel cucumber sandwich, and announce that she's own half-sister to a notorious criminal. Not that I know anything about William Mainprize myself. Murderers don't get themselves much remembered, thank goodness. I think the notion of dredging him up in this way is extremely . . . extremely repellent.' Young Coverdale, who had found this last word with some difficulty, sat back in his chair.

'Perhaps you *don't* know anything about William Mainprize,' Shand said harshly. 'But you would—although you mightn't exactly be aware of the fact—if you'd ever read *A Venation of Centaurs*.'

'What the dickens is that?'

'It's the title of Corderoy's last novel.'

'It sounds pretty affected to me. What's a venation?'

'Consult Sir Thomas Browne. Gnomic titles were fashionable. *The Golden Bowl, The Wings of the Dove*. But what was pretty well known at the time—'

'Of course!' Hilliard had broken his silence again.

'Corderoy took certain material for his novel from the Mainprize case. And the thing's done with extraordinary insight and compassion. It's regarded as an element in the book's being a masterpiece.'

'Nothing like it since *Crime and Punishment,* I suppose.' Coverdale had scarcely produced this when he blushed. He was prone to suddenly seeing himself as unmannerly. 'Sorry,' he said. 'Nothing to jeer at. I think it all sounds frightful.'

'You can now guess how I got on to this,' Shand continued. 'Studying the novel led me to studying the trial— and I suppose I know more about Walter Corderoy's life than anybody else who has ever done just that. Or, conceivably, than anybody else save one.'

'Ah,' Fenton said.

'Eventually something clicked. After that, only pertinacious detective work—I suppose "research" sounds more respectable—was needed. I rather wish I hadn't undertaken it now. Still, here's something the world must one day know. A great author's son—his unacknowledged son—ends his life in degradation and on the gallows. And the father faces it in a novel. Or should we say exploits it in a novel? At least it's a unique creative situation.'

'Did Walter Corderoy feel responsible for his illegitimate son's disaster?' Fenton asked. 'Did he feel guilty?'

'I don't know. There's nothing of the kind in the novel. The William Mainprize figure isn't described as a bastard, any more than the real man was in court. The facts have undergone a great deal of imaginative transformation. But of course he *must* have felt guilty.'

'How had he coped at the start with the consequences of seducing the girl?'

'Not in a way that commands our sympathy. I can find no evidence that he ever acknowledged the child, or had any personal contacts with him. Nor have I found out what, if anything, the boy ever came to know. The mother—

Martha Mainprize—died when her child was five years old. William—Bill, he was called—was handed over to foster-parents. Corderoy did recognise a continuing responsibility of a sort. He put up money.'

'A court could have made him do that,' Coverdale said. 'Rupert, isn't that right?'

'If there had been proof of paternity, most certainly.' Fenton turned to Shand. 'He kept the boy in his own neighbourhood?'

'Yes—which suggests that he *did* take an interest in him, and risk a glimpse of him from time to time.'

'Like Razumov's father, Prince Somebody, in *Under Western Eyes*.' It seemed rather to his own surprise that Coverdale produced this literary parallel. 'Did Corderoy plan to bring up the boy in anything like what he'd call his own station in life?'

'I'm not sure whether that's a fair question. Corderoy was never rich. Bill was sent to a local school, and at seventeen he was found a job as a clerk in a malting business. It was still near by.'

'Which seems to answer *that*,' Coverdale said contemptuously. 'The bastard was coped with on the cheap. What was he like—before, I mean, he took to murder?'

'Extremely attractive. He grew into an uncommonly good-looking young man, and he had a way with women.'

'Which was what led to his destruction in the end,' Fenton said. 'Too much of a way with too many women. But what happened after the malting-house?'

'I don't know much more. But I suspect he got into serious trouble, and that his father decided to pack him off to foreign parts. Money still went to him—I have no doubt of that—but it was to somewhere or other abroad. William Mainprize is over thirty before any further record of him turns up. And by that time the Old Bailey lies dead in front of him.'

'Charles, are you really going to give all this to the world?' It was Hilliard who spoke, and he was looking at his colleague in perplexity. 'At least, in the lifetime of this ancient daughter of Corderoy's?'

'If I don't, somebody else will.'

'I see.' But Hilliard's perplexity showed no sign of resolving. 'You wouldn't care to be beaten in a race?'

'One doesn't, I suppose. But it's obvious, surely, that I could scarcely think in such terms in this instance?' Shand was looking less hurt than astonished. 'Isn't it?'

'Charles, I'm sorry. We had this foolish talk about China tea and cucumber sandwiches.'

'Cucumber sandwiches? Ah, yes. Well, I've thought about it a lot, and I feel the old lady simply must be told. And the facts made known with dignity and decency. I've hinted there's another man on the trail. Not a scholar at all. An unprincipled sensationalist.'

Silence fell, and everybody looked suitably grave—so grave, that the small company rapidly broke up. There was a distracting noise in the quad—young men were shouting across it in the confidence of absolute ownership—and it was a moment before Shand realised that he had been followed into the open air by the Casaubon Professor of Greek. In the common room the Casaubon Professor hadn't uttered a word. But he did murmur now.

'My dear Charles, a rapid and judicious *protasis*. Should *epitasis* and *catastrophe* succeed, I hope we may hear about them.'

'A good many people will hear,' Shand said. And as he walked slowly through the darkness to his rooms he wondered just how competent he would be in the strange situation that had overtaken him.

2

Mrs Verity—unsuspecting half-sister of the notorious William Mainprize—lived in Cheltenham, since the modest landed property of her husband was now in the ownership of a grandson. It was only infrequently that she accepted her grandson's annual invitation to visit him. Although careful never to fail in giving the Veritys their due—they were good people, the men mostly in the army, and impeccably descended from one of the great Duke of Marlborough's commanders—Mrs Verity remained very much a Corderoy. It was no doubt gratifying to possess an ancestor who behaved not too blunderingly at Malplaquet; it was quite another matter to be honoured as the daughter of one of the most famous of English authors. Mrs Verity had maintained this attitude unflinchingly through the embarrassing discovery of Mr Corderoy the butler, and had even skilfully exploited that occasion to acquire from a shocked Corderoy brother-in-law what an older generation would have called Walter Corderoy's literary remains. One consequence of this was that the Cheltenham house had become something of a shrine. And Mrs Verity had become something of a priestess.

Charles Shand reflected nervously on these matters as he drove over from Oxford a week later. The fact that he was no stranger to Mrs Verity, that she knew of various aspects of his work and had furthered him in them, scarcely made the coming interview easier. Shand didn't quite get round to reflecting that he had very little sense of Mrs Verity's character—the dubiety was of a sort his mind didn't naturally focus—but he was uneasily aware that he had no idea how she would take the revelation of her kinship with a murderer. Shand's labours had been of the most orthodox kind, and conducted by a light than which there seems none cleaner : the clear hard light of a disinterested pursuit of knowledge. But this light—through, so to speak, no fault of its own—had suddenly found itself at play upon decidedly swampy territory.

Steering cautiously through the narrows of Northleach, Shand reviewed the stages of his luckless investigation. First there had been the thought to study the trial which Corderoy had so curiously made use of in a novel. Then there had been the turning to the earlier background of that trial's principal figure—normal if somewhat peripheral research which had brought up an interesting fact : the home of Martha Mainprize, the murderer's long-dead mother, had been in Corderoy's neighbourhood. There might have been nothing in that. It had been suggestive, all the same.

Then—Shand frowned over the wheel—had come the astonishing running to earth of an old woman who was Martha's niece, and the yet more astonishing discovery—in a cupboard in this old woman's hovel—of the little cache of Martha's possessions : the photographs, the locks of hair, the pathetically yellowed and almost illiterate diary, with the entry 'W.C., £10' recorded regularly every fortnight. Martha's niece had refused to part with these things for any reasonable sum; Shand had been prevented by some scruple from making an offer that would be exorbitant. What was going to happen when he told Mrs Verity all this? It had only been respectable biographical research all through— and yet was it not the very picture of 'private detection' such as one reads of in squalid law suits? And here was only the start of the story. Its conclusion was in Winchester Gaol.

Shand descended the long hill into Cheltenham more slowly than even his habitual care for road-safety required. A curious town, he thought. Stone flaking, stucco crumbling, paint weathered away. Behind these disgraced, these bleakly elegant façades did there still lurk the answering human detritus of an empire—the spinster daughters of retired admirals, the relics of the last administrators and defenders of British India? Shand didn't know, but he thought probably not. It all looked depressingly run-down, yet the shops in the centre told you there was something like affluence lurking around. He shook his head, acknowledging an insecure grip of recent social history. He parked his car, found in a grey deserted crescent Walter Corderoy's daughter's abode, and gave a moderate but adequate downward pull at the bell.

The hall had stone pillars and stone-coloured paint. It was lined with books. But the staircase had pictures, hung close together and themselves ascending in steps, like the advertisements on the escalators in London tubes. Only whereas the advertisements inclined to be indelicate, here a high propriety ruled. The pictures were mostly large photographs of gentlemen, and on their mounts or margins or neutral sepia spaces were written things like *Cordially Joseph Conrad* and *Comme un témoignage de profonde et affectueuse reconnaissance Marcel Proust*. Shand recalled being made uneasy by them on a previous occasion. They seemed to convey a slight intimation that a scholar was an outsider, after all. He would have hurried past them now. Unfortunately a very ancient parlourmaid—even more ancient than her mistress—was preceding him slowly and with creaking knees.

Mrs Verity received him in her drawing-room. It was large, with high windows through which there crept rather than streamed a cool grey light. There was perhaps nothing too obtrusive about Walter Corderoy's presence in the apartment. Here, almost, was an ordinary drawing-room of an upper-middle class sort: full of good taste and old furniture and faded stuffs and fabrics. But Corderoy by John Singer Sargent was over the chimney-piece, and in the big alcove where one might have expected a grand piano was Corderoy's writing-table with Corderoy by Jacques-Emile Blanche flanking it on the wall. There was a cabinet displaying various mementos of eminence: scrolls and diplomas, medals and patents and the insignia of foreign Orders, faded but gracious commands from exalted personages. There was a show-case frankly carrying some suggestion of a museum, with corrected galley-proofs and a few manuscripts. It was convenient—Mrs Verity would explain—to have such a small exhibition to hand when people with no special claim on one felt prompted to call.

'My dear Professor, I was delighted when you wrote that you could come. I am eager to hear how your work has been going on.'

Mrs Verity invariably addressed Shand as 'Professor', although she knew perfectly well that it was not technically correct. It was her way of remaining at a slight remove; in fact it went along with the signed photographs on the staircase. And although she was so piously devoted to Corderoy's memory—almost to a Corderoy legend, it might be said—she wasn't in the least the pathetic and teetering old person whom young Coverdale had conjured up. Shand himself found that, between visits, he was inclined to forget this; to forget, as it were, how much there was left of her. He took encouragement from it now. Perhaps, he told himself, the old girl was really quite tough. He ought already to have some better estimate of this in his mind. He must, he thought, have been remiss. It was rather as if he had failed to collate a relevant text. This time, he resolved, he would go away with Mrs Verity's character and temperament precisely noted down.

'I have heard again,' Mrs Verity said, 'from Professor Barthou of the Sorbonne. A charming man.'

'Yes, indeed.' Shand didn't feel worried about Barthou. 'Do you happen to have had any correspondence with a man called Fawdry?' He waited in suspense while Mrs

Verity appeared to make an effort of memory. She was still handsome—and uncommonly like the Sargent portrait of her father—but it was only to be expected that her mind might be going a little. 'Not a university teacher,' he prompted. 'Mr Fawdry is, I suppose, what is called a literary journalist.'

'No, the name hasn't come my way.' Much to Shand's relief, Mrs Verity had decisively shaken her head; Fawdry was the rather deplorable person who was also on Corderoy's trail. 'I receive, as you know, a good deal of correspondence about my father and his work. Much of it is from people of my own generation, who still remember him. You will recollect how much, in his later years, he came to relish society. He had a weakness for the great houses, had he not?' Mrs Verity's strong features appeared to be softening into an expression denoting affectionate acknowledgement of foible. 'Badminton, Chatsworth, Blenheim.'

'Yes, of course.' Shand couldn't in fact recall that bevies of cultivated dukes had been eager for Walter Corderoy's company. But the general proposition was correct. And Mrs Verity's so relishing her vestigial contacts with such social elevation as her father had attained made the coming revelation all the more grotesque and awkward.

'I'm afraid,' Shand said, 'that I have a painful communication to make to you.' He paused on this—'communication' had been a pompously chosen word—and didn't at all know whether to be encouraged by a glance of curiosity, swiftly veiled, which he had evoked. 'As you know,' he went on, 'I've been working chiefly on the biographical side of late.' He paused again, and it must have taken only a moment's silence to disconcert him. For instead of making a statement—which was certainly what was now incumbent upon him—he shied away into a question. 'May I ask if your mother,' he said, 'ever made you any confidence about the earliest period of her married life?'

'I scarcely know whether anything of the sort is to be expected between mothers and daughters.' Mrs Verity had started, as she well might. 'If you are referring, that's to say, to intimate matters.'

'Quite so, quite so.' Shand uttered these words without exactly knowing to what they applied. He was already feeling very upset. 'What I have to tell you isn't really startling,' he said. 'Or not,' he added conscientiously, 'the first part of it. I assure you, my dear Mrs Verity, that it wouldn't seem in the least surprising to any man of the world.' Shand wondered whether he himself at all measured up to this character. 'The fact is that Walter Corderoy had an illegitimate son by a village girl. He was very young. Scarcely beyond the stage of sowing his wild oats.'

'Why should my mother—?'

'But he had *married* very young. And I am afraid this lapse was in the early months of his marriage.' Shand produced a handkerchief and blew his nose. He had regretted that 'I am afraid' instantly. And 'lapse' had been bad too. The words touched in an unnecessary note of moral reprobation such as could scarcely have come into a man-of-the-world's head.

'My mother knew,' Mrs Verity said.

'You mean that *you* know?' It had taken Shand a moment to grasp the implication, and his first sensation was of sharp relief. 'I'm telling you nothing new?'

'My dear Professor, I didn't *say* that. Put it, if you like, that my mother *would* know. She was a remarkable woman.'

'Most certainly. She was widely felt to be so.' Shand made a clutch at his familiar decencies. 'A kind of Meredithian heroine.'

'Perhaps. But I think that Aeschylean would be my own definition.'

'Indeed?' It was only after a moment that Shand managed even this. Mrs Verity's last words had come to his ear like gibberish, so that he had been obliged to reach after them, consider them in phonetic terms, and finally make at least grammatical sense of them. Mrs Verity, he recalled, had been at Girton (in Miss Jones's time) and couldn't be wholly vague about the dramatist of the *Oresteia*. It seemed a batty remark, all the same. Not that Mrs Verity looked batty. She merely looked rather grim. It was a consciousness of this that prompted what Shand went on to say. 'I'm afraid you may judge me impertinent in bringing up this matter at all. But the man I mentioned—'

'A Mr Fawdry, I think you said? I quite understand.' Mrs Verity's countenance remained inexpressive. She was giving nothing away. 'Will you please tell me, Professor, just what you know?'

Shand began to do so, and his performance improved at once. He had an orderly mind. Once a week, during two terms out of three, he was a lucid if unexciting lecturer. With decent brevity he lectured now. William Mainprize was begotten, born, passed through his malting-house, and hanged—all within ten minutes. Even so, there had been a pause while the ancient parlourmaid brought in a tray. It was rather as when, in common room, the coffee had been brought in. *Pas devant les domestiques.*

'It will be backwards from *A Venation of Centaurs,* and from the trial, that this Mr Fawdry, too, will work?' Mrs Verity asked. She had, when one thought of it, a Girton way of phrasing things. And whether she had been staggered or not—whether, indeed, anything new had been broken to her—it was impossible to say.

'I'm afraid so. When it's a question only of the last hundred years there's almost nobody, whether gentle or simple, about whom the basic facts may not be discovered through dogged inquiry. Fawdry will have both William

Mainprize's parentage and his ultimate function in *A Venation of Centaurs* to play with. I can only suggest that the facts be first given to the world in a dignified way.'

'By yourself, Professor?'

'I would gladly avoid the task. But I am, conceivably, the most appropriate man to undertake it. I can assure you that I experience no pleasure in the contemplation of it.'

But Mrs Verity appeared not quite to have been listening. She had risen, and was crossing the room. Her posture was upright and her step firm. The movement revealed her as a very old lady, all the same.

'I have one or two things to show you,' Mrs Verity said.

3

With a twinge of discomfort, Shand recalled Martha Mainprize's relics. For he was being shown very much the same class of object now. Only whereas Martha's possessions had been retrieved from dust and mildew in a cheap deal cupboard, these were preserved in a formidably locked steel receptacle, leather-sheathed and velvet lined. For a moment something naked in the contrast shocked him, and then he concentrated upon the exhibits. Again there was a diary—this one finely-tooled and residually fragrant—and again there were photographs. Some of the photographs were small and primitive, others large and primitive. The more modern included both snapshots and formal studio affairs. There were various views of places and buildings too.

'My mother had the instinct of an annalist,' Mrs Verity was saying in her Girton manner. 'Whether in one medium or another, little was let pass unrecorded.' She picked out one of the oldest of the larger photographs and handed it to Shand. The surface had darkened in some places and in others faded, so that for a moment it suggested only a messy confluence of chocolates, milk and plain. 'The servants in 1871,' Mrs Verity said. She seemed to be quoting from memory some inscription barely decipherable in a margin. 'Martha Mainprize on the left in the back row.' She made a gesture which closed the quotation and allowed her to continue in her own person. 'So of course my mother knew. She knew everything. And of course I know. I must apologise, Professor, for having dissimulated. The record is only too clear about a number of things. Although some of the photographs, indeed, perplex me still.'

Shand had been regarding the stiffly posed group intently. There was a butler in the middle—in his early twenties the butler's grandson had attained to a butler—and two or three outdoor servants had been brought in. So it was a socially imposing affair. And there could be no doubt about Martha Mainprize; on the strength of a photograph glimpsed in the humbler collection, Shand recognised her at once.

'Martha Mainprize shortly before her death, with William aged five.' Mrs Verity handed another photograph. 'But I must make the tea, or Evans will be displeased.' And Mrs Verity turned aside. The tea-equipage which the decrepit parlourmaid had brought in was an elaborate affair, and ought to have been much beyond her strength. Mrs Verity absorbed herself with a silver kettle and fine china. Shand took a good look at William Mainprize aged five, and put the photograph down. There was something unnerving about this archive—and there had been something unnerving about one of Mrs Verity's remarks on it. She had said that some of the photographs perplexed her still. He felt a sudden irrational conviction that further revelation lurked here—matters still mercifully screened from Walter Corderoy's daughter, but the significance of which he himself, with his specialised knowledge, might discern instantly, and must be on his guard not to betray.

Obeying an impulse equally irrational, Shand thrust his hand into the pile of photographs as yet unexamined, and drew out one at random. It was of a stretch of landscape with some large structure in the middle. Before he had scrutinised this, before he had distinguished the stunted barred windows and the ugly octagonal tower, he knew what he was looking at. It was a prison. For a moment he lost his head, was on the point of crumpling the thing up and stuffing it into a pocket. Then he remembered that Mrs Verity *knew* what had befallen whom in Winchester Gaol; that this visit to her had been pointless, since she had nothing more to learn about the fate of her father's bastard son. But he continued to look at the photograph, strangely disturbed. It was sufficiently surprising that Corderoy's wronged wife should have assembled and preserved even those early memorials of her husband's peasant mistress and their child. It was surely a fantastic morbidity to have added that last grim pendant to the collection.

Something had gone wrong with a little spirit lamp required for the tea-ritual, and Mrs Verity was detained by it a moment or two longer. The diary he could not venture to open, but he turned over some further photographs. There was William Mainprize as a junior schoolboy and as a senior one. In the second of these phases William ought to have turned gawky, but hadn't. And in the next in the series—it must date from his malting-house days—he was a very hansdome youth indeed. He was also undeniably his eminent father's son. Shand picked up one further photograph. It had evidently been enlarged from a snapshot, and had something of an impromptu and even hurried air. The setting appeared to be a walled garden. A matronly lady was standing beside a rustic seat. Even in her elaborate costume—which might belong to the early 1890's, Shand supposed—it was evident that she was pregnant. Beside her was the unmistakable figure of William Mainprize, now really grown-up. His arm was familiarly round her waist, but his gaze was over his shoulder and out of the picture. He might have been poised to bolt. It was a displeasingly furtive scene.

An appalled sense of revelation came to Shand. Here *was* something which the old woman now tinkling her teacups had failed to tumble to. And she must never, never do so! But as he was about to thrust the photograph back among the others he found that Mrs Verity was again standing beside him.

'*That* one,' she said. 'I am perplexed, I own.'

'Indeed?' Even to his own ear, Shand's casualness of response sounded absurdly bogus. 'Probably it has drifted in accidentally and has no connection—'

'I mean that I am perplexed as to whom my mother could have trusted to take it. A confidential servant, no doubt. But it was extremely rash. Perhaps it was what actually led to the discovery.'

'The discovery?' Shand was conscious of the odd fact that his face had gone cold. It was as if somebody had poured ether on it. Presumably, he thought with dismay, it was betraying a deadly pallor. And now Mrs Verity was looking at him.

'We needn't lose our heads,' she said drily. 'It will be a long time before your Mr Fawdry lays hands on *that*.' And she pointed to the photograph.

'It's the only positive—?'

'There is also the diary.'

'Mrs Verity, ought you not—?' Shand had glanced at the comfortable fire burning in the drawing-room grate. 'Would it not be wise—?'

'Certainly not, Professor. I am not of a mind to destroy

any part of English literary history.' Rather strangely, Mrs Verity smiled. 'But I confess that, while I remain on earth, I am willing to sit on it.'

'That *is* your mother?' Shand had turned back to stare at the photograph.

'Certainly it's my mother. She was a remarkable woman, as I said.'

'Yes, of course.' Shand remembered the remark about Aeschylus. Clytemnestra, he dimly thought, didn't have much of an edge on Walter Corderoy's wife.

'While my mother was still a young bride in his house, her husband seduced one of the servants, Martha Mainprize. My mother waited, and herself seduced the young man who had been the fruit of that seduction. It is possible that she proclaimed the fact—announced to her husband that she was carrying William Mainprize's child. Certainly the young man was banished, as you know.'

'And the tragedy darkened again, long after.' Momentarily into Shand's head came the image of his colleague the Casaubon Professor of Greek, chattering about *protasis* and *epitasis*. But this was at once ousted by something else : a simple summoning up and comparing of dates, such as his work required of him daily. His eyes turned to the pregnant woman in the photograph, and then back to Mrs Verity. And on her they rounded. For Mrs Verity— Lavinia Corderoy—was not Walter Corderoy's daughter but his grand-daughter. And her actual father—Corderoy's illegitimate son and the lover of Corderoy's wife—lay in quicklime at Winchester.

But Mrs Verity, evidently for long cognizant of this remarkable parentage, was composedly pouring tea. She handed Shand his cup, turned round, and picked up a plate.

'Ah,' Mrs Verity said, 'cucumber sandwiches.'

A Change of Heart

'A CHANGE OF HEART.'

It seemed to Michael Firth that someone had spoken these words—or rather was in process of speaking these words—behind his left ear. The position had been chosen so that the speaker could remain invisible. He could remain invisible (the voice was a man's and sounded familiar) because Firth was for some reason unable to turn his head. There was a pain in Firth's head—suddenly a very bad pain.

The voice swam away into silence. For some time only a cunningly devised instrument (and the place was full of such things, hummed with them, had emanating from them the smell of dryness that complex electrical apparatus can produce) could have detected that anything at all was going on inside Firth. Then Firth was back being Firth, and aware of strange surroundings. Or he was aware of an astonishing discontinuity in his experience. Only a split second ago he had been doing he hadn't a recollection what. But nothing connected with *this*. *This* was grave attention centred on him, and figures in white clothes, and again that hum with its queer smell, and as well as the smell of the hum an ordinary *hospital* smell as well.

So that was it! 'I've had an accident,' Firth told himself— and knew that his split second might really represent days or weeks. 'A street accident,' he amplified. This time his own voice, which was rather like the other one, swam away. But now he was fleetingly aware of his consciousness as deliberately withdrawing within its inviolate subliminal intricacies. 'No more coma,' he told himself reassuringly. 'I'm merely falling asleep.'

A change of heart. . . . It surprised Firth—during another of the short spells of what he hoped was clear thinking— that the words were obsessing him like a small trickle of icy water from which it was impossible to edge away. It wasn't as if he didn't know why they were in his mind. They had been a joke, and if he himself hadn't liked the joke—well, that was only an instance of his being edgy these days. Overwork, he supposed. Back from the office late, and then, tiresomely often, one of Camilla's parties. And they had missed out on their routine winter cruise. He had told himself he was glad of that, since he had a feeling that a 'luxury' cruise, sold on the persuasions of glossy brochures, was a banal and vulgar way of easing off. But perhaps it had been a mistake, and he had succumbed to mounting fatigue. Perhaps the rubbery-smelling brochures were right, and business men really did so succumb unless they regularly performed those latterday pilgrimages of which the shrines were Pacific islands, and the rituals sticky nights in which you sat (decorously with your wife beside you) watching dusky beauties agitating their naked haunches in reputedly indigenous dances. However that might be, it is true that you can step off the kerb inadvisedly when dead tired. Probably a bus had got him—at least sometimes it felt as bad as that. He must ask them. So far as he could remember, they hadn't yet told him anything about it. Perhaps it was a memory of the bus that had been getting into his head every now and then as the sound of a roaring engine seemingly bearing down on him.

But about that other sound in his head : those insistently self-reiterating words. He and Camilla had gone down to Spindle, their country cottage, and at once there had been a party. Camilla was sensitive to the aspersion that they were mere come-and-go townees when at Spindle; that her husband was no more than a mini-version of a week-end squire. The dozen acres on which he let old Hayball (who pottered for them) keep goats and a straggly 'free-range' poultry, Camilla liked to refer to as the farm. He had even heard her refer to Hayball as the manager. Or had it been the agent? Camilla's distortions of reality, commonly small and dangerous like a distance marginally misjudged at night, occasionally became monstrous and rather funny, as if she were an animated hall of mirrors in a fair. Anyway, she always summoned the neighbours well in advance to a party to be held the moment the Firths themselves arrived at Spindle. This time, the guests had been upon them almost before Firth could get a fire going in the big fireplace. There was apple-wood, which gratified Camilla because it is supposed to be a pleasing and superior stuff to be in a position to burn.

Suddenly, as he remembered this, the smell of ether and disinfectants faded on Michael Firth, and the smell of the apple-wood was in his nostrils instead. Whether pleasing or not, there was too much of it, since the main chimney at Spindle was distinguished by picturesque rather than functional qualities. He was hurrying round the low drawing-room like a fumigated ferret, trying to coax away the smoke by opening one window and closing another, when people began to arrive.

Camilla was extending her territory. These were the gentry from about three miles around; when she got to ten miles, he supposed, she would start to feel that she was establishing herself on a county basis. Already there was the authentic week-end squire, who was a simple character comfortably niched in a harmless corner of a large family concern in the city. There was the squire's wife, who had written a book about being somebody's daughter in some embassy or other after the Kaiser's war or before Hitler's—

Firth could never remember which. There were people who trained horses, or bred horses, or—more grandly—owned horses and raced them : these tended, when not barking at one another briefly, to freeze into a glassy-eyed immobility, like children playing Grandmother's Steps. There were two commuting dons who worked in the University of London, men with an air of waiting, perfectly amiably and tolerantly, for something to be said worth saying; these had clever young wives, clothed in garments obtained in interesting foreign places, and with fast reaction-times and hostile impulses. There were several elderly couples, returned in a battered or at least discouraged condition from outposts of a disintegrating Commonwealth. There was Dr Roxburgh, the local G.P. And of course there was the vicar, Mr Baxendale.

Firth got all these people drinks as rapidly as he could. He had nothing against them except that they were a completely heterogeneous lot, brought together—like a random basketful of wild flowers and weeds and fungi—on no basis other than that of fortuitous topographical contiguity. Camilla liked this, and would refer to it as a challenge; she too hurried round, intent on making her party 'go'. Like the apple-wood fire, the party after a fashion went.

'Where the pigs be many the wash runs thin.' One of the horse-training characters said this as he accepted a drink. Firth thought it an odd sort of pleasantry; he was aware that there was a crush in the room, but was hardly prepared to have his martinis reflected upon in this way. It turned out, however, that he had got the bearing of the remark wrong. This often happened to him at parties. His guest was talking about Hayball's nephew, Luke Hayball, an able-bodied man now unemployed and alleged to have become scandalously disinclined for anything else. Luke had six children, and such were the iniquities of a socialist government that he got less wages when he worked than relief when he didn't. So the point was that the proverb no longer held true. The more numerous the pigs—meaning the little Hayballs—the thicker the wash provided for them by an over-indulgent community.

Firth couldn't feel much indignation about this; indeed, as the employer of the head of the Hayballs, he felt on the contrary a species of feudal obligation to stand up for the whole ramifying family. Certainly he didn't want to be bored by unintelligent and prejudiced generalisations based upon the supposed degeneracy of Luke. He was afraid, moreover, that one or other of the dons' wives would prove actually to *be* a socialist, and would plunge in with inappropriate political passion on the other side. So he turned to Dr Roxburgh, and asked him what was the news about Binchy.

There was an immediate hush among the people within earshot. It was almost a morbid hush, as if upon the expectation of some obscene exhibit, so that Firth wished he had thought of something else. At the moment Binchy (a man uninteresting except for his curious resemblance to a horse-fly, who ran the post-office and everything shop) was a national figure. You could read about him in your morning paper every day. But to have news of him from, so to speak, the leech's mouth was another matter. Binchy's success-story (as it might still currently be called) must have begun in Roxburgh's surgery—to which most of those present no doubt took their ailments from time to time. Hence the detectable *frisson* now.

Naturally enough, Roxburgh hadn't much to tell, even had the rules of his profession permitted him to be communicative. When a country doctor's patient vanishes into a great hospital, only a formal letter intimating his discharge (or death) is likely to be the sequel. Roxburgh, however, was at least in a position to say that the last newspaper yarn was true. Binchy had asked for a pint of best bitter, and been given a glass of dry sherry instead. And Binchy—although the activity is discouraged in hospitals—had smoked a cigarette.

So much, Firth thought, for Binchy, from whom he had been accustomed to buy stamps—now England's star transplant-patient of the moment, with his common man's common appetites returning to him. A man sitting up in bed, with a long, healing scar down his body, like a weal from a lash vertically laid on, and with somebody else's inside dovetailed and sutured neatly into him. . . . More gin, more vermouth, more ice, another lemon : Michael Firth was grateful for having to make a dash for them. In the kitchen Camilla's latest help from the village opened the refrigerator. She seemed a competent woman, but he had no notion who she was. She might be Mrs Binchy, for all he knew.

One of the young female academics, a Mrs Ruxton, *was* tiresome, but not about politics. She was writing a book, or perhaps what they called a thesis, about English rural life in the nineteenth-century novel. Far from being ashamed of this perfectly useless activity, she was evidently determined to run on it, and in its interest she was questioning poor old Baxendale about the murkier side of village *mores*. Some novelist, it seemed, had said he was far from darkening the picture in his presentation of such matters, and that had he been perfectly candid nobody would have stood for it. Was this true? Was it still true? Young Mrs Ruxton, with a solemn intentness evidenced only among the investigating classes in their female embodiment, put her questions to the Reverend Mr Baxendale with some insistence. Firth tried to head her off, even to shut her up. Was it not a firm principle of research, he interposed, that you got your information at first hand? Mrs Ruxton was a country-woman now, he went on, and a great accession to their small rural society. She must profit by her environment and enquire around among the villagers, like Wordsworth questioning his leech-gatherers and idiot boys.

This wasn't a success (and didn't deserve to be). Mrs Ruxton took the whimsical courtliness of Firth's 'great accession' gag for offensive irony, and she didn't like his attempted lightness of air about Wordsworth at all. She now showed signs, in fact, of going ahead for the hell of it. This made Firth think rather the better of her, but he listened in dismay, all the same. She was presently asking Baxendale (who was accustomed only to the smallest of small-talk) whether there was much incest among his parishioners. Was incest any longer proceeded against, unless it was mixed up with something else, such as rape? What *about* rape?

Quite a number of people were listening in on this cate-chism, and it wasn't making for the success of Camilla's party. The locals liked Baxendale, although the men at least hardly ever went near his church. He could be relied upon (except presumably from his pulpit) to keep clear of religion, and he was very much a gentleman of the old school. So the men addressed him as 'padre' on a note of jovial deference suggestive of a good regimental mess. Now they were looking bewildered as well as disapproving. The notion of any pursuit of general ideas was as inaccessible to them as the calculus would be to a tribe of decent and honourable Hottentots, and they failed to see that the young woman had at least started off with no offensive intention.

Firth, a successful solicitor, took it for granted that old Baxendale couldn't be at all clever. Clerics with any brains surely didn't grow old in obscure little rural benefices. But that Baxendale was perceptive as well as well-bred did now appear. He had become aware of the small current of philistine hostility towards his interlocutor, and he wasn't himself going to embark on it. He answered Mrs Ruxton's questions with an air of serious attention. It was unhappily true, he said, that no human society was likely to be without its areas of depravity. He believed that countryfolk were in the main untouched by some of the corrupting influences operative in towns. But rural communities had their special frailties. You might be doubtful about a child's paternity in London, but you had to move into darkest Kent to be doubtful about his maternity as well.

'Shocking state of affairs,' one of the London dons—not Mrs Ruxton's husband—interrupted cheerfully. He seemed to feel that, for the first time, something interesting had been said. 'A part of the world where only the horses can be guaranteed virtuous. Houyhnhm country, one might say.'

This remark—although the last part of it could not have been very generally intelligible—didn't go down well. But Baxendale maintained his frank dealing with Mrs Ruxton's curiosities. He had expressed himself extravagantly, perhaps, but every now and then one did hear of a grandmother going gallantly through a kind of ritual child-birth in order to cope with an awkward illegitimacy.

'Perfectly true,' Dr Roxburgh said briskly—and with a frank air of approving this break through the common bounds of conversation at Camilla's parties. 'Within my own experience. But no names, no pack-drill.'

'And are they really all pagans still?' Mrs Ruxton asked. Mrs Ruxton was herself presumably a pagan—if only because she wore suspended from her neck, much in the manner of an object of devotion, what was hideous enough to be a kind of miniaturised wooden fetich from the Benin States. Because she felt that she was at last having an intelligent conversation with an educated man, and vindicating her own character as a very much educated woman, this gauche and aggressive female was now quite happy. Moreover, the people round about had relaxed their disapproval. If the padre O K'd this sort of talk, it wasn't for them to object. Some of them looked round contentedly and expectantly for another drink. Firth ought to have realised the hitch was smoothed out.

'Still?' the vicar echoed, this time allowing himself a hint of humour. '*Ena, meena, mina, mo.* I suppose the children are still pagans when they do their "counting out" with that jingle. For these are the numerals of the Ancient Britons, I believe.'

'Professor Pfuhl disputes that.' Mrs Ruxton, plainly a devotee of learned journals, was happier still.

'Ah, yes. There is commonly a professor in opposition, is there not? But your main point is a most interesting one. I am myself inclined to think that it is only in novels that a paganism stemming from before our era remains a force amid the rural populace. Neo-paganism is another matter. It would be idle to maintain, my dear young lady, that people anywhere preserve their grandparents', or even their parents', regard for their religious duties.'

Dear old Baxendale—perhaps because he had been remarking the modish fetich dangling in the region of Mrs Ruxton's navel—had suddenly spoken out in his professional character; had, one might say, stood up to be counted. It was unprecedented, or at least unusual, so far as his party-going persona was concerned. Perhaps Firth overestimated the shock. He ought again to have realised that nobody was any longer much minding this particular piece of chit-chat. But he had a sense that here was an awkward moment —an awkward moment of a kind that Camilla (who was at the other end of the room) would deal with lightly and deftly, dissolving it and wafting it away on a small current of amusement which she would create on a basis of one-third wit and two-thirds silvery laugh. Firth was unequipped with a silvery laugh, so he had to rely entirely on something witty. He remembered the earlier talk about Mr Binchy of the post office.

'At least with Binchy's example before us,' Firth said, 'the vicar can hope for a change of heart.'

That had been the whole thing. The joke—not really a joke so much as a mere play upon words—had been his own. People had been moderately diverted—those who had tumbled to what he was talking about—and had drifted away to form other groups. But now, himself in hospital just as Binchy was in hospital, Firth was recalling his rather obvious quip as tasteless and humiliating. He worried about it a good deal. At times he even sensed in it something magical and ominous. He was doing so when he became aware of one of the white-coated figures looking with a wooden face at a clinical thermometer and then giving the instrument a discontented flick. Firth knew that his temperature had gone up.

And he supposed that his hearing had been affected. This would account for everybody's having been so uncommunicative. He seemed to have an ear only for interior voices, or for very small sounds like the hum (which might be air-conditioning and the like), or for that very big sound which intermittently shattered the place. For a long time he worked at disentangling the component parts of this big sound, rather as one wholly inexpert in music might work at disentangling the several instruments in an orchestra. He ended up by finding it very simple. There was always a roar, and usually there was a high whistling scream as well. When the big sound came while darkness was going on— and he was living or existing through nights and days, he supposed—it was accompanied by hurtling and blinking lights reflected on walls and ceiling. Eventually, and with an immense sense of intellectual achievement, he realised that only one explanation was possible of this fiendish outpouring of superhuman energies hard by where he lay. The hospital was sited beside a major airport.

It puzzled Firth that anybody should plant down a hospital so perversely. He could think of no rational occasion for doing such a thing.

2

They had told him something reassuring about his wife. At least he supposed it was that—for a great trouble was the way in which things kept slipping out of his memory. It was obvious that they had been at work on his head, and he was obliged to give them credit for stopping the very bad pain there. But sometimes he was angry with them for being careless. They must have left a hole in it, he reasoned, for things to keep dropping out of it as they did.

Several times he had thought about Camilla. Several times, while keeping hold of his general situation, which was that of a seriously injured man lying in hospital, he had reflected that she ought to be sitting beside him. She ought to be there holding his hand, or drawing grapes on a little cardboard tray out of a paper bag. But Camilla was never there, and one day he saw that there might be a very simple reason for this. Camilla was dead. Or perhaps she wasn't dead, but merely injured. They had been in a crash together, and now she was in a different part of the hospital, or in a different hospital altogether. This second hypothesis would account for whatever reassuring thing they had said.

But Firth could remember nothing at all about an accident. Along with much else, any recollection of it had trickled out through the hole. He would be a complete nuisance to himself and others until the hole was stopped up. He must locate it himself, he decided, and firmly point out their oversight to the white-coated surgeons and stiffly starched nurses. These people seemed concerned to do their best for him, and would take appropriate action at once. Cautiously and when he felt nobody to be looking, he put a hand up to his head.

Thus began the curious phase of Firth's covert exploration of his own person. He was like a schoolboy in a dormitory, apprehensive of disciplinary interference in his private affairs on the part of a puritanically minded prefect. The resemblance was accented by the fact that he now knew himself to have companions. This was a ward; there were several other beds quite close to his; the first thing he was aware of about their occupants (as was natural in an English institution) was their social standing in relation to himself. He must be in a public hospital, he realised, and not even in what was called an amenity bed, since his fellow sufferers so plainly belonged to the lower classes. Occasionally he heard snatches of their talk. They seemed well enough to be chattering together from time to time.

'Given 'im a pig's, they 'ave,' a voice said. 'And not even a take it or leave it, mark you. Unbeknownst, with 'im 'elpless under their bloody anesthekik. Right down there, too.'

'Gor!'

'Who knows 'ow things run into each other like—down there? Sniffing and grunting, 'is next kid will be, if yer asks me.'

'A scandal it is—a bloody scandal. Wot they got this place they call their catchment area for—eh, mate? Airport on one side, and bleeding speed-track on the other! Look at the ambilances, I say. Coming in all the time, they are—wot with one sodding crash following another. But the 'uman bits and pieces is all kep' for the bosses. Pigs' livers for you and me, mate—and not even served with bloody onions.'

Not unnaturally, Firth was filled with horror by this macabre (and subversive) talk. If, of course, it *was* talk. For he was having so many lurid dreams now that it was difficult for him to be quite sure about what were veridical reports of his senses. But he was prompted to step up, in a nameless apprehension, his stealthy fingering over of his own body. His first discovery was that he had only one hand, his left, available for the purpose. His head had been so obsessing him up to now, he supposed, that he had failed to be aware of his right hand and arm as bandaged and largely immobile. There was something almost reassuring in the discovery—or there would have been but for one isolated but acute perception that came to him. What had happened to his head must be far more serious than what had happened to a hand or arm, and it was clear that the white-coated figures understood this. But they were more *interested* in the state of his hand. He felt no pain there. But when the doctors or surgeons were present, it was there that a lot seemed to be going on. Perhaps his accident had resulted in his breaking a great many small bones in that part of his anatomy. All the same, there was something strange about it.

Lying flat on his back on the hard hospital bed, he was unable to explore himself below the line of his buttocks and genitals. But his fears extended no further, so this didn't greatly matter. The tips of his fingers, moving over his belly with the always slightly strange sensation of double touch, found the scar of his old appendectomy. At least he was almost sure it was that; that what his finger ran along was cicatrice and not a mere crease in a tummy no longer in anything like youthful trim. So that if anywhere else there was another cicatrice . . .

The depth of his irrationality, which he momentarily glimpsed as having to do with fever or delirium, stabbed into Firth's mind. And before his mind's vision—for his eyes were shut—there appeared, again only momentarily, the apparition of a monstrous horse-fly. Why a horse-fly? Firth hadn't a clue. But he was able to enunciate to himself a single word: *phobia*.

It is always comforting to be able to put a name to things, and the mere finding of this one relaxed Firth's tensions for a while. Then his left hand was fatuously at work again. He could get its thumb, he found, between his shoulder-blades, and zigzag it down a progressively broad area of his back. Short of his thighs, in fact, only a quite small scapular region remained beyond the reach of tactile investigation. Eventually his left arm began to ache as a result of its unaccustomed contortions, but by that time he really knew that his body—apart from what might have happened to his head and right hand—was unviolated.

So he reassured himself. Only he hadn't been able to *see*. Even when he undid the buttons of his pyjama jacket and the cord of his pyjama trousers, and so wriggled a good part of his torso naked; even when he did this and cautiously humped up the bed clothes into a little tent with his left forearm; even then, all that was visible was a shadowy and foreshortened projection of himself, like Rembrandt's *Anatomy Lesson of Doctor Deijman* viewed the other way on. At least he didn't seem to have lost weight as a consequence of whatever had happened to him. His protuberant abdomen showed as the segment of a circle—a circle the diameter of which suggested itself as not greater than the breadth of his hips. At its apex his umbilicus swam in a darkness taking the form of a crater, so that the whole of Michael Firth appeared to culminate in a small volcanic landscape, mysteriously softened beneath a surface of milky snow. But it was a landscape without a foreground. He could just glimpse his nipples as a species of *repoussoirs* moving the eye towards the navel which formed the centre of the composition. He was unable—perhaps it was because of the way his head was bandaged—to lower his chin so as to get any view of his chest.

He didn't bother to button up again, and of course he couldn't with one hand retie the cord of his pyjama bottoms. They would suppose that fever had made him restless. He lay back—or rather he simply relaxed, since he was always lying back. He glimpsed it as odd that this phobia—the word recurred to him—should momentarily have resolved itself in what was virtually an aesthetic experience : his own person as an artist might have taken a squint at it. He recalled, quite idly, that there had been a time when he wanted to be a painter. During his last year at school, and in bouts at Cambridge, it had been almost like an illness. Then, of course, he had entered the family firm.

He experienced a nightmare in which many swords pierced his heart. Although not a religious man, he was distressed upon waking up by the bad taste his unconscious mind had shown in trafficking with this particular icono-graphical *motif*. It was another instance, he supposed, of the bobbing up on him of that adolescent absorption in painting. But however that might be, it didn't help with the phobia. He now became obsessed with the idea of mirrors. He had fantasies in which, stark naked, he paraded the *Galerie des Glaces* at Versailles. Or he merely—what was better—visited his tailor (needfully enough, since nude still) and there manipulated the system of swinging mirrors which afforded one a view of oneself front, back and sides at once. Oddly enough, this embarrassing nonsense appeared to have a therapeutic effect. His anxieties gradually died away.

He was able to read. He became aware of this when he noticed that part of the hospital staff wore coloured buttons or badges on their jackets or aprons. The younger doctors (or perhaps they were students) did, and with them the plain colour appeared to afford all the information that had to be given. But the badges of some of the nurses were lettered as well, and it was one of these that Firth first managed to decipher. This was displayed by an elderly and responsible woman who appeared to do little except keep an eye on other people. Sometimes, however, she combed and brushed Firth's hair—or the half of it which was now free of the diminishing bandages. He had been horrified when first aware of this being done, but now he had come rather to like it. It seemed an action sufficiently marginal in terms of strict nursing necessities to afford him (with a decent tenuousness) the sensation of a man perversely pretending to be a small boy in the hands of a woman. And when he read what her badge said, he managed to be amused for the first time since all this had begun happening to him. The badge said: *After-care Sister*. He wondered whether this had been thought up by way of boosting morale. If it was after-care one was having, then things couldn't be too bad.

It was the After-care Sister, however, who brought about his relapse—his nervous or neurotic relapse, that is to say. She did this by carelessly leaving on the coverlet of his bed for a moment something which he was also able to read, at least in part. It was some sort of form or chart, he saw, upon which they wrote up his progress day by day, and he managed to make out one word of the last sentence entered on it. The word was *uneventful*. This, too, was reassuring. It must represent the official view of his recovery, convalescence, or whatever they called it. Feeling almost cheerful, he let his glance discreetly travel to the top of the form, where there was some sort of printed heading in small type. What this said was:

Graft and Transplant Unit: Male Ward

After this, Firth had another quite mad spell about mirrors. And eventually he managed to get hold of a real looking-glass. He did this by simulating a kind of fresh dawn of vanity during the hair-brushing business. The After-care Sister, doubtless pleased by this show of interest on the part of an ominously withdrawn patient, tactfully left the looking-glass beside him so that he could further admire himself in decent privacy. Firth felt his heart—*his* heart?—thumping in its cavern. No sooner had the woman turned away than he tore open his pyjama jacket and held the small looking-glass before his bared chest. He saw what everything sane in him told him he would see, what his finger-tips, indeed, had long since assured him of: an expanse of undisturbed white flesh.

He became aware that somebody was standing beside his bed—not one of the nurses, but an elderly man, vaguely familiar to him, and of formidable presence. It was plain that this was the boss of the whole show. Suddenly, for the first time, Firth's head was completely clear—even clear enough for him to feel embarrassed at having been detected in his small pathological performance.

'You see,' Firth said foolishly, 'It's Binchy. He's been on my mind.'

'Ah, Binchy.' The elderly man spoke as if he perfectly knew who Binchy was (as, indeed, he probably did) but was not particularly interested in Firth's remark. 'Things have been going very well, Mr Firth—very well, indeed.' He tapped Firth's right arm with great friendliness and cheerfulness. 'We can have the last of these things off now, I think, and tomorrow our friends here can get going on the exercises.'

'Yes—the exercises,' Firth said meekly, although he had no notion of what the man was talking about.

'I don't often risk prophecy, but this time I don't mind sticking my neck out.' The elderly man picked up the looking-glass and with what was apparently a profound unconsciousness put in a moment studying his own features with quiet satisfaction. 'It's going to be entirely successful—and for the first time in the history of surgery.'

'I congratulate you,' Firth said. Congratulations seemed, somehow, more appropriate than thanks when it was a matter of having been transformed into a historical object. 'But may I ask—'

The surgeon, however, was looking at his watch. It was with the air of a man who, although weightily occupied, finds rather against expectation that he has some small space of leisure at his command.

'My dear Mr Firth,' he said, 'shall we have a glass of sherry? They keep a very decent *fino* for one or two of us here.'

So they had a glass of sherry, and then Michael Firth was shown his new forefinger and thumb. Sir Horace Rumford (for that was the surgeon's name) explained to him that his old forefinger and thumb had been so crushed as to be useless. '*Absolutely* useless,' Rumford said with what was almost an air of reproach. 'Nothing whatever to be done with them. They simply had to be thrown away.'

'I see.' Firth felt apologetic. He also found himself (for he was now sitting up) glancing round the highly polished floor of the ward and even under the other beds—Rumford having concluded this part of his communication on a note of impatience suggesting that he might simply have chucked those abandoned parts of Firth into a corner.

'But it just so happened that we were deuced lucky in what came in. As neat as anything for months.'

'From the race-track?' Firth asked nervously, looking at the finger and thumb.

'No, no—not that kind of person at all. Will you have a cigarette, my dear Firth? Frowned on, rather, in these places. But why not?' He produced a gold cigarette-case and helped Firth light up. 'Now what were we saying?'

'There *is* a race-track—a circuit, or whatever it's called?'

'Dear me, yes. But you haven't been—um—linked up with it in any way.' Rumford spoke as if acknowledging that there would have been an impropriety in providing a member of a learned profession with such a linkage. 'The airport. A shocking business.'

'I see,' Firth said again. He was consulting his own inside, expecting it to tell him that he felt slightly sick. But this wasn't so. In fact, what he was chiefly conscious of was that he was enjoying his cigarette. 'Just what kind of person?' he asked.

'At first, I'm afraid, the exercises will have to be rather tediously elementary.' Ignoring Firth's question, Rumford spoke rapidly. 'Rolling bread pellets. Picking up pencils. Then picking up matches. That kind of thing. Our young friends here have it all worked out.'

'Yes, I see.' Firth was conscious of displaying himself as somewhat lacking in conversational resource.

'Then there will be the stage at which you attempt to recover your customary signature. I shall be most interested in that. Your bank manager too, eh?' Sir Horace laughed, and then appeared struck by a sudden misgiving. 'You're not left-handed, by any chance?' he asked.

'Definitely not.' Firth looked curiously at his hand. There was a hair-line in bright scarlet round the root of the thumb, but no other trace of surgery. Nevertheless, the thumb did faintly suggest itself as not belonging to the hand. And the index-finger did this much more definitely. With conscious caution, he placed his left hand side by side with his right on the coverlet of the bed.

'Pretty good, eh?' Sir Horace took it for granted that his patient was admiring what he saw. 'A modest milestone in surgical history, as I said. I dare say they'll call it Rumfordising—ha-ha!'

'Ha-ha!' Firth articulated. He remembered that there had been somebody called Count von Rumford who invented a patent chimney. The poet Coleridge—or had it been Wordsworth?—had been enthusiastic about Rumfordising. Perhaps Sir Horace was a descendant of the Count's. Noticing how idly he turned this over in his mind, and with how little effort he managed to laugh at the surgeon's not particularly scintillating joke, Firth realised the vastness of his own relief. His absurd morbidity—phobia, as he had rightly called it—had vanished. Now he had only to rejoice that, after all, virtually nothing had happened to him.

'But you haven't told me,' he said—suddenly remembering this—'what sort of person the donor was. I suppose that's the proper word?'

'My dear Sir, I must ask you to reflect.' Rumford was abruptly speaking in a changed voice. And with a changed manner, too. It was as if he had slipped a white gauze mask over his nose and mouth, and were speaking in a professional, almost a hieratic, character. 'It is in every regard desirable that anonymity should be preserved in these cases. We therefore make it a matter of etiquette.'

'I see.' Falling back on this expression yet again, Firth found that he imported into it a certain element of imperfect conviction. He hadn't intended to do so. Perhaps he had been slightly irritated by something portentous in Rumford's enunciation of 'etiquette'. But it was the chap's own business, and Firth was perfectly willing to drop the matter. Rumford, however, himself continued with it.

'Pray consider again,' he said severely. 'Were you to be made aware of the donor's identity, and then to encounter him socially, embarrassment might well ensue.'

'Encounter him!' There was stupefaction in Firth's voice. 'You mean he's *alive*?'

'It seems that I have inadvertently admitted as much.' Sir Horace was frowning majestically. He was also looking at his watch. 'I only beg that you will not communicate the circumstance to the press.'

'To the press! Whatever has the press—'

'We have kept them away, so far. But, of course, they will be interested. And very properly.' The milestone in surgical history was presumably in Sir Horace's mind. 'But this is something—'

'Of course I shall say nothing about it whatever.' Firth was indignant. 'I should consider it a monstrous invasion of privacy. But how did this unfortunate man—' Firth broke off, and looked at what he would have to come to regard as his finger and thumb. 'Why was it impossible—'

'The upper arm, Mr Firth. Pulp. Or perhaps a better word would be mush. Nothing whatever could be done about it, and we amputated at once. The finger and thumb, however, were eminently usable. And now, I am afraid I must leave you. Thursday is my regular day here, and I shall probably have the pleasure of seeing you once more before you are discharged. Good afternoon.'

Left to himself, Michael Firth noticed that the sherry was within his reach. He made haste to grab it and pour himself a further glass before the After-care woman came back again. He drank it off before taking another look at his hands. His left forefinger was tapering; the forefinger on his right hand was firmly square. His left thumb was slightly stiff; the thumb on his right hand, even in its unexercised state, was supple and curiously restless. For a moment he felt in danger of a recurrence of some foolish state of mind, and then he made an effort to reach out and grasp—that was the word—a due sense of proportion. After all, he told himself whimsically, if his right hand offended him he could always shove it in his trouser-pocket.

3

Firth and his wife came out of their respective hospitals on the same day. (It really had been a quite simple car smash.) Camilla's injury had not been dangerous, but it had immobilised her in a curious way and required a great deal of intensive medical care. Her nose had been sheared off, so that it was necessary to grow her a new one. For this purpose one of her arms had been positioned in a skilful manner, and she had been obliged to keep quite still and not to talk. The operation was very successful.

In fact, it was startlingly successful, just as her husband's had been. The plastic-surgeon had been provided with photographs (and even with an oil painting commissioned by Firth some years before from one of his artistic acquaintances). But the surgeon had found these guide-lines contradictory and unsatisfactory, and had been obliged to go ahead on his own. He had grown Camilla a really beautiful nose (which it isn't difficult for a plastic-surgeon to do). He had also (what is, on the other hand, tricky and dodgy) grown her a beautiful nose which quite notably harmonised with her existing features. The result was extremely striking. *'Tis not a lip or eye we beauty call*—the satisfied specialist had quoted to his pupils—*But the joint force and full result of all*.

The new Camilla was triumphant, and Firth himself was very pleased. Occasionally, however, he had to own to feeling a shade disconcerted. A childless couple, he and Camilla had contrived to remain fond of each other largely by developing a technique of unobtrusive inattention, and a certain effort of readjustment was required now that there was something novel and improved to look at across the breakfast-table. All the same, Firth was delighted. He resolved to have Camilla's portrait painted again by a better class of artist than before.

They recuperated in Switzerland. Firth himself had not much taste for those *papier-mâché* mountains, tinny lakes and tidy towns, but Camilla had been to school in Vevey and was fond of the place. Knowing that he would be bored, Firth contrived to smuggle out with him a good deal of work from the office. There were, after all, considerable arrears of stuff too important for subordinates to be let attend to. So he sat on the balcony of their enormous room in the *Hôtel des Trois Couronnes,* mulling contentedly over his papers, occasionally staring across the lake at the rocks of Meillerie and the spurs of the Dent d'Oche. Camilla went round shopping, or read *La Nouvelle Héloïse.* It was all pleasant enough. Yet Firth continued at times to be put out by Camilla's new look. It stirred up in him something from quite far back in his past, and this something was the more disturbing in that it didn't appear to be in the least amative. It was more like a prompting to some purely contemplative activity. Above all, it was elusive. Experienced in the dining-room of the *Trois Couronnes*— lofty, full of slabby marble, bizarrely peopled by an English upper middle class left over from the Edwardian age, productive on demand of roast beef and Yorkshire pudding or boiled rice and prunes: experienced amid this solid *ambiance,* anything elusive seemed altogether out of place. If it was merely the consequence of Camilla's nose—he found himself thinking just occasionally—it would be a relief if she could do with it as he did with his own recent acquisition. He had, in fact, formed the habit of going about with his right hand in his trouser-pocket.

But, of course, it had remained his working hand. His signature with it, if it was not quite his old signature, was yet firm and undeviating. As he scribbled notes in the margin of legal documents before returning them to London, it was with all his accustomed legibility and fluency. He enjoyed using the slim gold pencil he had owned for years; if anything, its fine chasing and its full weight in his hand afforded him a small sensuous satisfaction he didn't recall before. Whether with this pencil, or with a few coloured ball-points he had upon some prompting acquired in a cheap shop, he found himself coming to do a good deal of doodling. This had been no habit of his for years—but, of course, its reappearance now was simply a carry-over from that phase of constant controlled exercises through which he had been put by Sir Horace Rumford's young friends. He had enjoyed the exercises; had enjoyed his progressive ability to employ his new finger and thumb with precision. Now these doodles, which came from inside his head and were quite uninfluenced by the operatic prospects to be enjoyed from the superior apartments of a hotel on the Lake of Geneva, had themselves a quality of the precise. They didn't seem to have much else, and at times Firth found himself sufficiently attending to them to be aware of a feeling of dissatisfaction.

This was the state of affairs—ominous, although he had no notion of the fact—when he and Camilla returned to England.

Naturally enough, Camilla's London parties had a character quite different from that of the small affairs she organised when they were at Spindle. In the country she admired the lesser landed gentry, and provided somebody was of consequence within a couple of parishes, she didn't at all mind that he had never been heard of beyond them. She even expressed a high regard for Mr Baxendale and Dr Roxburgh, as men holding an appointed place in what she called a cohesive traditional society. But in town Camilla pursued larger game, and with considerable success. She had family connections which helped; and her husband, although he couldn't be called much of a draw, was properly unobtrusive, civil, and welcoming. On the whole, however, she deserved to have her little *salon* described as all her own work. She was very clever at bargaining with other women of similar mind, trading celebrities rather as small boys swop stamps. Jokes went round about this, and were sometimes retailed to Firth by unwary persons who supposed him to be merely one of Camilla's less noteworthy guests. For example, as a small girl at a Christmas party Camilla was supposed to have said to another small girl, 'You introduce me to Diaghileff, and I'll introduce you to Massine.' The 'in' character of this joke, although a shade *vieux jeu,* was judged to make it very funny.

Camilla's cards sometimes said things like (if not *quite* like) *To meet Monsieur Picasso,* or *For the honour of presentation to the Dowager Empress of China.* But she didn't overdo this, and it was generally understood that her special thing was less the positively first eminences than (as it were) second-string lions who for some casual reason were momentarily enjoying an enhanced celebrity. These people were commonly not put on the card, since the idea was that you were going to be surprised as well as delighted at meeting them. Camilla's taste was quite catholic. On one occasion there might be a visiting sheik, confidentially described as the richest man in the world; on another, it would be a pop singer who had suffered the misfortune of being led in manacles through the street; on yet another, one might find oneself endeavouring to converse with an Italian peasant or Belgian garage-hand who had won an international bicycle race. Certainly Camilla loved something up-to-date. She adored, she would tell you laughing, what her dear grandmother had called *le dernier cri.*

So Firth was a little surprised to find one evening that

his wife was in some excitement over having received an acceptance from Cyprian Windingwood. He had never met this well-established and quietly distinguished painter. But he knew his work and admired it—so much so, indeed, that it had been in his mind that Windingwood might be the man to do the fresh portrait of Camilla necessary now that she had her new nose. If he had hesitated to suggest this to his wife, it was because he felt that Windingwood was insufficiently of an *avant-garde* to make much appeal to her. It was odd, therefore, that the painter's coming to a party was being treated as something of an event. Firth was about to ask whether anything had happened to freshen up, as it were, Cyprian Windingwood's image, when Camilla was called away to speak to her caterer on the telephone. (Camilla's parties were always catered for by the same small and highly reliable firm.) Later, Firth did not pursue the matter. Just recently, without at all knowing why, a sense of unease and frustration had become increasingly common with him. This had the effect of making him rather inattentive, once more, to Camilla's goings on. And sometimes, when he had taken a piece of writing paper with the idea of getting off a personal letter, or of jotting down the heads of what he intended to say to a client or barrister, he would find himself staring at the blank sheet as if at an adversary. And he would feel a restlessness in his skilfully reconstituted right hand, and a sense that there emanated from it some subtle electrical impulse, impossible to block, which was seeking to make a desperate appeal deep in his brain.

4

As soon as the man with the empty sleeve came into the room, Firth instantly and mysteriously *knew*. Here was the moment of social embarrassment that Sir Horace Rumford had so sagely predicted. The donor had turned up, and in Firth's own house.

The guests were already numerous, and there was no need to step forward at once. Instead, he retreated into a corner and tried to argue with himself. There must be hundreds, if not thousands, of one-armed men in London. Indeed, alerted in the matter as he was, he had lately been conscious of quite a number as he moved about the City and the Inns of Court. Messengers of various sorts tended in particular to have only one arm. (Not that this man could be a messenger; he was simply some acquaintance of Camilla's unknown—as often happened—to Firth himself.) To suppose, therefore, that *this* man was *his* man was to predicate altogether too absurd a coincidence. Firth reminded himself of the totally irrational way in which his mind had sometimes worked when he was in hospital. What was threatening him now was something of the same sort.

Unfortunately he continued just to *know*—or at least to know that there was one way in which, without question asked or exposing himself in any way, he could obtain demonstrative proof. He moved out of the corner in which he had taken refuge, and edged across the room. Every now and then he had to stop and speak to somebody, and he was at once irritated by this necessity and thankful for it as postponing for a few minutes a kind of moment of truth. He didn't on these occasions have to carry round drinks himself, since the reliable caterer sent in an elderly man called Puckrup to do the job. (Puckrup had great skill in the role of family retainer; he usually addressed Camilla as 'Madam' but occasionally called her 'Miss Camilla', which somehow sounded extremely well.) Firth grabbed a drink from Puckrup—it was Camilla's usual undistinguished champagne—and then executed a flanking movement on the man with the empty sleeve. He too was holding a champagne glass—in his surviving hand, which was the left. He raised it to his lips just as Firth came up on his left shoulder. And there could be no doubt about it at all. Firth had perforce given a good deal of study to the forefinger and thumb on his own right hand. The forefinger and thumb holding the stranger's glass were a mirror image of them.

Obeying an absurd instinct for concealment, Firth transferred his own glass to his left hand, and thrust the right into a pocket. He reminded himself that the stranger could have no inkling of their bizarre relationship. It was even possible (Rumford had made no disclosure on the point) that he didn't so much as know that not every scrap of his lost limb had gone into the incinerator. If he, the donor, *didn't* know, this must mean that Rumford and his colleagues had allowed their professional zeal a little to sidestep their professional ethics. Or so Firth supposed. And if he didn't know, ought he now to be told? Firth had a momentary revolting vision of himself as stepping forward, holding a forefinger and thumb up in air, and embarking upon a dramatically or even facetiously toned disclosure.

Even as this undisciplined fancy was in his head, the man with the empty sleeve turned round and looked at Firth at close quarters. It was immediately evident that he didn't know he was in the presence of his host. Firth returned his gaze for the very brief space that politeness made possible without stepping forward and introducing himself; then he assumed the telegraphic smile, conventional at parties, of one who has made a pleasing recognition at the other end of the room, and moved away. He carried with him a vivid image of the stranger's features. The picture was of one about his own age, but notably handsome (Firth himself was rather undistinguished) and with an expression suggesting great concentration and strength of will. Firth looked round for Camilla, and at once saw that she was

the centre of so animated a group that breaking in upon
it in search of information would be awkward. But Puckrup
was passing, a bottle of champagne in each hand. Firth
saw with some surprise that his own glass needed replenishing; he hadn't been aware of gulping the stuff nervously
down.

'Puckrup,' he asked, as he watched the old man pour,
'do you happen to know the name of the fellow with a
missing arm?'

'Oh, yes, Sir. Yes, Sir, indeed. An artist, Sir. Mr Cyprian
Windingwood. A striking name for a striking gentleman
would be my manner of expressing it, Mr Firth.'

'I see.' Firth found this unexpected news strangely
staggering, as well as wholly unexpected. 'Do you know
how long he has been—like that?'

'Only since earlier this year, it seems. One of those
dreadful aeroplane accidents, Sir. Only a minute ago, I
happened to hear Mrs Firth talking to Lady Honeycombe
about it. Everybody wants to meet Mr Windingwood. On
account of its being so very sad, Sir. A great misfortune for
one who is, in a manner of speaking, a manual worker, Sir.'

'Yes, of course. I mustn't keep you from your good work,
Puckrup. Perhaps you should try Mr Windingwood. He
may need all that he can get.'

'Well, Sir, so one might suppose. But you will remark
that the gentleman's glass is still fully charged. Of an
abstemious habit, he would seem to be.'

Firth nodded, and again moved on. He supposed that he
continued talking to people here and there, but in fact he
was in a kind of dream. Once or twice he imagined himself
conscious of the smell of ether and antiseptics, so that he
feared some horrible disorder of the senses was going to
overtake him again. There was even a moment during
which he was convinced that Sir Horace Rumford was
standing in a doorway, looking at him severely—but then

Sir Horace's figure simply dissolved into that of a successful barrister whom he had known for many years. Firth decided not to have a third glass of champagne.

'Michael, darling, I don't believe you've met Mr Windingwood. And it is so *good* of him to have come.' It was clear that by *good* Camilla wished herself to be understood as saying *brave*. And she did seem to have a point. Windingwood had never been in the house before, and it was difficult to see why he should have turned up now. Camilla's latest lion—it was perfectly evident—was rating as a lion at all only because he was a *maimed* lion; and moreover her thirst for topical celebrity must be sufficiently well known, surely, to have given a hint of the fact in advance to an intelligent man. There was only one reasonable explanation, Firth told himself as he glanced once more at the composed and rather austere features before him. Windingwood was the kind of man who sets himself tests and carries them through. If this were so, he must have a good deal on his hands just at present.

Or on his hand, Firth was instantly obliged to add to himself. For as Windingwood uttered with gravity a conventional 'How do you do?' he set down his glass neatly on a passing tray, and took the initiative in holding out his hand to his host. He had thought this out, one had to suppose, along with a number of weightier things, and had got the small answer right. Moreover, he had perfected the movement he made. His hand came to you in such a way that you could without awkwardness take it in your own left hand or in your right. If you made a hesitating mess of this (which at least Firth managed to avoid), he would certainly betray no consciousness of noticing the fact.

'I'm sure you two must have something to talk about,' Camilla said brightly—and much as if her husband, equally with Windingwood, was a guest. She hurried off to a quarter in which languor appeared to threaten. For a moment Firth wildly supposed that there had been a sinister implication in her words; in fact, that she was up to something. But this was not really possible. Camilla had shown a disinclination to hear about his hospital period in detail, and there was no reason why she should connect it in any way with Windingwood's having been in an aeroplane accident. There was nothing except sheer fatality in her having taken it into her head to secure the painter as a principal attraction at this party.

'Can I get you another glass of champagne?' Firth asked. He couldn't, in these first seconds, think of anything better to say.

'That would be very pleasant.' Windingwood had the good manners to accept from a host who was a stranger a suggestion he might unobtrusively have turned down from a servant. 'I haven't,' he added, 'been to a party for some time.'

Firth went in search of a bottle. It gave him a further moment in which to think. It was possible, he realised, that Windingwood, far from having been kept in absolute ignorance by the doctors, had for some time known more than Firth himself did. Perhaps he had even come to this party out of a slightly morbid wish to glimpse what might be called his lost property. The grossness of this phrase, as it came unbidden into Firth's mind, brought home to him the inescapable grossness—or perhaps it was indecency—of the sheer physical fact which had elicited it. He asked himself what was the civilised thing to do. The answer seemed to be that he should have the few minutes' general conversation with Windingwood that courtesy required, and then take care not to meet him again. If, however, Windingwood knew the truth, or suspected the truth, and made the slightest tentative approach to it, Firth's only honourable course would be to acknowledge what—so to speak—lay between them. For Windingwood carried instant weight as a serious and truthful person, and one would be letting oneself down if one failed to meet him on that ground.

Firth found a bottle on Puckrup's buffet. He picked up a clean glass as well, for he remembered that Windingwood's had been carried off. His own glass was still on the mantelpiece where he had set it down, and he resolved, after all, to replenish that too. So he carried both bottle and glass back to the painter, and poured champagne for him. Windingwood watched him thoughtfully.

The party was now thinning out, and in particular there was nobody in the small inner drawing-room where Camilla kept her piano. But the two men were standing under the archway giving on this, and visible on the farther wall was a painting, softly lit, of a Breton fishing-village.

'How very jolly to have a Christopher Wood,' Windingwood said. 'May I look?'

'Yes, do. We're very fond of it. Camilla had it from an uncle as a wedding-present.' Firth, who had uttered these words many times at parties in this room, followed his guest round the piano. Now quite isolated, they studied the painting for some moments in silence.

'A wonderful talent,' Windingwood said. 'And so suddenly cut off.'

'Cut off?' Firth had rather forgotten about Christopher Wood, and the words jarred on him.

'Came the blind Fury with the abhorred shears. Not that it was anything so poetic. He just fell under a railway-engine. And he was still short of thirty.'

It was plain to Firth that Windingwood was in no sense consciously speaking in riddles. He was not that sort of person. Nevertheless the meaning of Windingwood's next words was instantly plain to him, even although in form they were a mere repetition of those spoken in another context only a couple of minutes before.

'May I look?' Windingwood asked gently.

Without a word, Firth held out his right hand.

'So you knew?' Firth asked presently.

'No, no—only that they had been made good use of. It was when you poured me this champagne. Perhaps it must be called an intuitive thing—although, after all, it would be an odd painter who didn't know his own finger and thumb. Say, if you like, that I was just making an outrageous guess. A fool I'd have looked if I'd been wrong!' Quite simply, Windingwood took Firth's right hand again, and turned it palm upwards, where the scarlet hair-line showed. 'It's a great wonder,' he said soberly. 'And I am so very glad.' He dropped Firth's hand, lightly touched Firth's shoulder, and then picked up his glass. 'Firth,' he said, 'shall we drink together in honour of this extraordinary thing?'

'Yes, of course.' As he uttered these words, Michael Firth had his first glimpse of the fact that he wasn't going to measure up to Cyprian Windingwood. He found himself, as he obediently raised his glass, trying to remember something in Shakespeare—something said by Macbeth, surely. And it came to him:

> *under him*
> *My genius is rebuk'd: as, it is said,*
> *Mark Antony's was by Caesar.*

That was it. He was in the presence of a man vastly more magnanimous than himself. He realised that this ought to be an edifying experience. It felt more like a disintegrative one.

5

Nevertheless Firth and Windingwood now became friends. It was on Windingwood's initiative, and sometimes Firth again asked himself whether an unconfessed morbidity in the painter was the basis of this continued, and surely very strange, association.

What chiefly happened was that he formed the habit of occasionally dropping into Windingwood's studio on his way home from the office. He had an open invitation to do this, and in time he came to believe that he had worked out why he availed himself of it. Whether or not Windingwood's attitude was morbid, there was a strong streak of morbidity in Firth himself. It took the form of an irrational feeling of guilt. Continuing to see the painter was a kind of penance. But he was also curious. Could Windingwood survive as an artist? The guilt, the sense of being a thief, would be a little dissipated, he supposed, if he could know that Windingwood was going to be able to draw and paint again. So was the loss of a right arm as absolutely fatal to a painter as it would be to, say, most musicians? Firth even found himself doing some research on this. But he didn't succeed in much more than turning up grisly records of arthritic octogenarians who had worked with brushes tied to their fingers, or of yet more unfortunate persons who had succeeded in extracting a livelihood from connoisseurs of the bizarre by selling them pictures painted with their toes.

At least there was an atmosphere of continuing activity in Windingwood's studio. It might literally be called an atmosphere, since it was largely a matter of smells—the immemorial smells of the painter's workshop which Firth remembered as exciting him when he had hankered after that sort of thing long ago. It was obscurely exciting him again now. Once, when he happened to retrace his steps from Windingwood's to his office to pick up some forgotten papers, he made the discovery that his office had a smell of its own : a smell of dust and ink and undisturbed calf-bound law-reports going slightly mouldy. And again a kind of baffled discontent stirred in him.

Windingwood was a bachelor, and his establishment—or visible establishment—consisted of an elderly manservant who seemed to have acquired skill in the odd jobs that fall to be done in a studio. It was clear that this man regularly laid out the various tools and materials which his employer might need, but there was never any actual sign of Windingwood's attempting to use them. Firth suspected that the attempt was being made, all the same, and that his own ringing of a doorbell on the occasion of these visits resulted in all signs of it being stowed away. He always came upon a Windingwood who was sitting or walking about in apparent idleness. Yet there was nothing embarrassing or (as there almost might have been) pathetic in this. For one had a sense of Windingwood's idleness as being, in some indefinable fashion, potentially creative; or at least that a process of severe thought was going on. The fact that Windingwood perceptibly *relaxed* when Firth appeared made this evident.

For the most part they talked about painting, but always in an impersonal way. Firth had little practical or technical knowledge of the subject—anything of that kind had long ago been overlaid in his mind—but he was a frequenter of the great galleries (he would have much preferred Florence to Vevey) and had a knack of recalling significant detail which made what he had to say not uninteresting to a professional. After a time, however, Firth came to feel that the oddity of their relationship—and above all, surely, it was *odd*—lent an artificial flavour to this scarcely intimate talk. And eventually he asked a direct question.

'Tell me, please. Are you going to be able to paint again?'

'It depends what you mean by painting, I think.' Windingwood was undisturbed by this abrupt challenge. 'For instance, a man can paint inside his own head, just as a musician can compose that way.'

'I can't think—'

'Don't you ever do it yourself?'

'Me?' Firth was disconcerted—perhaps only because Windingwood had never interrupted him before, but perhaps also on account of certain fantasies which had been coming to him of late. 'Why should I do such a thing?'

'You have this fondness for pictures.' Windingwood spoke with a lightness which didn't disguise a sense of being on delicate ground. And underlying this was a situation Firth found very hard to define. It might be called a perverse topsyturviness in Windingwood's attitude to him. Firth couldn't glance at his own right hand without knowing that he owed Windingwood the strangest of debts. Yet Windingwood seemed to regard *himself* almost as the debtor. At least it was as if he felt he owed Firth something he had no power to give. 'And you draw sometimes, don't you?' Windingwood was carefully preserving what was virtually a playful tone. 'Once or twice, I've noticed you.'

This was true. Frequenting Windingwood's studio, as he had come to do, on almost familiar terms, Firth had occasionally found himself picking up a pencil or a crayon and sketching with it on any scrap of paper to hand. But it confused him that this had been remarked, so that all he could now produce was an awkward mutter. Windingwood sheered off the subject at once.

'But to go back to your question,' he said. 'With me it's *the* question, I need hardly say. And it's early days to answer it, perhaps. But I'm discovering I must have been the most confoundedly right-handed person.'

'Have you thought, by any chance, of a change of medium?'

'Yes.' Windingwood had glanced up swiftly, and with a beautiful candour. He seemed to be able to take anything Firth said as making all for support and sympathy. 'It can sometimes be done, can't it? Think of Degas, taking to clay and wax in his old age! But that, of course, was because of failing sight. I doubt whether it could be my answer. Don't you think the most superb sculptors would have been those Indian gods with half a dozen hands apiece? They would be superb lovers too, of course. It's much the same thing.' Whimsically, he held up his left hand. 'So what can one hand do? Certainly not trim its own finger-nails! I suppose it might learn to cut out nursery silhouettes.'

'You mustn't think in terms of bagatelles,' Firth said. The awkwardness of this brought him to his feet. 'I must be getting along.'

'Must you? Then drop in again soon.' Windingwood spoke with his largest effect of simplicity. 'It gives me the greatest happiness to see you, my dear Firth.'

Firth now fell increasingly into the habit of thinking about Windingwood. He also 'got him up' (as it might have been called) as a painter. There were a number of canvases in the Tate as well as in other public galleries, and most of the better dealers had several either on show or tucked away. There was also a handsome catalogue of Windingwood's first retrospective exhibition from which a good deal was to be learnt about the development of his genius. And 'genius' came to seem to Firth at least approximately the right word. Windingwood had a high reputation and yet remained underestimated. He was a *great* painter.

This discovery or persuasion ought to have given Firth pleasure, since it was an assurance that Windingwood, before the terrible blow dealt to him, had achieved what must give him a secure niche in the history of his art. This seemed very wonderful to Firth, who retained in manhood

something of the adolescent's immature persuasion that it is
better to be among the thousands who linger for a time in
human memory than among the billions who do not. (Fame,
as Milton rather largely failed to say, is the first infirmity of
clever young men.)

But Firth thought of Donatello and Rembrandt and
Beethoven and Shakespeare : thought, that is, of all the
major artists to whom a 'third manner', an apotheosis at
once spiritual and sensual, had come. Of this, at least,
Windingwood had been cheated. And increasingly Firth
went about under the terrible burden of a conviction that
this cheating had been done by *him*. He knew perfectly
well that this belief came very near to madness; that the
'cheating' was non-existent, since mere fatality (which had
crashed Windingwood's air-liner) can play neither fair nor
foul. But this knowledge only added to what might be
called, with some mildness, his nervous distress. When he
looked at the finger and thumb on his right hand—above
all, when he *felt*, in a strangely physical way, what that
finger and thumb were itching to do—his intellectually
meaningless sense of guilt overwhelmed him.

At times it sought relief in idiotic ways. It seemed to him
(most absurdly) that Sir Horace Rumford and his unknown
colleagues had done something very wrong. He planned at
times to murder these blameless servants of humanity, and
at other times he had the strangest dealings with them in his
dreams. In one of these he was standing, palette in hand,
before a vast canvas, rather in the manner of Velazquez in
Las Meniñas. And suddenly at the back, in silhouette
within a brilliantly lit doorway, Sir Horace appeared. His
right hand was invitingly posed (this was Velazquez again)
upon a curtain. Firth, seizing his palette-knife, turned upon
him in some sort of Strewelpeter frenzy. But at this, and as
if through a wilderness of mirrors, the scene dissolved in a
whirling kaleidoscope of dwarfs and dogs and nuns and

elaborately dressed little girls. Only Firth himself was left, and he was naked, and there were two great transverse, blood-red gashes over his heart. 'The king,' he heard himself say aloud. 'The red cross of Santiago.' And he woke up.

But this murderous disposition towards an eminent surgeon was only (as a psychiatrist could have explained to him) a displacement. Without at all knowing it, Michael Firth had come to hate Cyprian Windingwood. And this shows that the role of benefactor can be extremely hazardous, even when one has been insinuated into it during the profound unconsciousness induced by an anaesthetic.

6

Not knowing about himself, however, except through the obscure intimations of dreams, Firth continued to call on Windingwood from time to time. He did so one afternoon when the painter (or *ci-devant* painter, as it was beginning to look to be) was out. He sat down in the studio to wait, and presently became aware of some almost imperceptible change in it. He looked around, and the change eluded him. He happened to sniff, and that placed it. Windingwood had been versatile and resourceful in his use of media, and the complexity of the studio smell had borne witness to this. Pigments, turpentine, acids, sundry experimental thinners, the queer smell of sodden blotting-paper employed in *peinture à l'essence,* even honey: all these had been involved. But now they had faded beneath a single predominant smell. And this, disconcertingly, was quite like one of the minor elements in the smell at Firth's office. It was simply a smell of gum.

But there was, after all, something else to attract attention. At the farther end of the studio, directly under one of the skylights, lay a broad shallow area which could be curtained off. On his previous visits the curtain had always been drawn back, revealing nothing but half a dozen canvases stacked face to the wall. But now the curtain was drawn to. Firth had noticed something like this in studios before. Sometimes, when a large work was in progress, or had recently been completed, the painter would screen it off in this way—partly against the casual observation of visitors, and partly, perhaps, that he himself should be able to achieve a fresh *coup d'oeil* after a useful interval. It seemed impossible that Windingwood had by any means achieved a work on a large scale—or for that matter even an easel-picture such as could be casually covered with a cloth. Firth was curious. But, although Windingwood's servant had disappeared after admitting him, he forbore to peep.

He doodled instead. He now found it necessary to admit that the habit was becoming compulsive with him. It interfered with his work. It disconcerted and offended clients. It irritated Camilla. But he went on doodling, all the same. Or rather he went on with his attempts at drawing, for that was what it honestly was. He had even, as far as he could judge, become quite good at it. The lines increasingly went precisely where he wanted them to go. All this would have been no more than the belated acquisition of an agreeable accomplishment but for the fact that it *was* so plainly compulsive. And magical as well. For there was no doubt that, having been given what of Windingwood's he had been given, he was under a curious constraint to employ that gift in Windingwood's way. And he was—he came to it again—*jealous* of Windingwood. He was jealous of Windingwood—who ought, in a sense, to be jealous of him, but who maddeningly appeared to be nothing of the sort.

The studio door opened, and the painter came in. Firth was instantly aware that some change had taken place in him. His expression, when he became aware of his visitor, was his habitual expression (which tended to irk Firth) of friendly concern. But there seemed not much *attention* behind it. It was rather as if there had come to Winding-wood a new purposiveness in which Firth had no part. His step was springy and impatient. Disconcertingly about him, indeed, there was something virtually manic. For a second Firth was at sea about this, and then he traced the impression to a very strange place. Windingwood had followed the common convention whereby men who have lost an arm continue to have their suits made with two sleeves, and he wore the cuff of his empty sleeve in the right-hand pocket of his jacket. Now it was as if this purely inanimate object had taken on an air of its own. The sleeve was tucked in the pocket, to an effect of confident negligence which was almost jaunty. Firth realised that only an abnormal con-centration of nervous eneigy in the man could play such a trick with his clothing.

'My dear Firth, I'm delighted to see you. But you ought to have got yourself a drink.' Windingwood strode rapidly over to a table on which a small collection of bottles and decanters was kept—a shade too rapidly, Firth ungraciously and even angrily thought, since the haste suggested a search for at least *something* Windingwood could do for the poor devil who had visited him.

'What's *that*?' It was with difficulty that Firth recognised his own voice, and with surprise that he distinguished him-self as in the act of pointing accusingly at the drawn curtain. 'What have you got hidden there?'

'Hidden?' The painter seemed to consider the word. 'You're perfectly right. I've been determined you should be the first person to have a look.' Windingwood, who had poured out a glass of sherry and handed it to Firth, now moved across the studio. 'It's our small private view,' he said. 'I have felt I owe you that much.'

'*Owe* me—?' The words died on Firth's lips. Winding-wood had drawn back the curtain.

It was *not* by Matisse. It was wholly different. Yet it was only Matisse in his last years who had produced, with just these materials, work of such vibrancy and on such a scale.

'It's a start,' Firth heard Windingwood say. Literally, of course, the words were true. It was a start, or at least a fresh start. At the same time, at least to Firth's ear, they had been spoken with a displeasing insincerity. For this thing was an achievement, and a very great one—nothing less.

'I always took a pride, you know, on doing a particularly neat job on the nails of my right hand. At least with scissors, almost an ambidextrous man.' Windingwood was now speaking with a whimsicality he certainly didn't feel. And a second later, indeed, he spoke on a different note. 'If your *matière* has to be coloured paper and gum,' he said, 'it means doing the devil of a lot of work inside your head.'

'I suppose so.' Firth had a moment of full aesthetic lucidity in which he perfectly understood this. 'I congratulate you,' he said huskily.

'But it has been enormous fun. And I see several ways of going ahead. The Master of the Snip-Snap—that's how I'll go down in the histories.' Windingwood had turned casually away from the triumphant *collage,* as if being careful not to make too much of it, and he had now strolled over to the corner of the studio in which Firth had been awaiting him. He paused, and gave a low laugh. 'Doodling again, I see.'

The laugh ought to have alerted Firth—even warned him. Windingwood was in a mood he hadn't met before. It was a mood of absorption in his own creation, in which he became careless about other things. But Firth failed to reflect on this.

'It isn't doodling,' Firth said. And again his voice surprised him.

'No—I know.' Windingwood had glanced with amusement at Firth's drawings. '*My* surgeon did a good job, I'm bound to say. But don't you think yours was an interfering fool?'

'What do you mean?'

'You didn't positively *need* two forefingers and thumbs, did you? They're not necessary for dictating letters, or even for eating a perfectly good dinner. And this particular finger and thumb—mine, that is—'

'Windingwood, please—'

But Windingwood appeared quite unconscious of having breached a delicacy which he had hitherto perfectly preserved.

'Your possession of them, if that's what it's to be called'—he went on—'has messed you up, really. Isn't that right? Hasn't it given a kind of ineffective prod to the artist *manqué* in you?'

'Yes.' Firth now had a weird sense that he might be speaking the last rational words ever to come from him. 'But it's more than that. It's a sheer physical thing. What's *there* now'—and he made a violent gesture towards his right hand—'tries to *use* me. And I'm no good to it.'

'I see.' For a couple of seconds Windingwood was soberly silent. And then, fatally, he touched once more his note of whimsical concern. 'There are more things in heaven and earth, eh?' He put out his hand, and lightly tapped that part of himself which Firth now carried around with him. '*My* tail wanting to wag *your* dog, I suppose one might say.'

'Well?'

'But the dog, my dear chap'—Windingwood, now glancing again at Firth's drawings, was frankly entertained —'is quite unwaggable.'

What now happened was very shocking, but might have

remained no more than that. Firth struck Windingwood hard across the face. For a moment the two men stared at each other in astonishment. And then, most unfortunately, Firth's mind and vision alike became curiously clouded. He was only aware of expending a great deal of physical energy. And he might have had no more than this awareness for rather too long, had not Windingwood's servant come into the studio and run protestingly if ineffectively forward. The man's cries just enabled Firth to see that he was strangling Windingwood. He relaxed his grip, and in a vivid moment glimpsed the two angry red marks on either side of the painter's windpipe. Then Windingwood scrambled to his feet—he had been flat on his back—and managed to speak, panting.

'Firth, my dear fellow,' he articulated, 'you're ill—a sick man. Will you let me call a doctor?'

Firth too was panting. But at these words he uttered a choking sob as well, and ran blunderingly from the studio.

7

He seemed to have forgotten that London traffic was so bewildering, and for a time he looked about him in despair. He supposed that Windingwood's servant was bound to call the police, so that at any moment he might become the object of a hue and cry. But presently he calmed himself sufficiently to get into a taxi and give the driver his address. Camilla—he thought absurdly—would be able to protect him. Then he remembered that Camilla was not at home. She had been away for some days. This meant, surely, that she was at Spindle. Still in great confusion of mind, he told the man to drive him to Victoria. He was in his train and rushing through the meaningless expanses of south London before it came to him that he had got this wrong. Camilla, of course, was in Paris, visiting some woman with whom she had kept up an acquaintance since their Vevey schooldays. There would be nobody at Spindle.

But it didn't much matter, he told himself later—as he stared unseeingly at the oast-houses that signalised the last stage of his journey. He had been the agent—and what he *did* see, with his inner eye, was those two terrible marks on Windingwood's throat—of a near-fatality unique in human history. In her silly way, Camilla wasn't a bad soul. But she certainly hadn't the imagination to grasp the horror of that.

Firth was still in the grip of this inflated view of himself (as many would have considered it) when he reached the little station at which, miraculously, trains from London did still occasionally condescend to stop. It was an antique place, decorated with battered tin notices commending Gold Flake cigarettes and the needs of anaemic girls, and was in charge of an old man whom Firth had never seen otherwise employed than in filling and trimming an array of oil-lamps which nobody ever seemed disposed to use. The old man greeted Firth respectfully, since he was of a generation to which this came naturally, and then stared in perplexity at the retreating back of so plainly distraught a passenger. Firth had hardly been aware of him, nor was he aware of the few people who glanced at him curiously in the village street. The anxieties besetting him became particularly acute as he walked past the police station. What if there had been a telephone call to Burbage, the constable, and Burbage was waiting to pounce? Was what he had always supposed to be a small coal-shed in Burbage's back-yard in fact a cell in which he could lock you up? No malefactor, so far as he knew, had ever been apprehended in the village, and he felt confusedly that this circumstance would render particularly shameful such a fate now befalling himself. He quickened his pace nervously. No Burbage appeared.

The short winding drive to Spindle was now in front of

him, and he strove to recall the small practical matters commonly in his mind as he came back to the place. Had Hayball cut the grass and attended to the wood-pile? Had Hayball's goats eaten Camilla's roses? Had both Hayball and his wife gone off on a reckless expedition of pleasure to the local market town, so that he would have difficulty in collecting milk and eggs?

Firth found himself incapable of addressing his mind seriously to these issues. What did come to him as some-how formidable was the fact that he would be spending an evening alone. Normally he rather liked this; now he found that the prospect terrified him. Was this still because of Burbage—Burbage who, with a decent tact, was going to await the merciful darkness before marching up this drive and knocking on the front door? With a sudden clarity, Firth saw that it wasn't so. The really dreadful thing had not, in fact, happened; and about what *had* happened Cyprian Windingwood was not the sort of man hastily to invoke the sanctions of the law. He was much more likely to contact Camilla and tell her that he had reason to fear her husband was unwell. This would be humiliating, but it wouldn't result in his being put in gaol.

Firth came to a halt—as abruptly as if a sabre-toothed tiger or other prehistoric carnivore had sprung up in his path. For with one of those sudden jumps by which his mind now seemed to move he knew the true reason why an evening alone was going to be unbearable. It was because he would have company through it, after all—the company of Windingwood's finger and thumb.

'It's that doodling and drawing,' he said aloud. 'It's the beastly magic of—what did he call it?—the tail wagging the unwaggable dog.' But something in his own voice told him that this was not the nub of the matter. It was true that Windingwood was a potent artist and he himself an artist *manqué*; that through some weird psychosomatic vagary what had been grafted on his own right hand was capable of urging a habit and will of its own; and that a black comedy of frustration and jealousy had been spinning itself from this. But these things merely disguised something far more radical : the mindless, primitive sense of what constitutes a selfhood and its integrity. Firth had somewhere read that all civilisation is erected on man's buried fear of being deprived of certain parts of himself. Perhaps there was a kind of inverse fear which had got hold of him now.

There is commonly supposed to be something therapeutic in successful self-analysis. It is an immemorial persuasion, indeed, and subscribed to by whoever caused the temple of Delphi to be engraved with the words γνῶθι σεαυτόν. But immemorial persuasions are often quite wrong. And the scrap of self-knowledge which had come to Firth served merely to throw him into a panic. He found himself running up the drive of Spindle. But not to that gentrified and adequately commodious cottage itself. When he came to a stop again, it was in the tool-shed.

He had the hatchet in his left hand and his right hand (or composite hand) on the chopping block, when there was a sound at the door of the shed. Or was it a smell? At least it distracted him (no doubt he wanted to be distracted) and he turned to look.

He had been visited by one of Hayball's goats. Goats belong, in a fashion, with panic, or at least they have associations with the god said to produce that disagreeable condition. But what this goat suggested was, on the contrary, a kind of animal tranquility in which, it dimly came to Firth, much wisdom reposed. Had the interests of science required, as they did now frequently require of the brute creation, some switch of limb or organ much more radical than Firth himself had suffered, this creature would doubtless have made do uncomplainingly with whatever such a one as Sir Horace Rumford had provided. Firth—at gaze with the goat, as the goat with him—felt rebuked. He looked at the hatchet, looked at Windingwood's finger and thumb, and wondered at the phrenetic folly of what he had been about. He recalled that Origen, supreme among the theologians of the early Church, had lived to regret executing upon himself a retrenchment yet more drastic than he himself was proposing, and also prompted by what might be called a dislike of doodling. Moreover, Firth told himself, it wouldn't be any good. He would simply be carried back to hospital, and Sir Horace would get going again. And with what might not the luck of the airport or the speed-track next equip him? He might wake up to find himself owning the finger and thumb not of an eminent artist but of an equally eminent forger, or a virtuoso exponent of some hideous instrument like the electric guitar.

There was considerable logical confusion in these thoughts, but at least they produced action. Firth threw down the hatchet, shooed the goat from the doorway, and staggered into the open air.

He found that he was making his way back to the village, but for some time he didn't know why. Was he going to 'give himself up', as people said, to Burbage? No, that wasn't it. On the contrary, he was engaged upon a sensible scaling down of the whole thing, and part of this process lay in realising that there wasn't anything to give himself up for. He had suffered a mere brain-storm, and certainly hadn't meant Windingwood any harm. If people got to know about the episode they would only conclude, perfectly justly, that he had suffered a nervous breakdown. Such illnesses are extremely unpleasant while they last, but it is their chief characteristic that they are regularly recovered from. One is constantly hearing of people who *have had* such a breakdown; one hears this far more frequently than that people *are having* one. And this proves their ephemeral character.

Thus muzzily cerebrating, Firth reached the post office. He now knew what was important. He must convey to Windingwood with all speed an apology for his rude behaviour. It wasn't that he wanted to propitiate the man, to head him off from taking legal action. It was simply that this was a civilised—you might say merely a gentleman-like—thing to do. He would send a telegram.

A little bell rang above his head, and there was a smell of paraffin and liquorice sweets and cheap news-print. There was a small counter, one half of which lay behind a symbolic little grille. The grille marked the post-office part, and at the other part you bought shoe-laces and packets of tea and shiny halfpenny-sized metal disks for mending leaking pots and pans. The place was empty except for a man behind the counter. Firth thought he looked like a horse-fly. Or rather he thought nothing of the sort; he simply remembered that this was what he was expected to think. Everybody said Binchy was like a horse-fly.

Binchy. Firth stared at the man in horrified recollection. Binchy had a sheaf of papers in front of him, and was banging alternately on these and on an ink-pad with a rubber stamp. This was a routine Binchy went into when anyone entered the post office; the papers were mere waste-paper, but the action impressed you with the importance of his official status. After the little bell went he invariably did a dozen bangs before looking up. The grandees of the district got precisely the same treatment as village children wanting a toffee-apple. Binchy was a man of finely democratic feeling.

'Ah, Mr Firth, good afternoon.' Binchy had made his final bang. 'Very pleasant to see you with us again, sir. Very pleasant, indeed. Quite recovered from your little operation, I hope.'

'Yes, thank you, Mr Binchy,' Firth said automatically. Everybody had, of course, heard of his accident and period in hospital, but 'little operation' suggested more information than there was any reason to feel Binchy ought properly to have. Binchy was not a perceptive man; it was unlikely that he discerned this feeling in his customer's mind; and his next words were therefore less suggestive of apology than of complacent self-regard.

'When one has associations in the highest medical circles, Mr Firth, one comes to hear of these things. And most interesting they are. Even, as you might say, the trivia, sir.' Binchy paused on this learned word. 'It was Sir Horace Rumford, I think? Quite a master, they maintain, of minor surgery of that kind.'

'I suppose so.' Firth's feeling was less of indignation—although it was clear that within Binchy's hearing some outrageously careless medical gossip had been going on—than of a confused bewilderment. This ineffably self-satisfied creature was the man down whose body must run a great scar like a zip-fastener; within whose flesh there beat—

Firth's phobia (or whatever his regrettable vulnerability was to be called) rose in him, and it had the odd effect of prompting him to answer grossness with grossness and get out.

'The heart doing well, Mr Binchy?' he asked.

'And lungs, Mr Firth.' Binchy was reproachful. 'Shockingly inadequate, the reporting was—although I'm bound to say the newspapers paid very handsomely for my own reminiscences. And here locally, sir, you wouldn't believe some of the slanders going around. Very malicious, often, is village life—particularly towards those with a certain position, if you understand me. It wouldn't apply, of course, to a private person like yourself. Do you know, now? There are those who go about saying it was a black.'

'A black?' Firth simply failed to understand.

'An immigrant or such like. Whereas the fact of the matter is that my donor was a young man of very good family. Of superior station, you might say, even to the people up there at the Hall.' Binchy paused impressively on this claim to vicarious social eminence. 'A college lad, too, Mr Firth, and very athletically inclined. But only taking that sort of thing in his stride, of course. Nothing to strain himself—nothing of that sort at all. A splendid constitution, they say. Now, what can I do for you, Mr Firth?'

For a moment Firth could find no answer. He did remember that he had been going to send a telegram to Windingwood, but he now realised that it would be a merely fatuous gesture. He had made a fool of himself, and wasn't going to mend matters by spending half-a-crown. But he had to spend something, since Binchy was looking expectantly at him.

'Stamps,' Firth said vaguely. 'I just want some stamps.'

'Your usual ten-shilling book,' Binchy said with authority. And he pushed aside a jar of assorted toffees and reached into a drawer.

Outside the post office Firth ran into the vicar, and they exchanged what he was blessedly aware of as perfectly normal greetings. Baxendale asked if Camilla was at Spindle. Firth explained she was in Paris. The two men were about to part.

'That fellow Binchy,' Firth said suddenly. 'He takes it uncommonly quietly, doesn't he? Thoroughly pleased with himself, in fact.'

For a moment the vicar was perplexed, and then he understood.

'Ah!' he said. 'The transplant. Yes, indeed. Like so much in life, these things are as one receives them, wouldn't you say?'